CW00553413

Workers' Tales

ODDLY MODERN FAIRY TALES

Jack Zipes, *Series Editor*

Oddly Modern Fairy Tales is a series dedicated to publishing unusual literary fairy tales produced mainly during the first half of the twentieth century. International in scope, the series includes new translations, surprising and unexpected tales by well-known writers and artists, and uncanny stories by gifted yet neglected authors. Postmodern before their time, the tales in *Oddly Modern Fairy Tales* transformed the genre and still strike a chord.

Kurt Schwitters *Lucky Hans and Other Merz Fairy Tales*

Béla Balázs *The Cloak of Dreams: Chinese Fairy Tales*

Peter Davies, editor *The Fairies Return: Or, New Tales for Old*

Naomi Mitchison *The Fourth Pig*

Walter de la Mare *Told Again: Old Tales Told Again*

Gretchen Schultz and Lewis Seifert, editors *Fairy Tales for the Disillusioned: Enchanted Stories in the French Decadent Tradition*

Édouard Laboulaye *Smack-Bam, or The Art of Governing Men: Political Fairy Tales of Édouard Laboulaye*

Michael Rosen, editor *Workers' Tales: Socialist Fairy Tales, Fables, and Allegories from Great Britain*

Workers' Tales

SOCIALIST FAIRY TALES, FABLES, AND ALLEGORIES

FROM GREAT BRITAIN

Edited by Michael Rosen

Princeton University Press   *Princeton and Oxford*

Copyright © 2018 by Michael Rosen

Published by Princeton University Press
41 William Street, Princeton, New Jersey 08540
6 Oxford Street, Woodstock, Oxfordshire OX20 1TR

press.princeton.edu

All Rights Reserved

LCCN 2018938282
ISBN (pbk.) 978-0-691-17534-8

British Library Cataloging-in-Publication Data is available

Editorial: Anne Savarese and Thalia Leaf
Production Editorial: Sara Lerner
Text and Jacket Design: Pamela Schnitter
Cover Credit: Cover illustration by Andrea Dezsö
Production: Jacqueline Poirier
Publicity: Jodi Price

This book has been composed in Adobe Jensen with Myriad

Printed on acid-free paper. ∞

Printed in the United Kingdom

1 3 5 7 9 10 8 6 4 2

■ Contents

■ Acknowledgments

I am indebted to Deborah Mutch for her work *British Socialist Fiction, 1884–1914* (London: Pickering and Chatto, 2013), from which I have taken many of these stories and their accompanying notes; and also to Caroline Sumpter's *The Victorian Press and the Fairy Tale* (London: Palgrave Macmillan, 2008).

Workers' Tales

■ Introduction

In 1974, I visited the mining area of South Wales to make a short educational radio programme about the nationalization of the mines, which took place under the Labour government of 1945–50. One miner and political activist, Chris Evans, gave me a long interview ranging across the history of locality, mining, work, and his hopes for a socialist future. In describing the nature of life and work, he moved into recitation mode and said:

I go to work,
to earn money
to buy bread
to build up my strength,
to go to work
to earn money
to buy bread
to build up my strength
to go to work ...

We laughed wryly. I enjoyed the way in which he had reduced the whole cycle of life and work into one rhythmic account. In literary terms, it turns the intricate interactions of existence into emblems, single vignettes that flow one to the other, contrasting with each other. It is, then, a particular kind of storytelling used with the intent of revealing or alerting a reader or listener to what the speaker thinks is an unsatisfactory state of affairs. The fact that the story doesn't end with a conclusion hits the button because through its never-ending form (rather than through words themselves) it reveals the folly, drudgery, and wrongness of what is being critiqued.

Fig. 1. A child's birthday card from a Socialist Sunday School.

Since that encounter, I've often also thought about that word 'bread' and how it sits in what was a piece of late twentieth-century political talk. It is of course symbolic and carries with it the reference to the Lord's Prayer, 'give us this day our daily bread', in which 'bread' represents all food, all sustenance. Yet, that image was on its last legs: in British schools, daily recitation of the Lord's Prayer was coming to an end, and a more religiously diverse society was taking shape. Whoever it was who coined Chris Evans's homily knew that they could draw on the prior knowledge of a particular religious image.

This symbolic, emblematic, rhetorical way of speaking, drawing on shared images, can be found again and again in the stories in this collection. They were written by people who were part of a project—socialism—that they hoped would transform society. Though this can be described in economic terms, it is a mistake to imagine that this was purely a matter of, say, changing the ownership of the coal mines, or even a revolutionary change in the ownership of all the 'means of production', as Karl Marx put it.

William Morris, the great artist, designer, and socialist activist, and author of socialist-fantasy novels such as *A Dream of John Ball* (1888) and *News from Nowhere* (1890), wrote:

> Whatever system of production and exchange we may come to, however justly we may arrange the relations of men to one another we shall not be happy unless we live like good animals, unless we enjoy the exercise of the ordinary functions of life: eating sleeping loving walking running swimming riding sailing we must be free to enjoy all these exercises of the body without any sense of shame.[1]

As he said in many different ways, 'I do not want art for a few, any more than education for a few, or freedom for a few'[2]—and, 'Nothing should be made by man's labour which is not worth making; or which must be made by labour degrading to the makers.'[3]

The language of necessity and desire that Morris used here—we shall not be happy unless …; we must be …; nothing should be …—indicates the level of emotion, commitment, and urgency that many socialists of the time poured into their writing, speaking, and activity.

British socialists in the period 1880–1920 produced millions of words in print. A good deal of this is what we might call political rhetoric. One part, though, consisted of various kinds of nonrealist tales. The main body of these involved a recycling of the traditional literary forms like the fairy tale, the fable, the parable, the allegory, and the moral tale. Along with these, we find a few examples of the mystery tale. The home for most of this output was in the newspapers, magazines, and journals of socialist groups and parties. These mostly appeared as weeklies, which, as can be seen from the notes at the rear of this book, blossomed, were reinvented, or died out at quite a rate. The tradition of socialist journals is that the publication in question could represent a sectional interest, as with, say, the *Miner*, or a 'tendency' within socialist thought, as with William Morris's *Commonweal*.

This tradition of journalism was not simply a matter of an exchange of opinions, because the ideas were intertwined with crucial but much-disputed questions of action (When? How?) and organisation (Group? Movement? Trade union? Party?). Behind every strike, demonstration, petition, or movement activity lay questions of whether the action would or would not achieve its objectives, or do anything greater than itself in terms of consciousness and political power. Then, as now, differences found shape within journals that could easily grow into antagonisms, rivalries, and splits, though the particular moment of these tales is marked by an extraordinary act of unity: the founding of the Labour Party in 1900, an organisation that has overcome many divisions and splits and thrives today. The ideas fought over in the period covered by this book live on both in the Labour Party and outside, and much of the landscape of present-day groups, ideas, and actions was laid out in that time. With specific reference to the tales here, any of us who listens to speeches or reads articles circulating today can call to mind socialists who've used some of the literary tropes and genres in this book.

The leading figure in one of the socialist groupings in Britain, for example, used to regularly tell an old joke-fable about a rabbi and a goat, in which a poor man goes to the rabbi to tell him how terrible life is, what with the little home being so overcrowded. The rabbi tells the man to put his goat in the house. A few days later, the man goes back to the rabbi and tells him life is worse, the goat has made it even more overcrowded, and it's eating all the food and leaving its droppings everywhere. The rabbi tells the man to sell the goat. A few days later, the man returns and thanks the rabbi profusely: life is so much better, there's more room, and everyone's happy! It's a little morality tale about how easy it is for people (politicians?) to look as if they are changing something when in fact it stays the same. Other left-wing speakers have, for example, cited 'two bald men fighting over a comb' (pointless war) or 'one of two cheeks on the same arse' (seemingly different views that are in reality the same). My great-grandfather, born around 1860, used to explain to my father what a trade union is: 'Like a box of matches. One match, you can break. Two matches you can break. Three matches also. But a whole box, you can't break. That's a union.'

There are no simple explanations for why the political activists responsible for the tales in this book thought that such stories were an appropriate way to talk about and reflect on politics, to win sympathy for socialist ideas, or to sustain the allegiance of those already committed. Some, but by no means all, of the output was directed specifically toward children, just as the Socialist Sunday Schools movement had adopted and adapted the form of the Christian Sunday School for socialist purposes. In the 1830s, people like the utopian socialist Robert Owen (1771–1858) established some Sunday training schools for children. These died out, but such secular, socialist schools for children started to reappear in the 1880s, and by 1909 the National Council of British Socialist Sunday Schools Union was set up to bring together the 120 schools that had developed all over the country. The implication behind socialist tales for children and adults was that just as Bible stories were thought to make Christianity comprehensible and appealing, so socialist stories would do for socialism. In its own way, behind this lies a literary theory: that literature (narrative and story) transmits ideas through its 'figures' (its representational devices, motifs, scenes, interchanges between protagonists, and outcomes), as these have the power to engage a reader's empathy.

The writers of these stories would almost certainly have all attended schools, chapels, churches, or synagogues where stories were told to illustrate and exemplify ideas for children and adults by way of winning people to a cause, or set of beliefs, and some parts of the British socialist movement embraced a religious aspect, exemplified by the name of one influential organisation, the Labour Church, founded in 1890 by a Unitarian preacher, John Trevor, who also edited its journal, *Labour Prophet*. This is not a change or aberration but a continuation of the strand of Christian communalistic and egalitarian thinking found amongst the Levellers and Diggers in the radical parts of the parliamentary side in the English Civil War (1642–51), in the poetry of William Blake (1757–1827), and in Methodism, with its overly populist message of salvation for the most lowly, an ideology that informed the Tolpuddle Martyrs, a group of men transported to Australia in 1834 for trying to organise an early form of a trade union.

In the period of this book socialists were setting up organizations: political parties, 'leagues', trade unions, and agitational movements and groups (like the suffragettes) in addition to the 'Mechanics' Institutes' and the social organizations that came under the wing of *Clarion* (see below), where ideas from literature, religion, politics, science, and philosophy circulated in the form of talks, discussions, pamphlets, newspapers, and books.

The urgency for this output came from the historical context: Britain at this time was in a country made up of England, Scotland, Wales, and, importantly, the whole of Ireland, with the issue of Irish independence being a intermittently a matter of fierce struggle and war. This national entity had an international component: varying degrees of control over a majority of the world's land surface. The material base of Britain, then, was both British and imperial and involved a global interchange of finance, raw materials, and finished goods, with enormous benefits primarily for the wealthy of Britain but also for colonial ruling groups. Within Britain, both the industrial and rural working classes were largely poverty-stricken, though this period also saw the growth of a white-collar working class; a supervisory, managerial caste; an expanding layer of retail tradesmen; and professional classes such as teachers and industrial designers along with 'tradesmen' servicing this growing middle class.

Over this period, suffrage widened, but universal suffrage for all twenty-one-year-olds was not reached until 1928; so government was, for many, still something that was done to them, not by them. (The facts are these: The Second Reform Act [1867] extended the vote to the skilled urban male working class; the electorate increased to one in three men. The Third Reform Act [1884] extended the vote to working-class men in the countryside; the electorate rose to two out of three men. The Representation of the People Act [1918] gave the vote to almost all men over twenty-one years old, and women over thirty years old. With the passage of the Representation of the People [Equal Franchise] Act in 1928, effectively all women and men over twenty-one had the vote.)

Christianity was the dominant belief and practice for most people in Britain, but class, culture, nation, and history manifested themselves separately, sometimes antagonistically, in the various Christian sects. Given that Christianity was the official religion of the state, it could be used to justify the ruling order in Britain along with an order over many other peoples of the world, yet at the same time—and of great importance, in relation to the tales in this book—the same sacred texts could be used to justify revolt, reform, millenarianism, equality, and communitarianism.

Official education was delivered in differing quantities according to class, with the wealthy able to acquire the most, the poorest the least. Through this period, however, state education for all was on the march, so that by its end there was universal, free education for children between the ages of five and fourteen, along with selected access to more education for a minority. This was not the only vehicle for literacy, numeracy, and taught skills: a popular literature of newspapers and magazines, of which the socialist newspapers and magazines were one part, took over from the street literature of the previous era. Working-class associations such as the 'institutes', trade unions, and sporting clubs were important and influential ways in which people began or widened their literacy. An elaborate system of guilds and apprenticeships taught high-skill trades that also involved forms of literacy. This too was 'education'.

The period was marked by a series of colonial wars in Africa and the Middle East involving, in total, hundreds of thousands of men on all sides and, toward the end of this period, the cataclysm of the First World War. Millions of British people at this time—including thousands of socialists—were recruited into a powerful allegiance to nation, empire, and racial hierarchies. The issue of whether British socialists should or should not welcome this allegiance led to division then and has done ever since.

Almost all care of children was carried out by women, whether in the home or in schools. Working-class mothers, grandmothers, or sisters not only were the sole caretakers for their own children but often cared for the children of middle- and upper-class women too. The working-class child was becoming 'noticed' in the sense that key figures such as Margaret McMillan (1860–1931) began to think of more enlightened ways of creating interesting, pleasant, and kindly places for young poor children to learn and play. Large numbers of older poor children were educated or punished in militarized institutions such as 'naval colleges' or 'reformatories'. Key changes were taking place in middle-class women's education, particularly as employment for women was expanding into retail, education, and 'clerking'. Places for women in teacher-training colleges and nursing courses, and in a very small way at universities, were expanding throughout this time.

Alongside the growth of popular newspapers and magazines came lending libraries and an explosion in the sale of sheet music and song. There was a vibrant music hall culture supporting and supported by the sheet music trade, while older 'folk' forms thrived in pubs and clubs and on festive occasions. 'Literature' was stratified in ways that are familiar to us now, read and consumed, if not directly along class lines, then along the lines prescribed by a class-determined education. Categories such as 'children's literature' often disguise these divisions, but it's worth remembering that authors like Lewis Carroll or Frances Hodgson Burnett were read in their original editions almost entirely by middle-class children during this time, though popular editions, sometimes abridged, appeared soon after. An avant-garde created a private coterie for the circulation of sexually explicit and/or foreign literature. At times, the personnel within the socialist movements included people who frequented this avant-garde, such as Edward Carpenter (1844–1929), a socialist, poet, and early activist for gay rights; see Sheila Rowbotham's *Edward Carpenter: A Life of Liberty and Love* (2008) and Stephen Marcus's *The Other Victorians: A Study of Sexuality and Pornography in Mid-nineteenth Century England* (1974).

In Britain, the ideas of socialism embodied many strands of intertwined thought and activity, owing their thought to very different—sometimes contradictory—traditions, which ebb and flow throughout this period, including dissenting, nonhierarchical Christianity; the Christian socialism of clerics within the Church of England; universalistic ideals expressed in the founding documents of the

American and French revolutions; utopian notions of what an ideal society could look like; the actions of organized groups of working people; agitation for the rights of nations to be free of being dominated by another; pacifism; antislavery and anticolonialism; the theories of Marx and Engels—including total revolution; the birth control and eugenics movement; agitation for universal suffrage; a belief that the move toward a better society could come only through gradual reform; secularism; the cooperative and 'guild' movements; one particular branch of the arts and crafts movement; the antiracist ideas pioneered by Émile Zola, passed into the French socialist movement and then to Britain; the working-class education movement; sexual liberation; feminism; pastoralism ('back to nature'); the temperance movement; scientism—a belief that the use of science and technology would lead to social progress; and Fabianism, syndicalism, and anarchism. One central conflict between these ideas was over whether socialism was something that could be brought about by the activity of working people or whether it would be ushered in by the actions of enlightened leaders.

It is from within all these contexts, material and ideological, that the socialist fairy tale, allegory, fable, moral tale, and mystery tale were written and read. Incorporating the wide variety of ideas that the socialist movement had gathered up, the tales looked to critique the world and agitate for a better one. Each of the first four literary forms mentioned had precedents stretching back thousands of years. The fable owed a good deal of its popularity to the nebulous figure of Aesop; the allegory to Greek philosophy; the fairy tale to the Renaissance literature of Italy; and the moral tale to the exempla of sermons. Fables and allegory had always held within them the potential of being overtly political, the fairy tale showing its politics less overtly, often as personified social conflict. Editions and revisions of Aesop were always in print; two great allegorical texts, *Pilgrim's Progress* and *Gulliver's Travels*, had immense popularity preceding and throughout this period; and the fairy tale had developed out of Italy, moved out of the salons of French upper-class women, and combined with the folk tales of the largely rural classes of Europe. In written form, its most popular appearances at this time were in the collections of the Brothers Grimm, Hans Christian Andersen, and Andrew Lang, and in the brand new, and specifically national, collections of Joseph Jacobs. Indeed, Jacobs produced two collections of what he called 'English Fairy Tales' in this particular period (1890, 1894), which lay down a canon of tales—not all of them English and not all of them 'fairy tales', but which were distinct from Perrault and Grimm. Though most of the tales had appeared before, Jacobs created what came to be seen as definitive versions, and these have remained key features on the British child's cultural landscape ever since. Several, such as 'Jack and the Beanstalk' (1890) and 'Tom Hickathrift' (1894) (the latter is included in this collection), though not specifically 'socialist', do represent the kind of tale that symbolically enacts an element of the class system in a wish-fulfilling way—the poor little person who gets the better of the gigantic wealthy one. The Jacobs version of 'The Three Little Pigs' story ('The History of the Three Little Pigs', 1890) sees the two improvident pigs perishing at the hands of the wolf, before the third gets revenge and finishes him off. On offer here was a warning about what to do if you're weak in the face of danger or annihilation: be well prepared and cunning. Perhaps it's no coincidence that Jacobs was someone who was active in several of the issues and campaigns in which socialists were active too: women's rights, and the conditions of the poor—in particular, in his case, the plight of the persecuted, indigent Jews of Eastern Europe.

Another genre had prevailed throughout the nineteenth century: the moral tale. Overlapping with the fable, its origins lie in the parables of the Pharisees of the Middle East (who were in reality street preachers rather than the high priests of the New Testament), reaching the world through Jesus's parables, while the tales of Petrus Alphonsus's 'Disciplina Clericalis' (c. AD 1100), itself a borrowing from the Middle East, furnished preachers across Europe with yet more fables and moral 'exempla'. The use and popularity of the moral tale was given a twist and a huge boost by the Religious Tract Society (est. 1799), which explicitly created a vast literature of such tales. The Religious Tract Society was designed to compete with what it saw as the amoral 'low' literatures of the street, with their motifs of giant killing, wild women, miniature men, and the like. Just as socialist and agitprop songs of the period of this book drew on the shared repertoire of hymns and carols, so this moral literature offered pre-texts to socialist writers alongside the fairy tale, allegory, and fable.

In addition, several writers experimented with the mystery tale. The most widely known, but by no means the only, exponent of these prior to this period was E.T.A. Hoffmann (1776–1822), but Hans Christian Andersen had attempted writing a handful of them too (e.g., 'The Shadow'). The largely French 'symboliste' movement had continued the tradition in the late nineteenth century. The essence of such tales is that they are unsettling and unresolved. Features of nature in the tales may well have symbolic or, as we might say now, 'expressionist' overtones, and the central protagonist is likely to face an existential dilemma.

A further context for the tales in this book is the strong tradition of morally and socially critical fairy and fantasy tales, as exemplified by John Ruskin's 'King of the Golden River' (1841), Charles Dickens's *A Christmas Carol* (1843), William Makepeace Thackeray's *The Rose and the Ring* (1855), and Oscar Wilde's *The Happy Prince and Other Tales* (1888). As Jack Zipes points out in *Victorian Fairy Tales: The Revolt of the Fairies* (1987), such literary tales, alongside those of Laurence Housman (1865–1959), George Macdonald (1824–1904), and E. Nesbit (1858–1924), represent a body of literature that critiqued greed, materialistic attitudes, and dominant ideas, often from a 'purer' or 'truer' Christian viewpoint. It's reasonable to speculate that the writers of the tales collected here came across at least some of these literary tales and saw themselves as part of that tradition. In a broad sense, though, the socialist tales in this book swim in all these historical, ideological, and literary contexts and constitute a critical, resistant literature intended to alert, reform, enlighten, provoke, and educate.

Genres, with Examples from the Book

I) TALES THAT USE TRADITIONAL STORIES OR TRADITIONAL STORY FORMS—FAIRY TALE, FOLK TALE, MYTH, AND LEGEND

i) In 'Little Red Riding Hood' (from the *Labour Leader*, 26 October 1895), C. Allen Clarke relies on his readers to know the story, so that they can enjoy the modern references, asides, and jokes that he has inserted into what appears at first to be nothing more than a slightly verbose retelling of the traditional tale.

ii) F. J. Gould, in 'The Man without a Heart' (from *Labour Prophet—Cinderella*, October 1893), uses the fairy tale form to construct a story along the lines of Ruskin's 'King of the Golden River' to arrive at a Tolstoyan conclusion in relation to the dignity of labor.

iii) 'Tom Hickathrift' (from *More English Fairy Tales*, 1894) comes from outside the socialist journals and is included here because of the way in which its author-collector, Joseph Jacobs, makes explicit the socialistic outcome of the hero's exploits: "The ground that the giant kept by force for himself, Tom gave part to the poor for their common land, and part he turned into good wheat-land to keep himself and his old mother, Jane Hickathrift." This illustrates how an egalitarian, communitarian thread was kept alive in fairy tale collections by anthologists, collectors, and retellers of traditional tales.

2) ALLEGORICAL FAIRY TALES AND FABLES

These are the forms that writers of socialist tales most preferred.

iv) In 'The History of a Giant: Being a Study in Politics for Very Young Boys', by Keir Hardie (published in *Labour Leader*, 8 April 1893), the figure of 'Labour' is analogous to Christian in *The Pilgrim's Progress* (first published in 1678), as he moves historically and geographically through the kingdom discovering and revealing how capitalism and the political system work, and how in the great battle ahead 'Labour' will win, thanks to the "INDEPENDENT LABOUR PARTY".

v) No less a figure than William Morris published 'An Old Fable Retold' in *Justice* (19 January 1884). It's a sophisticated retelling of the tale in which protagonists discuss the best way that they will themselves be executed.

vi) The slightly arch, know-better tone of the allegorical fable emerges in 'Fables for the Times—II: The Political Economist and the Flowers' from *Justice* (18 October 1884), which strikes at the heart of the nature-nurture debate that followed the appearance of *On the Origin of Species* (1859).

vii) 'A Dream of Queer Fishes (A Modern Prose Idyll)' (*Commonweal*, 19 November 1887) by H.S.S. is a warning tale about deceit over home rule for Ireland, which involves the Old Man of the Sea and a shoal of mid-Atlantic fish!

viii) Dan Baxter in 'The New Shilling' (*Justice*, 23 March 1895) uses the fable form to reach forward to a utopian money-less future, a theme to be found in a good deal of utopian thought and revived by some reflections on Marx and his famous citation from *Timon of Athens* about gold.

ix) Joseph Grose in 'The Golden Egg' (*Justice*, 13 July 1901) revives the classical and Renaissance 'dialogus' (dialogue) or even perhaps the 'disputatio' (dispute) in which 'The Cynic' and 'The Person of Good Intentions' debate the economic system.

x) Frank Starr in 'The Doll Shop' (*Labour Leader*, 15 August 1903) uses the metaphor of shopping for dolls to dissect class and certain types of 'Man' whilst finding room at the end to take swipes at fellow socialists who had been unsuccessful in convincing the masses.

xi) R. B. Suthers, in 'The Peasants and the Parasites' (*Clarion*, 24 January 1908), is more direct than Keir Hardie with his *Pilgrim's Progress* approach to the travails of the class system, naming his types according to their social position.

xii) "Happy Valley." A Fairy Tale' (*Justice*, 20 July 1907) (anon.) leans heavily on pastoralism as a way of critiquing the system, whilst naming characters as 'Monopoly' or 'Fairplay'.

xiii) W. Anderson, in 'The Fool and the Wise Man' (*Justice*, 13 August 1910), returns to the dialogue form in order to unlock the absurdity, contradiction, and unfairness in the class enemy's position.

xiv) The most elaborate of the tales of this type, 'Jack Clearhead', "by Keir Hardie, M.P.", appeared in the *Labour Leader* weekly from 1 September until 27 October 1894. This is a thirteen-chapter Swiftian allegory with 'Dullards' and 'Plumheads' and the like.

3) MORAL TALES

xv) Socialist writers and editors attempted the moral tale with stories such as 'Elfhome (Charlie's Garden)' (from the *Labour Prophet*, April 1897) but really didn't achieve anything more socialistic than a homiletic about making things nice!

'The Man without a Heart' (discussed above) is also in its own way a moral tale.

4) MYSTERY TALES

In this section, we can place, for example:

xvi) H. Bellingham's 'Chips' ('*To-Day*', September 1888), in which a conversation between Chips and a numinous frog (!) undercuts the figure of God as nothing more nor less than 'Love', which itself is belied by the existence of poverty.

xvii) M. Winchevsky—a notable Yiddish poet—produced 'He, She, and It' for *Social Democrat* (April 1906). Set in London, social realism sits alongside a kind of magical realism analogous to Oscar Wilde's fairy tales. Here an apple tree and a streetlamp have thoughts, while 'the scavenger' sweeps the leaves and leans on the apple tree.

xviii) 'The Scarlet Shoes. (The Story of a Serio-comic Walking Tour and its Tragic End.)' by Harford Willson (*Teddy Ashton's Northern Weekly*, 3 March 1906) appears at first to be simply an odd story, but it draws on references to Grimm and H. C. Andersen and symbolically enacts in an unsettling way societal attitudes to eccentricity.

xix) In 'Nightmare Bridge' by Glanville Maidstone (*Clarion*, 15 July 1910), our route into an urban hell is along a road and over a bridge that present themselves in a dream. The hell is, of course, London, a subject and theme that obsessed reformers, nonfiction writers, and journalists of the era, puzzled and appalled as to how at the heart of Britain's huge empire so much poverty, disease, and crime could exist just down the road from the City of London's financial institutions.

xx) Schalom Asch looks back to E.T.A. Hoffmann and prefigures Kafka's 'In the Penal Colony' with 'Behind the Wall' (*British Socialist*, 15 December 1913). People are in prison, but imprisonment is more a state of being than a punishment or an act of justice.

In trying to assess how effective these stories were, I would suggest that for many of them, it's pointless trying to use narrowly literary criteria, any more than one would for the 'Good Samaritan'. The question we can ask is, were such stories convincing to people at that time? Evidence for that is scant, but Carolyn Sumpter, in *The Victorian Press and the Fairy Tale* (Basingstoke: Palgrave Macmillan, 121), cites enthusiastic young readers of Keir Hardie's tales, writing in 1894 to tell him that they were 'very highly appreciated by the mothers and fathers' as well as the by the youngsters, and this enthusiasm impelled him to write more. It is interesting to note that part of the currency of political speeches by socialist leaders since that time is the biblical allusion, the joke-fable, and the apocryphal tale, and one might say that even if we have no way of saying whether any individual tale 'convinced', there is a more general way in which they contribute to a long-standing and international rhetoric.

Taken as a body of fiction, the stories reveal the fault lines and viewpoints that ran through the world of socialists then, but which persist today. It's not as if inequality, injustice, exploitation, poverty, and war have been abolished—nor indeed have the hugely powerful agencies for sustaining this state of affairs. These tales sought to describe, critique, and agitate against this. I think they show signs of being 'green': that is, part of a young movement, confident in the certainty that the end point can be achieved, often using stories to make things seem self-evidently necessary. This is socialism at its most hopeful, perhaps at its most innocent, untouched by world war, Stalinism, or the Holocaust. That innocence is hard to recycle, and it may be unwise to try, but I think there is another way in which these works have contemporary potential: in their apparent desire to lay bare the processes that make the majority of people's lives such a struggle. We can read in the stories the idea that the display of these processes would educate and motivate readers to join movements and work toward making a fairer, more just world.

A Note on the Illustrations

Along with the rise of socialism and explicit socialist stories for young people at the end of the nineteenth century came a wave of socialist art and visual reinterpretations of classical folk and fairy tales. Most of the tales in this volume were not illustrated, yet many referred to well-known fairy tale books and plays. This book includes a sampling of fairy tale illustrations and political images of the era by such artists as William Morris, Walter Crane, Charles Folkard, and Laurence Housman.

TALES

■ An Old Fable Retold

William Morris, 1884

In the days before man had completely established his domination over the animal world, the poultry of a certain country, unnamed in my record, met in solemn conference in the largest hall they could hire for their money: the period was serious, for it was drawing near Christmas, and the question in the debate partook of the gravity of the times; for, in short, various resolutions, the wording of which has not come down to us were to be moved on the all important subject, 'with what sauce shall we be eaten?

Needless to say that the hall was crowded to suffocation, or that an overflow meeting (presided over by working-class leaders) was held on the neighbouring dung-hill.

All went smoothly; the meeting was apparently unanimous and certainly enthusiastic, abundant wisdom was poured out on the all-important question, and the hearts of all glowed with satisfaction at the progress of the race of—poultry. The very bantam-*hens* were made happy by the assurance that their claims to cackling were seriously considered.

But when the hands of the clock were pointing to ten minutes to ten the excited audience, as they recovered from the enthusiasm produced by one of the great speeches of the evening, saw on the platform beside the chairman a battered looking and middle-aged barn-door cock, who they perceived was holding forth in a lugubrious voice, praising the career and motives of every advanced politician of the poultry yard. This bored the audience a good deal, but being used to it they stood it with patience for some time, till at last the orator's voice got rather clearer and louder, and he spoke somewhat as follows:—"Sir, I know I have little right to air my own theories (cheers) after the remarkably and clear exposition of the rights of poultry, which has been delivered in various ways on this platform to-night (loud cheers), but I am free to confess that one idea has occurred to me which seems to have escaped the more educated minds of our leaders to-night; (cries of Oh, Oh)— the idea is this!" Here he stopped dead, and amid ironical cheers tried nervously to help himself to water from the long-ago emptied decanter, then at last blurted out in a trembling, shrieking voice not without a suspicion of tears in it; "In short *I don't want to be eaten at all*: is it poss—"

But here a storm of disapproving cries broke out, amongst which could be heard loudest the words 'practical politics!' 'county franchise,' 'great liberal party,' 'municipal government for—Coxstead!' which at last all calmed themselves down into a steady howl of 'question, question!' in the midst of which the ragged, middle-aged cock withdrew, apparently not much more depressed than when he first stood up.

After his departure the meeting ended in all harmony, and a resolution was passed with great enthusiasm that the conclusions come to as embodied in the foregoing resolutions should be engrossed and forwarded to the farmer's wife (or widow was it?) and the head poulterer.

A rumour has reached us that while there were doubts as to the sauce to be used in the serving up, slow stewing was settled on as the least revolutionary form of cookery.

Moral: Citizens, pray draw it for yourselves.

Fig. 2. Notice by Walter Crane and William Morris for the Arts and Crafts Exhibition Society in Hammersmith (1890).

THE MONKEYS AND THE NUTS
'Utile Dulci', 1884

A colony of monkeys, having gathered a store of nuts for the winter, begged their Wise Ones to distribute them. The Wise Ones reserved a good half for themselves, and distributed the remainder amongst the rest of the community, giving to some twenty nuts, to others ten, to others five, and to a considerable number none. Now, when those to whom twenty had been given complained that the Wise Ones had kept so many for themselves, the Wise Ones answered, "Peace, foolish ones, are ye not much better off than those who have ten?" And they were pacified, and to those who objected, having only ten, they said, "Be satisfied, are there not many who have but five?" and they kept silence. And they answered those who had five, saying, "Nay, but see ye not the number who have none?" Now when these last made complaint of the unjust division and demanded a share, the Wise Ones stepped forward and exclaimed to those who had twenty, and ten, and five, "Behold the wickedness of these monkeys! Because they have no nuts they are dissatisfied, and would fain rob you of those which are yours!" And they all fell on the portionless monkeys and beat them sorely.

Moral.—The selfishness of the moderately well-to-do blinds them to the rapacity of the rich.

THE POLITICAL ECONOMIST AND THE FLOWERS

Anon., 1884

A Political Economist, grown tired of writing books, bought a garden and resolved to devote himself to growing flowers on economic principles. The soil was very poor, but he sowed seeds and planted flowers, and bade them grow. They did their best; but in the summer they were but a sorry spectacle compared with those of the Ignorant Man in the next garden. The Ignorant Man, looking over the fence one day, and seeing a heap of manure in the Professor's garden, said to him, "Sir, why do you not improve the soil of your garden by spreading over it that manure in order that your flowers may have strength and beauty?" "My good fellow," responded the Professor, "you are a most immoral and unscientific gardener, though I forgive you on account of your ignorance. What! Would you treat all the plants alike, the strong and the weak, the good and the bad? Nay, but let them contend among themselves for the soil which they have, and when I see plainly which of them flourish best in this poor soil, to them will I shortly give more manure than they will know what to do with!"

Moral.—It was the Ignorant Man who took the prize at the Flower Show.

■ Aristos and Demos

D. F. Hannigan, 1887

Once upon a time there lived a mighty monarch whose name was Aristos. He ruled over millions of subjects by whose labour he acquired enormous wealth. He dwelt in a gorgeous palace, where hundreds of white slaves attended on him, and the honour of men and the chastity of women were sacrificed to his all-devouring passions. Though in his life he ignored every moral law, Aristos considered it indispensable to have an established religion in order to awe and intimidate the multitude by impressing on their minds the belief that there was a connection between monarchy and the divine government of the world. A crowd of obsequious priests paid homage to the sovereign, and urged upon the people the necessity of blind obedience. The monarch's authority was further strengthened by the intrigues and sophistries of cunning lawyers, who invented a number of false maxims calculated to deceive the credulous masses, and to bewilder even the wise and virtuous. Amongst other things they laid down that "the king can do no wrong"; and that even to conceive the idea of dethroning the reigning sovereign was an offence more heinous than murder, to punish which the most horrible form of death should be devised.

By this system of monopoly and self-deification, Aristos kept the toiling millions down, and it was only when some terrible calamity, such as famine or pestilence, aroused the people to a sense of their miserable condition that anyone dared to question the right of the monarch to oppress, tax, murder and degrade his subjects. So strong is the influence of custom that many of the poor and weak who were ground down to the earth by tyranny of Aristos looked upon him as something more than a man: else (they asked themselves) how could he have such unlimited power? A curious notion took possession of some minds as to the very colour of the royal blood. Inasmuch as the blood of common people was red, they assumed that the blood of a king must be blue, though they might as readily have assumed that it was yellow or black. A privileged class sprung up in the course of time which owed its social eminence to the favour of Aristos. This class consisted mainly of persons who devoted themselves to upholding the royal authority. Titles of nobility were conferred upon these persons and they were known as the aristocracy. Though they possessed no great or noble qualities and were, as a body, ignorant, cowardly and sensual, the aristocracy looked down on the rest of the king's subjects as their inferiors, and only addressed them in terms of opprobrium or contempt. As the greater portion of the population was kept necessarily in a condition of abject poverty in order that Aristos and his parasites might live in luxury and splendour, all who did not belong to the privileged class had to earn a wretched livelihood by work of the most distasteful and exhausting description. Some of them were employed in sweeping the streets of large cities; others worked as miners in the bowels of the earth; many had to become the hired slaves of the aristocracy, who treated them worse than horses or dogs. Gradually a few of the toiling multitude yearned for some change in their condition, and, in the effort to emancipate themselves from the thraldom of the aristocracy, they were sometimes driven into acts of violence. These manifestations of discontent were punished as crimes, and the toilers who indulged in them were either put to death or immured in prison for the rest of their lives. The result of this repression was to strike a temporary dread of the law into the hearts of the masses who lived, or tried to live, by menial work. The king had a large army for the maintenance of which he taxed his subjects, exacting payment from the poor as well as the rich. He also employed many thousands of police and gaolers to enforce the criminal code, by means of which he had succeeded, for a time at least, in intimidating the discontented workers. To the latter, under these circumstances, the struggle to free themselves from the misery of their lot seemed a hopeless one. Many of them in despair abandoned their ordinary occupations and enlisted as soldiers in the king's army, deeming it better to die on the field of battle than to perish by disease or starvation. If they had not been plunged in the densest ignorance, the masses would, no doubt, long ere this, have risen up in revolt against the system which enslaved and degraded them. To educate them would have been the first step towards freedom. For this reason, Aristos and the aristocracy made education such an expensive luxury that no poor man's child could afford to learn anything except merely to read and write. Even this scanty modicum of knowledge was shut out from most of them. Finding no other means of softening the bitter hardness of their lives, the toilers, in a wretched fashion, began to imitate the vices of the aristocracy, and too often lowered themselves to a greater depth than poverty could ever lower them to by drunkenness and debauchery. Thus arose a trade by which intoxicating liquors were supplied to the unhappy beings who could only procure those vile stimulates by depriving themselves and their families of food. Other trades sprang up, too, in the course of time, through the exigencies of the toiler's lot, such as that of the petty usurer, the pawnbroker, and the auctioneer. The extravagant tastes of the aristocracy gave rise to other departments of commerce such as the sale of jewellery and lace. Most of these traders were a hybrid race consisting of persons who had made some money by pandering to the aristocracy, while a few of them were members of the privileged class, who had from some cause or another become impoverished. The growth of a commercial class instead of improving the condition of the toilers made it much worse, for the traders imitated the vices of the aristocracy, and compelling those who were poorest in the community to work for them, ground them down until life became perfectly intolerable. Suicides amongst the toilers or their children were common occurrences; and when the aristocracy read of such things in the newspapers they only laughed.

It happened, however, that in spite of evil laws, young men amongst the toiling masses learned some of the truths of science almost starving themselves to procure books; and at length a few of them had the courage to publish their thoughts and to denounce the oppression of the privileged class. These young men were prosecuted and severely punished, but the seed they had sown bore fruit. The people's hearts had been stirred and they thirsted for liberty.

The time arrived when an emancipator was born in the midst of the struggling, starving multitude. His name was Demos. He was poor and apparently helpless, but a spirit of divine energy inspired him. He was strong, courageous, intelligent, loving and indomitable. Some people said he was an archangel and compared him to St. Michael,[1] but this was an idle superstition. He was only a man, but ah how much there is in that! Because he was a man he had no fear of Aristos and his myrmidons.[2] He defied and despised them. He saw that the vile monarch who had kept his brethren so long in bondage had relied altogether on the power of money. With money Aristos had hired soldiers and police to terrify and coerce the millions whom he called his subjects; with money he had bought the support of his parasites, the aristocracy; and by monopolising all forms of wealth he had left the multitude no resource but slavery or death. There was one thing, however, that Aristos had forgotten, namely that labour is the origin of all wealth, and that without it no wealth, however enormous, can be preserved. This great fact flashed on the clear brain of Demos. He grasped the whole problem with his far-seeing intellect, and he saw the true remedy for all the evil wrought during the long reign of Aristos. He called some of the other young men around him and spoke to them earnestly.

"My friends," he said, "let us organise labour! That is the lever which moves the world! No king, no tyrant, no capitalist, can compete with organised labour. Let these wealthy despots coop themselves up in their palaces and their mansions, without us they cannot exist; their luxuries, their food, their lives depend on us. They have trampled on us for years. They have treated us as if we were inferior animals. They shall do so no more! We are men; we are workers; we inherit as men this earth and its produce. Let us crush this fabric under which we have groaned! Down with Aristos and his minions!"

Those who heard him cheered, and soon a great multitude had assembled. Demos showed them how by organisation they might destroy the artificial structure which, as if in mockery, had been called "society," and he taught them, in simple but eloquent language, that until now they had lived in the vilest slavery, because they knew nothing of the rights of man.

No apostle in olden days had ever more enthusiastic followers. The millions raised a mighty shout of exultation. They knew their power at last, and they resolved to level Aristos to the dust. Demos, who was as prudent as he was brave, saw the necessity for caution as well as courage. He had already prepared his plans. He had provided money and arms by agencies known only to himself and his trusted confederates. The multitude were undisciplined, but what are a few thousand soldiers and police against millions with arms in their hands.

The struggle was short lived. The aristocracy, most of whom were large landowners, feebly cried out to the police to help them. The police laughed and after firing into the air surrendered to the revolutionists at discretion. Not many lives were lost. Aristos shut himself up in his palace, but the people, in spite of the bayonets of the soldiery, forced their way in. They found him lying on a luxurious couch, stone dead. The system had perished along with it.

"Let us burn his vile body!" cried the people wildly.

"No comrades," said Demos solemnly. "Remember he was a man like each of ourselves, and if he trampled on his fellow men he will do so no more."

Some of those who followed Demos grumbled at these words, and the more fiery spirits suggested, as a sort of compensation for this disappointment, that all the aristocracy should be massacred.

"What?" burst out Demos with flaming eyes, "would you commit murder the very day you have gained your freedom?"

"They murdered our kith and kin," shouted several hoarse voices together.

"True," said Demos, "but we have destroyed the system. Is not that enough? If they submit to human laws we will pardon them; and they like us shall honourably toil. The goods of the earth are for all. Those only shall suffer who refuse to work for the good of all. The happiness of the whole community must be our only aim and object. The tyrant has passed away, and it now becomes our duty to erect upon the ruins of tyranny the Republic of Man."

■ A Dream of Queer Fishes (A Modern Prose Idyll)

H.S.S., 1887

"As the sleeping hound dreams of the chase, so the fisherman dreams of fishes." Thus says the old Greek poet Theocritus;[1] and that the same thing is true even to the present day may be seen from the strange dream dreamed by Joe, the Commissioner of Fisheries, as he was on his way to America to manage the fishy business of the firm of Salisbury and Co.,[2] whose service he had lately entered. Now Joe was thoroughly familiar with every kind of bait and fishing-tackle, having been apprenticed as a youth to a grand old fisherman, a regular old piscatorial hand, who carried on certain deep-sea fisheries, in which Joe soon became very expert, and was regarded by his master as his right-hand man. But unfortunately Joe had been always on the look-out for bettering himself, until at last he and the old man had words, and Joe rashly gave a month's notice and left the service in which he was doing so well. After this Joe had set up service on his own account, but finding it did not prosper, and being still very bitter against his old employer, he had become commercial traveller to the rival firm above-mentioned—a post for which he was specially qualified, through his proficiency in the piscatorial language usually known as "Billingsgate."[3]

So Joe was now in mid-voyage for America; and it happened that one night, after thinking a great deal by day of the fishy business on which he was embarked, he dreamed that he had fallen overboard and was surrounded by a vast multitude of fishes. Herring, mackerel, mullet, whiting, turbot, cod, haddock, soles, eels, oysters—every fish, great and small, was there, from a whale to a sprat. It was, in fact, a Public Meeting of sea-fish into which Joe had suddenly entered and just at that very moment the chair (a relic of a sunken vessel) was being taken by the Old Man of the Sea. It was a great annoyance to Joe in his dream to find that there was an Old Man even in this submarine assembly, especially as he seemed to detect in his features a lurking resemblance to his old employer; but what alarmed him still more was the hostile feeling which evidently animated the scaly meeting against himself. Each fish as he sailed round to his seat rolled a glassy eye on Joe with a very sinister expression; but Joe, smart fellow that he was, cocked his eyeglass in return and did his best to stare them out of countenance. Now fish, as we all know, are dumb; so in this Public Meeting there could not, on their part at least, be any delivery of speeches; yet, strange to say, Joe's conscience told him clearly enough what was the object of the meeting and how he himself was concerned with it. These fish were met for the purpose of demanding Home Rule, which he, as Commissioner of Fisheries, had the power of giving them—nay, more, which he had formerly pledged himself to give them (such was the extraordinary conviction by which he was possessed in his nightmare) and had since broken his promise.

Every eye now turned on Joe, and there was a twinkle on the features of the Old Man of the Sea as he invited him by a courteous gesture to reply to the complaints which, though unspoken, were plainly understood. What was Joe to say, and in what language could he address a company of fishes? Suddenly the happy thought occurred to him that he might address them in Billingsgate; so, leaping on an old fragment of a wreck, he poured out one of his vigorous harangues. The upshot of his speech, as far as it could afterwards be remembered—for, as is the way in dreams, it was rather vague and illogical—was that the Home Rule he had once promised them was not what they now demanded, but *Canadian* Home Rule, and that as they were a shoal of rascally, gaping, cold-blooded conspirators, he was now determined not to give them any Home Rule at all. He further managed to recommend them, in choicest Billingsgate, one and all to go about their business—the herrings to be cured, the mackerel to be pickled, the oysters to be scalloped, the cod to be crimped, the lobsters to be potted, and the eels to be skinned alive. Such was Joe's spirited oration; but if the truth be told, he soon repented of it, for he quickly found that he had got a pretty kettle of fish on his hands. So far from knocking under to Joe's bluster, the fish had one and all got their backs—or rather, their dorsal fins—up, and came round him in vast numbers, with the evident intent of making him food for fishes. In vain poor Joe, who now inwardly cursed himself for his temerity, entreated them to shake fins and be friends again, promising to use his influence with his new employer to obtain for each one of them three acres of good submarine pasturage and a sea-cow.[4] But they would have none of it—nothing but Home Rule would satisfy them, and it seemed even that was now to be preceded by the execution of Joe. For at a signal from the Old Man of the Sea, whose face wore a stern yet half-amused expression, a sword-fish appeared on the scene, while two large eels, even more slippery than Joe himself, began to pinch Joe and lead him towards a block of water-logged timber which lay on the ocean floor. It was a fearful moment; for, as is usual in nightmare, Joe could stir neither hand nor foot, and even his voice failed him as he tried to call aloud to his old pals to come to his assistance. However, just as the sword-fish was about to strike, Joe woke with a cry and found himself once more in his comfortable cabin.

Such was Joe's dream, which he remembered for a long time afterwards, the thing which dwelt longest in his memory being perhaps the sort of pitying half-smile on the face of the Old Man of the Sea when poor Joe, in the extremity of his despair, offered three acres and a sea-cow as a substitute for Home Rule which he had first promised and afterwards refused.

■ Chips

H. Bellingham, 1888

It was a very strange world for Chips. He had made up his mind long ago that he, Chips, was a mistake in it. Chips' world was a very small one; it reached from the cellar where he slept to the crossing that he swept, but he found no room in it for him, he was elbowed out of it. Had he known how big the world really is, he might have wandered away to find the place in it that he was intended to fill. But he would not have found it, for the grown men had not yet made up their mind about Chips's place, and until they could do so, Chips must live and die in any out-of-the-way corner. Chips had at one time thought it not unlikely that some one might make room for him, but he knew better now: clearly he was one too many in the world, for the people who had a right to the places in it paid a policeman to keep him away from them. He had his crossing, but he had had to fight for that, and now his broom was worn to the stick, and the weather was often dry for weeks together. When it was not he made a few more halfpence, but he got soaked through and this made him ill, and now he was very ill indeed with a deadly fever and could not go out at all. Another boy, as wretched as he, had stolen his broom and taken his crossing, so that Chips if he could have got out would have found still less room left for him. There was nothing for Chips but to stay where he was, and to this he was reconciled by the companionship of his friend, the frog.

His friend, the frog, had been brought out of the green lanes by the big boys who went out on Sunday mornings to snare birds, and finding its way into Chips' cellar it had become the only plaything of the sick boy.

"Froggie," thought Chips, "is as much out of place as I am." And he felt for the frog the same pity he had always felt for himself.

Chips and Froggie had exchanged confidences, and in the saddest fashion they came to know that for neither of them could there be any more a place in the world.

And one bright morning when the good sun was struggling to send a broken ray down into the dim cellar to cheer the sick boy, Froggie who was lying panting painfully in the hot hand of Chips said on a sudden:—

"Dear little boy, I am very sorry to leave you all alone, but I feel as I did when I changed from a tadpole to a frog, and I know that I am going to leave my frog's body and go away out into the bright air."

And then Froggie's legs went very shaky and all in a minute he turned over on his back and lay very quiet, and Chips knew he was dead.

Chips would have cried over the loss of his companion, but just at that moment he felt as it were an icy hand at his heart which made him shut his eyes in pain, and when he re-opened them he found that he held in his hand instead of the frog a quivering beam of light. And the hand itself was not the poor thin grimy hand he knew, but bright, transparent, and shapely, and all his body had undergone a similar change. The pain was all gone too and he could stand up, and he felt a strange desire to float or fly. Then he became aware of the presence of a beautiful boy, who glittered like a sunbeam and who held out his hand to him, and kissing him on the cheek led him out of the dim cellar. But instead of climbing the broken ladder they floated out into the sunny street, and instead of walking along on the hot pavement they went up high in the air above the heads of the people. But strangest of all, the air, so far as Chips could see, was peopled with a host of bright beings like himself who came and went hither and thither, in and out of the houses, and hovered round the passengers in the streets.

Said Chips, "Pretty boy, I have lived ten years in the world and I never saw anything like this."

"How could you when you were alive?" said the pretty boy, laughing a soft silvery laugh that was like a forest of silver bells ever so far away.

"Pretty boy," said Chips again, after he had thought for a minute or two, "am I dead?"

At this the pretty boy laughed again and still holding Chips's hand drew him swiftly back to the cellar door. And Chips looking in, saw himself looking very white and motionless, and understanding that he was dead, said very solemnly:—

"Poor little boy! He has got out of the way at last. There never was any room for him—And Froggie?" he asked.

"Its spirit is in your hand," said the boy. "No life perishes, but when it quits its earthly being, it roams the wide universe as a tender thought of the great God. Let it go, to do its appointed work."

Chips loosed the spirit of the frog which rapidly sped away.

"What is God?" said Chips.

It had been nobody's business to teach him anything, and Chips in seeking that place in the world which he never could find, and in thinking what mistake he must be altogether, had not got so far as to imagine Who had put him there. He knew what churches were, but of their purpose nothing. Hard-pressed for a night's lodging he had sometimes looked longingly at the deep-vaulted porches, but the iron rails kept him out. Churches were not for Chips. Of Book and Priest and what they wonderfully taught, he knew nothing. Ancient Record and adored Mystery, which were lights to the groping soul of Man, had not penetrated the crowd that wedged in Chips, else might he have caught a faint glimmer of the truth that flows there, reflected in all distorted fashions by men's vain fancies.

"God is Love".

"And what is Love," asked Chips.

Have you never heard men of soft lives with gracious women and sweet children round you, have you never heard the agonised cry of hundreds of thousands of yearning for the hand and voice and the kiss of love? The cry of these desolate, of poor women, of poor children! While you sit with your pockets buttoned polishing some rough poor law, content to be ruled by a demon called Expediency, these are wading through the sloughs of infamy and misery, fainting for a word of sympathy, lost for want of an outstretched hand. Are they nothing to you, these gloomy men and these hollow-cheeked women, the sisters of despair, these white-faced children born into hell?

"What is Love?"

His glittering guide drew him gently downwards till they hovered only a few feet above a crowded thoroughfare.

"Why, there's my crossing," cried Chips, "and there—there's that Bob that stole my broom."

And stooping he kissed the dirty cheek of the wretched Bob.

"Ah!" said Bob, turning up a grateful face towards the sun, his cheek flushed with Chips' kiss, "we do get the sun for nothink."

That was Chips' first love-lesson in God's other world.

■ Nobody's Business

Elihu, 1892

Upon a heap of straw, in a bare garret, a man lay dying. It was in the heart of one of the richest cities in England. Within a stone's throw of where he lay in that last dread struggle the merchants' exchange was thronged with busy traffic, and huge wealth flowed in an unmeasured stream; and this man was dying—of hunger. Whilst they bought and sold there, making an increased babel of sound, he lay in silence yonder. His glazing eyes, moving wearily over the mouldering walls of the den in which he lay, lighted for a moment upon the window in the roof, and upon the glimpse of blue sky that showed through the broken panes. A sudden gleam of recollection passed over his sunken face, and he lifted a hand towards the light, but it fell back again upon the straw. His eyes closed, and a faint smile passed over this feature, and he lay in perfect stillness. Was he dead? No, not dead yet; but he was dying. Upon one side of him, unseen, knelt Death, gazing on him with dread, sightless sockets, with grizzly, unseen hand choking his breath. Upon the other side knelt Hunger, weird and gaunt, with cruel, sunken eyes, crueller than death. And there, unseen of mortal eye, whilst the blue sky lay overhead, and the noise of children at play, and the busy hum and rattle of a city's traffic floated up from the streets below, these two dealt with him after their kind; and there was no hand reached out to save him.

There was a merchant on 'Change as this man lay dying who, in one stroke of business, made a thousand pounds, and went home and thanked God, and was glad, for his wife and children's sake, that things prospered with him. But he knew nought of the man who lay dying of hunger within a stone's throw of him as he buttoned up his pocket book;[1] did not know that Hunger and Death were staring in grim silence so in to the face of a fellow-man.

Ten thousand men and women passed to and fro on that day, near where the man lay dying of hunger, but none turned aside down the narrow court, nor mounted the dark stairway that led to his garret. It was no business of theirs; they had each their own affairs to look after. They did not know the silent tragedy that was being enacted so near them; it was nobody's business to know. He had had money once, and friends and wife and children, but his wife and children were dead, and his money gone through a stroke of misfortune that beggared him, and in his old age he was cast helpless upon the world; but that was nobody's business. He struggled hard for a time to maintain himself, but who would employ an old man when young ones offered? The sickness came, and misery, and abject want; but, of course, that was nobody's business, and now he lies dying, and it is nobody's business yet. And nobody knows; it is nobody's business to know.

He lies yet perfectly still. His eyes remain closed. The faint smile has not died away from about his mouth. He is dreaming of his childhood. He sees the old homestead, the trees, the river, the high hills stretching away height beyond height until they merge and melt into the blue sky. See! His lips move. He "babbles o' green fields."[2] It will soon be over.

A quiet shudder passes through his frame, and with a sigh the soul is freed of its burden. The grinding, heartsick misery is past now and forgotten. Death loosens his hold of the man's throat, and Hunger glares no longer on him; they had "business" with him, but it is done now; and silent and unseen they pass on their way and leave him lying there; and with fixed glassy stare he lies stark and rigid, unwept, unpitied, unhelped, unknown. As a man might have died in the midst of some lonely and uninhabited desert, so has he died in the midst of a city full of people.

No man saw it; but in the broad daylight an angel came down from God and passed over the city—over the thronging streets, over the factories and churches, and houses and shops, and, entering the garret where the man lay dying, the angel, too, knelt beside him. But Hunger and Death were not afraid of the angel, for they were also God's messengers. The angel watched and waited, and when their work was done he bore upward the spirit they had freed from its weary bondage and stood with him at the foot of God's throne; and God wiped away all the tears from his eyes.

And God said, "It is a great city from whence thou art come; are there many that dwell therein that serve me and keep my commandments?"

And the man bowed his head in the presence of God's glory, and answered Him, and said, "Yes, Lord; and they have built many temples in Thy name."

And God said, "I have given them much possessions and great riches in that city, and yet thou hast died of hunger and want."

And he answered, "Yea, Lord; for I was solitary and alone, and where so many strive together I could find no footing, because that I was stricken with age and infirmity, and none had compassion on me."

When he had spoken it was so, that there was suddenly a great silence in heaven for a space, and the songs of the unnumbered multitudes were hushed.

And God said, "What hearest thou?"

And he answered and said, "I hear the cry of them that are oppressed, and of them that suffer hunger and want, and that are in bitterness, rising up from all the land."

And God said, "Even so, for their cry cometh up before me continually. This people build temples in my name, and worship me with their lips, but their hearts are far from me. I have opened wide mine hands for nought, and poured out riches upon this nation, so that there has been none like unto them until now in all the earth, and lo, they strive greedily together as men that have not enough; and they that lay hold my riches say, 'Lo, it is all ours; it is we that have made it; and as to these multitudes they are not truly our brethren. God has created them poor to labour for us.' And they blindly seek every man in his own gain and are heedless of one another, even as the beasts that perish."

■ The History of a Giant

BEING A STUDY IN POLITICS
FOR VERY YOUNG BOYS
Keir Hardie, 1893

Chapter I.

Once upon a time a young giant set out to seek his fortune. He travelled from the east westwards and wherever he went Beauty and Plenty followed in his train. Cities sprang into being through his efforts; deserts were turned into fertile plains and fruitful gardens. He fought down with his sharp sword all hindrances to his onward progress, and even captured the elements and made them his servants. Wind, water, and fire were his handmaidens, and the whole of creation living or dead, were his to command. The young giant's name was Labour. It so happened that Labour one day in his wanderings met in with a strong hulk of a fellow who was much given to scheming and had a perfect hatred of work. This fellow's name was King. "Look here," said King to Labour, "you are a fine brawny chap, but you have no brains. You need someone to think for you; someone to improve your manners and give tone to society. Now I am just the man for that kind of job. I am good-looking, and know how to dress well, and besides am a good hand at law-making, and will undertake the whole job for my keep."

Good-natured Labour did not quite see what he wanted with laws or tone to society, but he thought there must be something in it, and at any rate he could afford to give King a trial; so without bothering his head much about it he told King to go ahead and he would see that he was well fed and cared for.

For a time Labour did not feel the extra burden much, but by and bye King began to breed a rather numerous family, whom he named Earl, Lord, Baron, Count, Knight, and so on, and these too had to be fed by Labour. As they grew up they began, as children will, to quarrel one with the other, and finally to grumble at their father not allowing them to help him to boss Labour.

By degrees their clamour grew so loud that King in order to keep them quiet, agreed to form them into a committee, and not to do anything without consulting them. Then there was great rejoicing among the family, and they named the agreement Magna Charta. The committee they called Parliament. Labour was pleased as Punch,[1] thinking that now he would be relieved of some of his burden.

But it was not so. The first act of the committee was to declare that the land (which had hitherto belonged to the whole people) all thereon and therein, was theirs. Labour found himself burdened as sorely as ever, and he puzzled himself a good deal as to the meaning of it all. Sometimes he had a glimmering suspicion that his troubles were connected with King and his offspring, and on these occasions Labour would lay about him lustily, and frighten the whole crowd who pretended to rule him; but by one method or another means were always found to quieten him, and even to fix the burden of maintaining King and his offspring more firmly upon his shoulders. By this time children innumerable had grown up round Labour and some of these began to develop wonderful gifts. They dug in the earth for metals and turned them into fresh giants and fed them on coal. The wonders these new giants— Machinery was their family name—performed are too wonderful for my poor powers of description. Suffice it to say that those who created them, being clever and unscrupulous, claimed ownership over them and added the burden of their upkeep to those already borne by Labour. Not only so, but the wealth these new giants produced was pocketed by their owners, who in time grew to be very wealthy. And now Labour was in sore straits. He was not allowed to grow food on the land without asking leave and paying high tribute. He could not perform work without the aid of the new giants, and these were all owned by the clever men who had created them; and so perforce he had to hire himself out as a slave to the men who owned the land or to those who owned the machines, and take in return what they were pleased to give, which was just sufficient to keep him in food of the poorest kind. Then the owners of the machines who called themselves capitalists said to Labour, "All your troubles arise because we are not allowed to sit on the committee which makes your laws. Help us to get seats thereon and then—well you will see what you will see." Labour good natured and stupid as of yore shouted hurrah! and set to work to frighten the King and his committee, so that in alarm they granted his demand and admitted the manufacturers and a few of their friends to a share in the selecting of the committee, and this they called the first Reform Act.[2]

Labour was not long in discovering that the Capitalists on the committee, which was now named a Parliament, were even worse friends to him and his than the old gang had been. The two sets, who had hitherto been called Landlords and Capitalists, and who saw that unless they could hoodwink Labour he would speedily drive them both out, hit on the ingenuous method of dividing themselves into two camps, the one named Liberal and the other Tory, and having a sham fight occasionally which would amuse Labour and perhaps keep him quiet. The plan succeeded admirably, for not only was the attention of Labour diverted from his own interests, but he and his offspring began to take sides at these sham fights, and take as much interest in them as if they had been real battles in which their interests were at stake. For it was always a characteristic of Labour to do whole-heartedly whatever he undertook, and his good nature made him an easy prey for the unscrupulous. But while he and his fellows fought with might and main to secure victory for their side, Capitalist and Landlord winked at each other and chuckled hugely. By and by Labour began to weary of his thankless task of fighting sham battles, especially as the fun began to pall on him. But his masters were alive to this possibility, so that they threw into the ring a prize called Franchise which was to be fought for, and which when won would infallibly end all Labour's troubles. After fifty years of fighting, Labour succeeded in winning the Franchise prize, and then he found it was of no use since he was expected to use it in helping Liberal to fight Tory or *vice versa*, but not to help himself in fighting both Liberal and Tory. The poor fellow scratched his towsy[3] head a good deal over this. His slow wits told him there was something wrong somewhere, but where it was he could not exactly discover. Here he was in possession of a vote, and had good Liberals and good Tories ruling him turn about, and yet somehow he got no "forarder." It was all very strange, and the big strong easy-going chap sat down one day to have a big think over a smoke. He then made a discovery which I will tell you about.

Chapter II.

This is what Labour discovered. He could not live without food, and to procure food land was necessary. All the land however was owned by people who did not till it themselves, and would only allow others to do so on condition that the produce was handed over to them. Thus for his food supply Labour was dependent on the landlords. He required clothing, furniture, and a house to live in; but the machinery and materials for making these were owned by the capitalists, who claimed the whole of the clothing and furniture that was made, and all the houses that were built. What puzzled poor Labour was that he tilled the land, ground the grain, tended the herds, wove the cloth, made the shoes, and built the houses, and after he had done all this he and his children were often hungry, and naked, and homeless, whilst others who did not toil had more than they could consume. He found that the men who called themselves Tories and the men who called themselves Liberals and Radicals in Parliament were the owners of these things, and whether they were Liberal or Tory they jealously guarded their own interests, and combined their forces in exploiting Labour. Besides, while Labour had been toiling and moiling in mine, and mill, and forge, and factory, these cunning fellows had been making themselves secure by laws passed to protect themselves, and had organised a force of police, and an army of soldiers, to prevent him from laying hold of the work of his hands. It was clear to Labour that the men who made the laws and administered the affairs of the State were the masters of the situation, and that until he and his children made and administered the laws for themselves they were helpless. When Labour made this discovery he at once hied off to his friends, or at least those who profess to be his friends at election times—to wit Liberal and Tory—and in the innocence of his heart pointed these things out to them and said:—

"Now, my friends, I want to put your friendship to the test. I am working beyond my strength, and my food is so bad that my children cannot live upon it; my housing accommodation is such that my poor wife is heartbroken in trying to keep things clean and nice. On washing and cleaning days and other such occasions, I am glad to escape to the publichouse where I learn habits which are not good for me. I believe I can change all this if only you allow me to make and administer the laws. Will you therefore please clear out, both of you, at next election, and make room for some of my sons?"

This proposition seemed to afford much amusement to Liberal and Tory, whereat Labour began to scowl ominously. This so frightened them that they began, with one consent, to prove to Labour how outrageous his proposal was.

"Here," said Tory, "is your enemy, Mr. Liberal, who wants to split up this glorious empire of yours, pull down all your churches, destroy your foreign trade, bury law and order, and otherwise injure your interests. No, good Labour, first help us to beat this dangerous fellow and then, my dear sir, you will see what we will do for you."

But Liberal, who was more cunning, took Labour aside and said, with many mysterious nods and winks:

"You know what an enemy Tory is to Labour. Before you can fight him we must first perfect the machinery of Government. You must have improved registration, payment of members of Parliament, you must disestablish the church, and do a great many more things, and if you help us to do all these and beat Mr Tory, then you will see what we will do for you."

"But," said Labour timidly, "might we not use the machinery of Government as it is now, at least to the extent of its powers, to ease the burden which Landlordism and Capitalism imposes on me and mine. If we had waited for cloth till the mule and the spinning jenny[4] and the steam loom[5] had been invented, we would still have been naked savages; and if we had waited for the linotype machine[6] before we had printing, we would still have been writers of letters, and might have raised writing to the fine art which it has become in the hand of Cunninghame Graham."[7]

This was spoken sarcastically, but no sooner was it said than both Liberal and Tory shouted:

"That name, ah! now we know the secret of this discontent. Beware, foolish Labour, that ye be not led into the wiles of this crafty scheming man. We will not, no, we cannot, stand quietly by and see you led to your destruction by him. We are your friends. For hundreds of years we have proved that we are, and we will stand between you and the ruin which lies in the Labour Party."

This outburst so frightened Labour that he was glad to make his escape and think the matter over slowly and quietly, which he did. And having done so the truth became clearer to him, which he had almost forgotten, that having empowered King and his offspring, who were now known as Liberal and Tory, to rule over him, the only remedy for his present evil was to rid himself of them, and as they had given him a vote, for his amusement as they thought, he would use that to undo the mischief which the carelessness of generations had brought upon him. True, his children were very much divided; some being misled by the honeyed promises and fine words of Liberal, and others frightened by the alarms of Tory. Still giant Labour made up his mind that either he must be master in his own household or die in the attempt. He saw that it was necessary to gather together all those who were on his side and who could be relied upon, so that when next Liberal and Tory came out to have their sham fight he might fall upon both and perchance destroy them. To this end he built a huge tent, the centre pole of which was set in Bradford,[8] a village amidst the hills, and inhabited by the kindliest and trustiest of Labour's children, while its ropes had fixings in the fertile plains of the sunny South of England, in picturesque Cornwall, amidst the rugged hills of bonnie Scotland, and in the valleys of gallant little Wales. The good and the true are flocking thither in a great and goodly company. They are of all ages and both sexes. The learned, the wise, the fair, the witty, are all there furbishing their arms and strengthening their hearts for the coming conflict. And ah! such hearts as theirs! Hearts that can and do throb with indignation at the suffering which injustice produces; eyes that grow bright when children are happy, and sadden and grow moist at the sight of the waifs and strays of the slums. And throughout all that camp there is the joy of service and pleasurable thrill of comradeship. And there enthroned sits Labour. Heavy and worn and weary, with grizzled locks, and gnarled fingers, and bent back; but the fire of youth is beginning to flash from his eye occasionally, and the spirit of revolt against brutality to fill his soul. He looks on wistfully, and wonders whether this gathering throng will really free him. He knows by sad experience the forces which are arrayed against him; but, strong in the consciousness of the justice of his cause, he awaits the coming conflict.

■ ■ ■

There endeth my story. Some day you will read for yourselves the result of the battle. But you too will be called to take part in it. On which side will you be?

High over the Tent of Labour a gallant standard is floating proudly in the breeze, and on it are emblazoned in letters of gold the words—

"INDEPENDENT LABOUR PARTY,"

and under that flag will be found those who love Humanity more than material greatness.

■ The Man without a Heart

F. J. Gould, 1893

There was once a man who had no heart. You would not have known it by looking at him. His eyes were bright, his arm strong; and he was always well-spoken. But, if you had watched him closely, you would have noticed some strange things. There were never any tears in his eyes, even when he saw a little babe lying dead in its cradle. And he never laughed, for people without hearts do not know what it is to be merry. And he never blushed if he did wrong or made a mistake.

Yet all the time he wished to have a heart. He thought he ought to be like other folk, and feel a beating at his breast, and be able to cry and laugh, even though he had heard that people sometimes died of a broken heart.

So he went to a Wise Old Man who was a Wonder-worker. The Wonder-worker lived on a mountain, where he kept goats, and made butter and cheese. He was sitting in front of his cottage door one evening when Silvanus approached; for Silvanus was the name of the man who was in search of a heart. Silvanus told him all his story, and then said:

"Though I look like a man I am no better than a marble statue. Tell me how I may become like other men. It seems foolish to dwell among them, and yet not feel as they do, and never weep or smile. What shall I do to win a heart, even if it be only one that breaks?"

"There are many things I can do for you," answered the old Goatherd. "I can make you a king, or a scholar, or an artist, or a man of wealth, or a woodcutter—"

"Not a woodcutter!" cried Silvanus. "A man who fells trees all day long has no time to weep or laugh. His heart, if he has one, can only be small."

"Then," replied the Wonder-worker, "would a king's crown suit you better?"

"Yes," said Silvanus; "a king sees many people, and governs great countries, and can travel whither he pleases, and his heart ought to be the noblest in the land."

"When you wake to-morrow morning, you shall find yourself a king."

■ ■ ■

When the next day broke Silvanus leaped from his bed, and hastened to the window. Down below he saw an open square, where the guards of his palace were gathering, in glittering helmets and breastplates, at the sound of the bugle. Beyond that he saw a wide park, in which the deer, with their beautiful antlers, came in and out among the trees.

As he descended the stone staircase, servants in shining liveries walked before and behind. After he had breakfasted, King Silvanus rode out to review his troops. Ten thousand horsemen drew their swords and saluted him, and the people of a great city hung banners across the streets and shouted as he passed along.

Day by day King Silvanus did mighty works. He built harbours for ships, and made towns and markets. When robbers were caught he had them hung, and their heads cut off, and placed over the city gates. And when he thought himself strong enough, he marched his army into the country of another king, and took his land away.

Then he came home, and his heralds played on silver trumpets, and girls strewed flowers before him in the road.

As he could not keep up his splendour without money, he made the people heavy taxes to his officers. But the officers never told him how some of the poor folk wept because they had to pay their last farthing, and had nothing left to buy clothing and food.

With some of this money King Silvanus erected a lofty pyramid, made of huge blocks of granite, and here he meant to be buried when his time came to die. Then he looked round on all his works, and said to himself:

"I have been a good king, and my courtiers tell me there never was so noble a man."

But he could not feel any beating in his breast. He could not be sorry, neither could he feel glad. So he judged that all was not well.

■ ■ ■

One evening he left his palace, and rode away to the hills where the Goatherd dwelt. He found the old man binding up the broken leg of a bleating kid.

The Wonder-worker listened to the King's confession, and said:

"You may try another kind of life. Will you be a woodcutter?"

"Oh, no," exclaimed Silvanus, "I have been on the throne too long to care for such a lowly occupation. But I should like to be a great scholar."

"To-morrow," said the Goatherd, "you shall wake up in a quiet country house, where you will possess a library full of books new and old, and maps, and instruments. And though you will know more than any man living, yet you will go on learning every day."

■ ■ ■

All this came to pass. The servants of Silvanus were now fewer in number, and all they had to do was to keep his house in order, give him his meals, go up and down ladders to fetch books for him from the high shelves, and write out what he told them on large sheets of paper.

Sometimes he would go away and examine the ground to learn how the earth was made, and how coal and iron and lead were formed. Or he voyaged over the sea, and learnt how the fish lived, and the history of seals and whales. Or he mounted in a balloon, and watched the clouds and storms. Then he would return home, and put all his knowledge into books, which were read in many countries, so that he became quite famous. But for all that he never laughed or cried or blushed. Nothing moved within his breast.

At last he grew tired of his books, and left them alone till they were covered with dust.

■ ■ ■

Again Silvanus went to the old Goatherd. The Wonder-worker was putting up a shed to shelter his goats when the winter brought snow, and no grass could be cropped on the mountain side.

"So you are still without a heart," said the Goatherd, when Silvanus came up and greeted him. "What say you to being a woodcutter?"

"Not yet," answered Silvanus. "I have been writing books, and my hands are white and delicate, and are not fitted for such rough work."

"Will you be an artist?" asked the Wise Man, "and carve statues, and paint pictures? I see you are willing. To-morrow you shall wake up an artist."

■ ■ ■

It came to pass as the Goatherd said. Silvanus had beautiful white stone fetched from Greece and Italy. With chisel and mallet he cut figures of men on horseback, and hunters slaying lions, and boys wrestling, and women braiding their hair, and mothers carrying little children, and girls weaving garlands of flowers. These statues were put up at street corners, and in temples and gardens, where people could flock round and admire them.

Silvanus also painted pictures of battles, and feasts, and reapers cutting corn, and weddings and funerals, and sunshine and storm. Rich men paid large sums of money for his pictures, and had them watched at night lest they should be stolen. But while many tongues praised the artist, and students came from far and near to copy his works, Silvanus was all cold and dead within. He could not even feel glad when his work was applauded.

■ ■ ■

One day Silvanus threw down his chisel and mallet, and took the road to the Goatherd's cottage.

The old man was giving milk and butter to a woman whose husband had died, and who was much troubled to obtain food for her little ones. The Goatherd was smiling kindly, and the woman's eyes were wet with tears.

When the widow was gone, Silvanus said:

"I am obliged to seek your help again, for I have failed again. I think the reason must be that I have not mixed enough with the common people, for their hearts seem to feel more than the hearts of the people of rank. When I was a king I was always surrounded by soldiers, and I have heard it said that it would never do for a soldier to have too much heart. When I was a scholar, I had little to do with anything but books. And when I was an artist, I used to observe people so that I might copy them for my statues and pictures; but I did not say much to them, or stay long in their homes."

"And what do you wish me to do now?" replied the Goatherd. "Shall I change you into a woodcutter?"

"Ah, no," cried Silvanus. "I have painted pictures of woodcutters, but I do not want to be one myself. Give me riches, and I will go and help the poor, and serve them every day of my life till my heart begins to beat."

"To-morrow you shall be rich," said the old man.

■ ■ ■

And this came to pass also. Silvanus went wherever he saw ragged children and broken windows and scanty furniture. As he drove about in his carriage, he flung money into the beggars' outstretched caps. If he saw a boy or girl with bare feet, he had them to the nearest bootmaker's, and fitted them with a stout pair of boots. When a poor man's house was burned down, Silvanus would give him a purse of gold to repair the loss. In time of famine great crowds of hungry men and women and children stood outside his gates, and Silvanus fed them all. Sometimes he would go out at night, and peep into doorways, to see if any poor creatures were sleeping on the steps, and he would have them carried to a warm and cheerful place.

Then he would stop to thrust his hand under his comfortable fur coat, and was greatly puzzled when he found there was no gentle pulse in his breast.

After many days he fastened down his money-boxes, and resolved once more to present himself before the Wonder-worker.

■ ■ ■

The Goatherd was teaching the widow's sons how to milk the goats and make cheese.

When he saw Silvanus, he inquired:

"Have you no more money?"

"Yes," said Silvanus, "plenty of money. But I have no heart."

"Perhaps you think of turning woodcutter?" quoth the old man. "But woodcutters have very little money to give away."

"That is true," spake Silvanus. "But I have gone high without gaining what I sought, and I cannot do worse if I take the lowest place."

The Goatherd looked earnestly at Silvanus, and then said:

"To-morrow you will wake in a thatched cottage by the forest. Your wife will rise at dawn to prepare you a bowl of porridge. You will see the axe hanging behind the door. Your children will bring you your dinner, and you must eat it while you sit on the trunk of a tree. If you do not find a heart there, you never will find one."

■ ■ ■

All this likewise came to pass. The next morning the air was cold and frosty. Silvanus would rather have lain in bed, but his wife called to him that there was another day's work to be done before he would be paid his week's wage, and he must be up betimes. So he swallowed his porridge, seized his axe, and hastened into the forest. There, all the morning, and all alone, he plied his heavy tool. He was getting very hungry when he heard the shouts of his little son and daughter, who were bringing father his dinner. Silvanus waved his hand to them.

Suddenly the girl slipped on some damp leaves, and fell. Silvanus hurried to lift her up, and quite forgot his hunger while he bound up her bleeding forehead.

As he did so, he felt a fluttering in his breast and something moist in his eyes. After the children had gone back he wondered whether, at last, he had a heart.

It was nearly dark when he reached home. When the little ones called out for joy, and his wife came to kiss him, Silvanus smiled. And that was the first time in his life.

Yes, every day he was more and more sure that he had a heart. He felt it beat when he found a neighbour fallen in the snow and benumbed, and carried him home to his own hearth, and made him warm and able to set out on his journey again. He felt it beat when his good wife was ill, and he nursed her, and had so little money to buy the things she needed.

And once he felt it almost break when his little son was drowned in the stream that ran through the forest. But even then Silvanus the woodcutter did not wish to have the heart which he had so long waited for.

His home, in time, became more cosy and bright; but he did that himself with his hard toil and his axe.

And, after all, he was still a rich man, still an artist, still a scholar, and still a king.

He was RICH, for he had a heart, and his heart loved others, and was glad to be loved.

He was an ARTIST, for he cut trees with care and skill, and he took pleasure in the beautiful flowers of his cottage garden, and the pretty ornaments he made for the walls.

He was a SCHOLAR, for he knew how to live and work, and how to act justly towards his neighbour, and he loved to watch and talk about the birds and beasts and trees of the forest.

And he was a KING, for he was master of himself, and earned his own livelihood and was not afraid to look all men in the face.

■ A Terrible Crime

Dan Baxter, 1893

"I give you a kiss as a guarantee that I shall tell it in such a manner as will save you all tragic emotions."

"Well, proceed," said she.

"In the days," began he, "when the desires of a free people were controlled by men and women who were trained from their infancy to deal only with results, and could not, or would not, look deeper than results, there lived a man who became so wealthy that neither dukes, nor even clergymen could stand upright in his presence.

"Philip Bullion was his name, He lived in a house like yours, surrounded by lawns, and gardens, and forests, and streams.

"The source of his wealth was a mystery to the whole people, until one day the report was flashed all over the world, along with the intelligence that he had been found dead on a couch.

"In each some two hundred rooms of his palace, and some outhouses, were found plaster casts and dies, and machinery of all kinds for producing every coin of the various realms of the world. Not only that, but in four of the largest rooms were found expensive photographic and lithographic[1] plants adapted for the making of all descriptions of paper money.

"Ha!" cried everybody. "Then Bullion was a maker of counterfeit coins, and notes—a forger, a scoundrel."[2]

"All that I know," cried one man, "is that had it not been for Bullion, a great many thousands of our respectable people would not be such large shareholders in the railways, mines, and other company concerns formed for the purpose of sucking the life's blood out of the people."

"Now it happened that the free, generous, good-natured slow-to-anger people, who lived in those days, were so careful to guard against any tampering with their money stamps, that they had proclaimed forgery to be one of the vilest of crimes, and punishable even by death.

"It had been made a crime to order that individuals might not become possessed of the power to command the products of the people's labour, without giving products of their own labour, or some appreciable equivalent in exchange.

"So, when it became known that Squire Bullion was not only a forger, but had made thousands of men and women wealthy by giving them gifts of the money he made, and in that way enabling them without working to procure what the people had sweated to produce, the whole population turned out, and in their wrath were preparing to burn his body, when a more highly developed man than the rest stepped on to a chair and cried:

"Friends, listen to me before you set fire to these tar barrels.

"You are cursing Mr. Bullion and his satellites. Why?

"Yesterday you would have gone, hat in hand, to beg of them to be allowed to toil for your means of life!

"Is it because thousands of your fellows have, without your knowledge, accumulated large stocks of forged coins and notes, and are going amongst you with them, forcing you to supply them with food and clothing, forcing you to dig coal and make gas and build fine houses, and repair these fine houses, and provide them with all the other comforts and luxuries, without their doing a hand's turn in the work?

"Is that what makes you angry? Is it because they are giving you *forged* money instead of good money for the products of your labour, that you are so angry?

"If these thousands, tens of thousands of idle men and women, gave you what you call 'current' coin of the realm, what would be the difference to you, you asses?

"Would they not be idle all the same?

"Would you not be doing all the work that requires to be done without their help, forged money or good money?

"There are many thousands giving you good money.

"Lord Rent, Squire Tax and Messrs. Profit and Interest and their flunkies are giving you good money. They do no work. You do it all.

"Why, then, curse Forgery without at the same time cursing Rent, Profit and Interest?

"Your anger, friends, shows that you have got a glimpse at the truth. You shall have a good look at it.

"See. Who is that at the castle door? He is no other than Squire Bullion. He was not dead—only pretending. He filled his rooms with the implements of the forger, in order that you might rise in your wrath against a system that permits a poor type of men and women to live lives of idleness and wrong-doing by obtaining large stacks of your money-stamps—the token of your labour—in a way that is no more honourable than it is to forge them.

"Mr. Bullion is a convert to the truth—to Socialism—and has taken this way of showing it to you."

"Yes," cried Mr. Bullion, stepping from the door of his castle, "I have taken this way of showing you why you should take charge of your own affairs; why you should take back to yourselves the money, the keys to the products of your own labour; the articles you, as a people, put your stamps upon; the articles that were intended to measure the value of your own labour, but which have not served that purpose since your fore-fathers introduced the use of coal and machinery. These money stamps (the money) are your own. You must take them. And if you do not need them, to make ornaments for your wives and daughters, place them under the control, the distributive control, not of irresponsible anybodies who have the cunning and greed to do nothing but keep them from your reach; place them under the control, the distributive control, of men and women whom you can trust to distribute them in such a way as to make sure that every man, woman boy, and girl, shall not only get what they need, without crime, but also be placed in a position that will enable them to give what Nature alone will force them to give."

◼ Tom Hickathrift

Edited by Joseph Jacobs, 1894

Before the days of William the Conqueror there dwelt a man in the marsh of the Isle of Ely whose name was Thomas Hickathrift, a poor day labourer, but so stout that he could do two days' work in one. His one son he called by his own name, Thomas Hickathrift,[1] and he put him to good learning, but the lad was none of the wisest, and indeed seemed to be somewhat soft, so he got no good at all from his teaching.

Tom's father died, and his mother being tender of him, kept him as well as she could. The slothful fellow would do nothing but sit in the chimney-corner, and eat as much at a time as would serve four or five ordinary men. And so much did he grow that when but ten years old he was already eight feet high, and his hand like a shoulder of mutton.

One day his mother went to a rich farmer's house to beg a bottle of straw for herself and Tom. 'Take what you will,' said the farmer, an honest charitable man. So when she got home she told Tom to fetch the straw, but he wouldn't and, beg as she might, he wouldn't till she borrowed him a cart rope. So off he went, and when he came to the farmer's, master and men were all a-thrashing in the barn.

'I'm come for the straw,' said Tom.

'Take as much as thou canst carry,' said the farmer.

So Tom laid down his rope and began to make his bottle.

'Your rope is too short,' said the farmer by way of a joke; but the joke was on Tom's side, for when he had made up his load there was some twenty hundred-weight of straw, and though they called him a fool for thinking he could carry the tithe of it, he flung it over his shoulder as if it had been a hundred-weight, to the great admiration of master and men.

Tom's strength being thus made known there was no longer any basking by the fire for him; every one would be hiring him to work, and telling him 'twas a shame to live such a lazy life. So Tom seeing them wait on him as they did, went to work first with one, then with another. And one day a woodman desired his help to bring home a tree. Off went Tom and four men besides, and when they came to the tree they began to draw it into the cart with pulleys. At last Tom, seeing them unable to lift it, 'Stand away, you fools,' said he, and taking the tree, set it on one end and laid it in the cart. 'Now,' said he, 'see what a man can do.' 'Marry, 'tis true,' said they, and the woodman asked what reward he'd take. 'Oh, a stick for my mother's fire,' said Tom; and espying a tree bigger than was in the cart, he laid it on his shoulders and went home with it as fast as the cart and six horses could draw it.

Tom now saw that he had more strength than twenty men, and began to be very merry, taking delight in company, in going to fairs and meetings, in seeing sports and pastimes. And at cudgels, wrestling, or throwing the hammer, not a man could stand against him, so that at last none durst go into the ring to wrestle with him, and his fame was spread more and more in the country.

Far and near he would go to any meetings, as football play or the like. And one day in a part of the country where he was a stranger, and none knew him, he stopped to watch the company at football play; rare sport it was; but Tom spoiled it all, for meeting the ball he took it such a kick that away it flew none could tell whither. They were angry with Tom, as you may fancy, but got nothing by that, as Tom took hold of a big spar, and laid about with a will, so that though the whole countryside was up in arms against him, he cleared his way wherever he came.

It was late in the evening ere he could turn homeward, and on the road there met him four lusty rogues that had been robbing passengers all day. They thought they had a good prize in Tom, who was all alone, and made cocksure of his money.

'Stand and deliver!' said they.

'What should I deliver?' said Tom.

'Your money, sirrah,' said they.

'You shall give me better words for it first,' said Tom.

'Come, come, no more prating; money we want, and money we'll have before you stir.'

'Is it so?' said Tom, 'nay, then come and take it.'

The long and the short of it was that Tom killed two of the rogues and grievously wounded the other two, and took all their money, which was as much as two hundred pounds. And when he came home he made his old mother laugh with the story of how he served the football players and the four thieves.

But you shall see that Tom sometimes met his match. In wandering one day in the forest he met a lusty tinker that had a good staff on his shoulder, and a great dog to carry his bag and tools.

'Whence come you and whither are you going?' said Tom: 'this is no highway.'

'What's that to you?' said the tinker; 'fools must needs be meddling.'

'I'll make you know,' said Tom, 'before you and I part, what it is to me.'

'Well,' said the tinker, 'I'm ready for a bout with any man, and I hear there is one Tom Hickathrift in the country of whom great things are told. I'd fain see him to have a turn with him.'

'Ay,' said Tom, 'methinks he might be master with you. Anyhow, I am the man; what have you to say to me?'

'Why, verily, I'm glad we are so happily met.'

'Sure, you do but jest,' said Tom.

'Marry, I'm in earnest,' said the tinker. 'A match?' ''Tis done.' 'Let me first get a twig,' said Tom. 'Ay,' said the tinker, 'hang him that would fight a man unarmed.'

So Tom took a gate-rail for his staff, and at it they fell, the tinker at Tom, and Tom at the tinker, like two giants they laid on at each other. The tinker had a leathern coat on, and at every blow Tom gave the tinker his coat roared again, yet the tinker did not give way one inch. At last Tom gave him a blow on the side of his head which felled him.

'Now, tinker, where are you?' said Tom.

But the tinker, being a nimble fellow, leapt up again, gave Tom a blow that made him reel again, and followed his blow with one on the other side that made Tom's neck crack again. So Tom flung down his weapon and yielded the tinker the better on it, took him home to his house, where they nursed their bruises, and from that day forth there was no stauncher pair of friends than they two.

Tom's fame was thus spread abroad till at length a brewer at Lynn, wanting a good lusty man to carry his beer to Wisbeach went to hire Tom, and promised him a new suit of clothes from top to toe, and that he should eat and drink of the best, so Tom yielded to be his man and his master told him what way he should go, for you must understand there was a monstrous giant who kept part of the marsh-land, so that none durst go that way.

So Tom went every day to Wisbeach, a good twenty miles by the road. 'Twas a wearisome journey, thought Tom, and he soon found that the way kept by the giant was nearer by half. Now Tom had got more strength than ever, being well kept as he was and drinking so much strong ale as he did. One day, then, as he was going to Wisbeach, without saying anything to his master or any of his fellow servants, he resolved to take the nearest road or to lose his life; as they say, to win horse or lose saddle. Thus resolved, he took the near road, flinging open the gates for his cart and horses to go through. At last the giant spied him, and came up speedily, intending to take his beer for a prize.

He met Tom like a lion as though he would have swallowed him. 'Who gave you authority to come this way?' roared he. 'I'll make you an example for all rogues under the sun. See how many heads hang on yonder tree. Yours shall hang higher than all the rest for a warning.'

But Tom made him answer, 'A fig in your teeth; you shall not find me like one of them, traitorly rogue that you are.'

The giant took these words in high disdain, and ran into his cave to fetch his great club, intending to dash out Tom's brains at the first blow.

Tom knew not what to do for a weapon; his whip would be but little good against a monstrous beast twelve foot in length and six foot about the waist. But whilst the giant went for his club, bethinking him of a very good weapon, he made no more ado, but took his cart, turned it upside down, and took axle-tree and wheel for shield and buckler. And very good weapons they were found!

Out came the giant and began to stare at Tom. 'You are like to do great service with those weapons,' roared he. 'I have here a twig that will beat you and your wheel to the ground.' Now this twig was as thick as some mileposts are, but Tom was not daunted for all that, though the giant made at him with such force that the wheel cracked again. But Tom gave as good as he got, taking the giant such a weighty blow on the side of the head that he reeled again. 'What,' said Tom, 'are you drunk with my strong beer already?'

So at it they went, Tom laying such huge blows at the giant, down whose face sweat and blood ran together, so that, being fat and foggy and tired with the long fighting, he asked Tom would he let him drink a little? 'Nay, nay,' said Tom, 'my mother did not teach me such wit; who'd be a fool then?' And seeing the giant beginning to weary and fail in his blows, Tom thought best to make hay whilst the sun shone, and, laying on as fast as though he had been mad, he brought the giant to the ground. In vain were the giant's roars and prayers and promises to yield himself and be Tom's servant. Tom laid at him till he was dead, and then, cutting off his head, he went into the cave, and found a great store of silver and gold, which made his heart to leap. So he loaded his cart, and after delivering his beer at Wisbeach, he came home and told his master what had befallen him. And on the morrow he and his master and more of the towns-folk of Lynn set out for the giant's cave. Tom showed them the head, and what silver and gold there was in the cave, and not a man but leapt for joy, for the giant was a great enemy to all the country.

The news was spread all up and down the countryside how Tom Hickathrift had killed the giant. And well was he that could run to see the cave; all the folk made bonfires for joy, and if Tom was respected before, he was much more so now. With common consent he took possession of the cave and everyone said, had it been twice as much, he would have deserved it. So Tom pulled down the cave, and built himself a brave house. The ground that the giant kept by force for himself, Tom gave part to the poor for their common land, and part he turned into good wheat-land to keep himself and his old mother, Jane Hickathrift. And now he was become the chiefest man in the countryside; 'twas no longer plain Tom, but Mr Hickathrift, and he was held in due respect I promise you. He kept men and maids and lived most bravely; made him a park to keep deer, and time passed with him happily in his great house till the end of his days.

■ Jack Clearhead

A FAIRY TALE FOR CRUSADERS,
AND TO BE READ BY THEM TO
THEIR FATHERS AND MOTHERS
Keir Hardie M.P., 1894

Chapter I.

Once upon a time two tribes of people inhabited an island in the western ocean. It was said that originally they had sprung from the same parents, but neither of the tribes believed this, the difference between them being too great. One of the tribes was known as Sharpheads, and the other as Dullards. They were of much the same colour and build, and it was this fact which made people say that they must have come originally from the same parents. If they resembled each other in appearance, they differed in nearly everything else. For the Sharpheads were masters and owners of everything. All the land on which the people grew their food; all the roads by which food was taken to the market; all the fine houses, and good clothes, and all the stone which built the houses, and the sheep on whose back grew the wool, and the machinery which turned wool into cloth. All the streams in which were speckled trout and silver salmon; all the birds and hares and rabbits, all the water which fell from the clouds, and all the minerals, such as coal and iron, which were hid away down in the earth till man should need them. In fact, they owned everything which Sharpheads and Dullards alike needed to keep themselves alive. The result of all this was that the Dullards were slaves to the Sharpheads. They did not call themselves slaves, and in fact used to sing that "Dullards never, never, never shall be slaves."[1] All the same they were slaves. For they required food to eat, and the Sharpheads owned all the food; they required clothes to wear in the cold weather, and the Sharpheads owned all the clothes; they required houses to live in, and the Sharpheads owned all the houses. Before the Dullards could either eat or sleep or lodge, they had to obtain the consent of the Sharpheads, which made the Sharpheads the masters and the Dullards their slaves, since the Dullards were bound to do as the Sharpheads wanted or perish of hunger and cold. In fact, thousands did perish in this way—some because they would not do everything the Sharpheads wanted, and others because the Sharpheads had no use for them. It was these facts which made both sides scout the idea that they were drawn from a common stock. The Dullards said it was impossible, because if it were true, they and the Sharpheads would be brothers, and no brother could treat another as the proud Sharpheads treated them, whilst the haughty Sharpheads looked at the poor Dullard with his bent back and cringing voice, begging to be allowed to work for bread, and said "That my brother—ho! ho!! ho!!!".

Chapter II. The Great Pow-Wow
and the Plumduffs and Piecrusts.

Now the affairs of this people were managed by a committee which they called the Great Pow-Wow, and those who were members of the Great Pow-Wow were called Chin Chiners. The Great Pow-Wow, like everything else, belonged to the Sharpheads, but there was one difference. Every five years the Chin Chiners had to come out from the Great Pow-Wow, and wait outside until they got a number of Dullards to hoist them on their shoulders and carry them back in. The Dullards could carry anyone in they pleased, either one of themselves or one of the Sharpheads, and if they had carried Dullards in then all the land, and the machinery, and the food, and the fine houses, would have been theirs, since whichever tribe sat in the Pow-Wow was the master of the other. But the Sharpheads had guarded themselves against being turned out— or thought they had, by dividing themselves into two divisions one of which was named Plumduff,[2] because it was thought to be very dull and stupid, whilst the other was named Piecrust,[3] because it made promises intending to break them when necessary. When Dullard carried Plumduff into the Great Pow-Wow all the Piecrust Chin Chiners spent the next five years in telling him he had made a mistake, since the Plumduffs were too stupid to do anything for them. The poor Dullards hearing this said without ceasing, would come at last to believe it, and when the five years were up they would carry in the Piecrusts and leave the Plumduffs out. Then the Plumduffs would spend five years in pointing out how many promises the Piecrusts were breaking and say they are deceiving you, we never deceive you, send us to the Great Pow-Wow and see what nice Chin Chiners we will make. Poor stupid Dullard with his short memory would believe this tale also, and at the end of five years he would leave the Piecrusts out and put the Plumduffs in. What he forgot was that Piecrusts and Plumduffs were Sharpheads, and that no matter what they called themselves so long as they ruled the Great Pow-Wow they were the masters and the Dullards were their slaves.

POOR STUPID DULLARDS!

(More next week. Telling how little Jack Clearhead taught the Dullards sense, and what happened).

Chapter III.

Now it so happened that on the Island was a cave, in which dwelt the good fairy Common Sense. She had at one time dwelt with the Dullards, but they had driven her from them, and now she dwelt in a cave. Near the cave was the house of a Dullard who had married a clever wife, and who had one little boy named Jack. One day Jack's mother sent him with his father's dinner, and off the brave little fellow set, whistling and singing all the way. After his father had eaten his dinner he said, "Here, Jack, there's a piece for you, which you can eat on the way home."

"Thank you, dad," said the little fellow, as he tied the bread up in a handkerchief and started for home.

On the way home he came to a spring, and sat down to eat the piece of bread which his father had given him. After eating a little while he felt thirsty, and knelt to drink of the cool water as it welled up out of the ground. When he lifted his head he saw a little old woman standing by the spring, and she said, "Good afternoon, little boy, would you give me a piece of your bread, I am hungry?"

"Oh, yes, lady," said Jack, and he gave her all he had.

Now this old lady was a fairy, but Jack did not know this; and she was willing to befriend him. She had asked him for a piece of the bread which his father had given him, to see if he was greedy or no. When she found that he was willing to share his bread with her she was very much pleased.

She had an old bag with her which did not look as if it had anything of value in it, and Jack was greatly astonished to see her take out of it a nice, bright, bright sword.

"Now, little boy," said the old lady, "you have been kind to me, and in return I am going to be kind to you. Take this sword, and whenever you are going to fight, take it with you and use it. You will find yourself in many battles as you grow older, and this sword will always help you to victory so long as you remain on the side of honesty and truth, and when you are going to use it, you must always repeat the following rhyme:—

"Sword, sword fight for me,
I belong to the I. L. P."

And then before Jack knew where he was she had disappeared.

Chapter IV.

I have not yet told you that a number of great giants lived in the land in those days, and these, like everything else, belonged to the Sharp-heads, who used them to oppress the people. One of these giants was named Mon-o-Poly, and the other Com-pe-Tition. Cruel monsters they were, who devoured men and women and great numbers of little children every year. The Sharpheads knew how valuable these giants were to them, and so they pampered and fed them and got the Pow-Wow to pass laws to protect them. The poor Dullards had grown so used to these giants that they actually believed them necessary to their welfare, and allowed them to trample on their bodies and bruise and maim and kill them, and even went so far as to feed them with the bodies of their own children. Every year these giants killed thousands of grown-up people, and ate hundreds of thousands of little children, some of them only a few weeks old.

Com-pe-Tition was the eldest son of Mon-o-Poly, and it so happened that if the parent was destroyed the son could not live without him. Mon-o-Poly was an ugly, big-bellied monster, with fat cheeks, low forehead, small eyes, short legs, and flat feet. He waddled like a duck when walking, and spoke with a rasping voice, like the noise of sharpening a saw. His greed was insatiable, and he clutched everything which came within his grasp. His pockets were full of stones, and his hair was matted with earth which he had stolen. A dirty, gluttonous monster, who was hated by everybody who saw him.

Com-pe-Tition was of a different kind of ugliness. His eyes bulged out of his head, his cheek bones were high, and when he opened his big thick lips he showed a mouthful of cruel teeth always white and glistening. His arms and legs were long and bony, and for feet and hands he had claws like a bird of prey, with which to tear his victims in pieces. Sometimes these two used to sing after this fashion:—

Mon-o-Poly—"Bang the coffin, beat the bones,
   Break the skin and drink the blood;
How I love the shrieking tones

Of the children of the flood.
    Ha, ha, ha!
    He, he, he!
Happy, happy giants are we."

Com-pe-Tition—

"Tear the children limb from limb,
    Break the hearts of man and wife;
Tell them to repine is sin—
    Death to them to us is life.
    He, he, he!
    Ha, ha, ha!
Jolly merry giants are we."

One day as they were singing together, little Jack suddenly appeared before them.

Chapter V. Jack Gives the Giants a Drubbing.

"Hullo!" said Jack, going up to the two ogres as they sang their ugsome[4] ditty, "what are you two fat heads up to?"

"Ho! ho! ho!" laughed Mon-o-Poly, "you are a fine imp, you are, to call us names. Do you know that if I liked I could get Com-pe-Tition to tear you with his claws and then crunch your bones with his teeth. So, ho! ho! ho! get out of my way at once."

"Aha!" said Jack, "you think you could, but you just try it on," saying which he drew his sword, and brandished it within an inch of Mon-o-Poly's nose.

"That's mine!" shrieked Mon-o-Poly. "Everything is mine, and unless you give it me at once I will eat you, I will."

Jack meets a Giant with two heads.

Fig. 3. Illustration for "Jack the Giant-Killer" from *Routledge's Nursery Book* (1865). Stories of tiny Jack, Jack the Giant-Killer, Jack and the Beanstalk, or Jack Clearhead had great appeal for young readers. Private collection © Look and Learn / Bridgeman Images.

"All right greasy pouch," laughed Jack, "you try and take it from me," and he began to frisk round them, hitting Mon-o-Poly with the flat blade and touching Com-pe-Tition in a tender place with the point. The two began to dance, and howl like tamed bears with pain and anger, trying all the time to lay hold of their tormentor. "How do you like that, old big belly?" said Jack, as he gave Mon-o-Poly a smack on the stomach with his sword.

"Ow, ow, ow!" yelled the monster, "hit him Com-pe-Tition, hit him."

"All right dirty head," said Jack, "I'll give him leave to hit me when he catches me."

Com-pe-Tition here made a desperate lunge at the little warrior who, jumped aside and the monster fell headlong to the ground. Jack laughed and began to cut off with his sword some big carbuncles which were growing on Com-pe-Tition's nose.

"Ow, ow," yelled the giant, "come and help me daddy, come and help me. He's cutting me all to bits."

"Ow, ow," answered Mon-o-Poly, "he's hurt my stomach, my poor stomach, oh my stomach."

"Now," said Jack, as he turned to go off, that's a touch of what you will get every time we meet.

For, my pretty sword and me
Belong to the I. L. P.
We've joined the Crusaders,
To wipe out all traders
In crime and tyranny.

Each Dame and Knight agree
To fight big ghouls like thee,

We'll harry and worry
And some day will bury
'Tition and Mon-o-Poly."

Saying which he went home leaving the giants nursing their sore places, and cursing him and his I. L. P. sword.

Chapter VI. The Giants Hold a Council and Get a Fright.

After the two giants had rubbed their sores down a bit, they went home to their big castle to plan out their revenge on Jack. All the way they kept talking about what they would do with him, when they caught him.

"Yes," said Com-pe-Tition, "but how are we to catch him? That I. L. P. sword of his is a warmer. If we could only break that or steal it from him, we'd be all right. And then wouldn't we give him beans."

"I wonder," said Mon-o-Poly, "what I. L. P. means. Let me see now; it might mean 'I Like Porridge.'"

"Nonsense," growled Com-pe-Tition, "only Scotchmen like porridge. It means 'I Like Power.'"

"Or 'I Love Property,'" said Mon-o-Poly.

"Well, whatever it means, said the youngest of the two, we must get hold of it, or it will take both power and property away from us, and our friends the Sharpheads."

"Look here," said Mon-o-Poly, "you know these dogs we keep, I mean the Press Curs, let's set them on to this Jack. They'll soon tear him to pieces, see if they don't."

"Well," said Com-pe-Tition, "if they don't tear him to pieces, they'll keep snarling and barking at him, so that the Dullards will say 'There must be something amiss with Jack, or the giants' curs wouldn't bark and snarl at him so,' and then Jack will be left alone, and will be powerless."

"Ha, ha, ha, he, ho, ho, he, he, he!" laughed both giants together, "'pon our breeches pocket that's a capital plan," and having settled the matter to their own satisfaction, they went home in great glee and called a meeting of Sharpheads and told them of their plan.

"Capital," said one of the Sharpheads, "and while the Press Curs are barking we will lay some traps for him to fall into, and then we will seize his sword and break it and he will be harmless again."

"Very good," said another Sharphead, "and if the dogs and the traps both fail, we will try to buy the sword from him. For, he whispered, if the Dullards get to know that Jack Clearhead has a sword like that, and that he can defy us, they may ask him to be their leader, and them what will become of us."

At this thought the giants and Sharpheads began to tremble so violently that the castle walls were shaking, and an old owl who had her nest among the ivy, got so frightened that she began to sing out "Te-wheet-oo, te-wheet-ooo."

When the giants and Sharpheads head this, they thought it was Jack after them with his sword, whereupon they all began to beg for mercy, thus:—

O Master Jack, good Master Jack,
    Don't hurt us now we pray,
We'll call the dirty Press Curs off,
    And what you ask we'll pay.

Here's Com. and Mon. and Sharpheads all,
    Your faithful slaves will be,

Tag, Rag, and Mob, and Parson Bob,
Will join the I. L. P.

"Tu-wheet, tu-weet, tu-woo-oo-oo," sang the owl, more frightened than ever.

"Why," said Mon-o-Poly, "it's only the owl we've been scared of."
Whereupon they all felt so much ashamed, that they slunk home to bed.

Chapter VII. Jack Has Another Fight, and Rescues a Pretty Maiden.

One day Jack was out walking by himself, thinking and planning how to fight the giants successfully. His heart was very sore and heavy when he looked upon the poor Dullards and saw how they were robbed and cheated by the Sharpheads, and how cruelly the giants Mon-o-Poly and Com-pe-Tition treated them, and what annoyed him most was that if the Dullards would only combine their forces and carry the right kind of Chin-Chinners into the Pow-Wow they could free themselves from the Sharpheads and bury Mon-o-Poly and Com-pe-Tition and all the other giants a thousand leagues under the sea, there to be food for the fishes. Thinking of all these things, poor Jack was very sad, and though he had a brave, strong heart, yet he was at that moment quite downcast.

He had wandered for miles over wood and hill, through deep glens, and by the side of clear streams, and though the birds were singing their best and the streams were making their sweetest music, Jack had no ears for them that day. Just as he was thinking about turning back he heard a loud scream. Jack stood still to listen, and again and again the scream was renewed, and appeared to come from a thick wood, and for the first time Jack noticed that he was in the neighbourhood of the giants' castle. He at once felt for his sword, and drawing it rushed in the direction from whence the sound proceeded.

On and on he ran, and the screaming was becoming fainter, and Jack feared he would be too late to make a rescue, when he suddenly entered a green glade right in the heart of a thicket, and there he saw a beautiful maiden who had been bound by Com-pe-Tition and Mon-o-Poly, and who was being carried off by a number of other giants, while the Press Curs followed, trying to tear pieces out of her dress, which was trailing on the ground. Evidently the maiden was much exhausted by her struggles, and her screams were low and faint. At her head was a big bully named Ig-no-Ramus. Like all bullies he was a rank coward. His head was a turnip, his body a big bladder full of wind, and his legs a bundle of rushes loosely tied together. Super-Stition had hold of her feet, and he was a long thin scarecrow, tied up with white bands and red tape to keep himself from falling to pieces. Besides, a number of little elfs and goblins, the children of the giants, were running here, there, and everywhere. With a great shout Jack rushed at the lot and sent his sword right through Ig-no-Ramus' body, whereupon all the wind rushed out and he collapsed on the ground, where he lay moaning helplessly. Super-Stition, the moment he saw Ig-no-Ramus fall, gave a shriek and ran off as fast as his rickety legs could carry him, while the Press Curs, the elfs and Goblins, and even Mon-o-Poly and Com-pe-Tition followed suit, and thus Jack found himself alone with the maiden, who had fainted through fear and exhaustion.

Chapter VIII. Jack Falls in Love.

When Jack had brought the maiden round by means of water from a spring, she fairly overwhelmed him with gratitude for his brave rescue. She told him her name was Social-Ism, that her mother's name was Truth and her father's Justice, but that the giants had carried these off and locked them up in the dark dungeons of their castle, and she had not seen them for years. At first they did not think of taking her, because she was such a tiny creature she could do no harm. But when she began to grow into womanhood they became alarmed when they found that she was as strong as her father and mother put together. Then they said to one another—

"O, ho! If Truth and Justice were free they would soon kill us. Here is their daughter, Social-Ism, who is growing as strong as her parents, and unless we capture her and lock her up beside them we shall be destroyed." And so they had watched her when she went out for her morning walk, and would have captured her but for Jack's timely intervention.

Jack had never seen anyone so beautiful as Social-Ism, and the more he looked at her the more beautiful she seemed. Her clear eyes and flowing hair, and the fearless, frank, open way she looked at him made him feel that she was as good as she was beautiful. Her dress was pure white, whilst a bright green sash encircled her waist, and on her head was a red cap, from underneath which her wavy hair fell all round her shoulders.

"But," said Jack in astonishment, "had you no friends to protect you from these monsters?"

"Oh," she answered, "there were some who thought they loved me, and even called themselves by my name. But these only cared for me because they thought I could give them more bread and perhaps more beer. Their love was too gross to satisfy me, and so I fled from them, and thus fell into the hands of the captors from whom you have just rescued me."

Falling on one knee Jack drew his sword, and raising it over his head said—

"Then, accept me as your knight, and I pledge you to fight your cause against all comers; to rescue your parents, Truth and Justice, from the dungeons where they lie; and finally to overthrow the giants Mon-o-Poly and Com-pe-Tition and all the hateful brood who follow in their train, and in the end to make you queen of this empire, even as you now are queen of my heart."

"And I," said Social-Ism, placing her hand on his shoulder and gazing steadfastly into his eyes, "plight my troth to be leal[5] and true to you, until your great task is accomplished.

"And see," she said, taking a rosette from her breast and fastening it on his, "wear this for my sake. The three colours which you see are Red, White and Green, representing, Red for myself—Social-Ism, White for purity, and Green for nature.[6] Go forth among the Dullards and try and get them to wear your colours, and fight under your standard, for when my parents, Truth and Justice, have been freed, then the wrongs of the Dullards will soon be put right."

"Then," said Jack, "come with me to my home and share its humble protection, and when I grow weary or down-hearted in the great battle which lies before me, I will look upon you and remember your parents in the dungeon, and my arm shall be strengthened and my heart nerved, for any struggle which the future may have in store."

And so arm in arm, linked together for life, these two set out for home, as full of happiness as it is possible for two human beings to be.

Chapter IX. Preparing for the Fight.

As the time drew near for the Chin-Chiners to break up their Pow-Wow and ask the Dullards to carry them back in again, the Plumduffs and the Piecrusts were as usual pretending to vilify each other, and all the while they were meeting in private and laughing at the way they were fooling the Dullards. For, as I have already told you, the Chin-Chinners were all Sharpheads, and it was because of this that their power over the Dullards was so great. But one thing alarmed the Sharpheads seriously. Jack and his fair companion Social-Ism had been at work among the Dullards, and had been telling them of the way in which the Sharpheads and the Giants had carried off Truth and Justice, who had always been on the side of the Dullards, and had tried to kidnap Social-Ism also. But the Dullards were hard to rouse. They had almost forgotten that Truth and Justice had ever lived; and, in fact, some of the young men amongst them said that the stories about them were old wives' fables. When, however, Jack brought Social-Ism into their midst they could doubt no longer. Her beauty won every heart; and when she told them in glowing language that their lives could be as beautiful as hers, they were filled with astonishment. But Social-Ism proved her case in this way. "Here," she said, "is old Mother Earth. She is kind to everybody who is good to her. You have only to tickle her skin till she laughs, and as a reward she will fill your barns with golden grain, and your chests with rosy apples. She will send you flowers to make your homes and gardens beautiful, and provide food for sheep and kine[7] and horses, and all manner of useful animals."

"Oh," said the old Dullard, interrupting "we know, Miss, what you are saying is true; but Mother Earth belongs to the giant Mon-o-Poly, and she gives all her good things to him and his friends the Sharpheads."

"Just so, said Social-Ism; but if she belonged to you, you would treat her more kindly that Mon-o-Poly does, and then she would yield you treasures and abundance of good things of which you have never dreamt in your wildest dreams. And then," she continued, "there is the poor, blind giant Cap-i-tal, Mother Earth's husband. He, too, is in bondage to Mon-o-Poly and Com-pe-Tition. You know how they use him to oppress you and your children. But if you destroy Mon-o-Poly and Com-pe-Tition then Cap-i-Tal will become your share, and toil for you morning, noon, and night. Then, instead of children being destroyed by him in smoky, dirty dens, they will be at play all day long in summer, in meadows, among the daisies and buttercups; and their mothers, instead of being the poor drudges so many of them are to-day, will love and be loved, and have their lives filled with sweet joy. And their fathers will again grow strong and brave and fearless, and not be crushed down by grinding toil and the dread of poverty as they are to-day."

"Ah, but," said the Dullards, "how is it to be done?"

"In this way," said Jack, drawing his bright I. L. P. sword. "I will lead you and fight for you against the giants. We will go out together to rescue Truth and Justice from the dungeons where they lie buried. When the time comes to carry Chin-Chinners to the great Pow-Wow, get some of your own men on your shoulders and carry them in, and refuse even to look at the Sharpheads, whether they call themselves the Plumduffs or the Piecrusts. Then when you have done as I tell you, we will make short work of the giants Com-pe-Tition and Mon-o-Poly, for this sword cannot fail when used against them."

At these words the Dullards send up a great cheer and said—
"We will follow you and your I. L. P. sword wherever you lead us."

Then Jack made them kneel down, and with uplifted hand pledge themselves never to carry any Plumduff or Piecrust into the great Pow-Wow, after which he and Social-Ism went home to rest for the great battle which they knew lay before them. Next week we shall see what happened.

Chapter X. The Big Procession.

At length the day of election to the Pow Wow came round. Two great crowds of Sharpheads were gathered on the banks of a stream waiting on the Dullards to carry them over and make them Chin Chiners. One of the crowds were Piecrusts and the other Plumduffs. They were separated from each other by a rope of sand, and a number of them seemed not to have made up their mind on which side of the rope to stand. If they thought the Dullards were going to carry the Piecrusts, they went on to their side; then if they heard that it was the Plumduffs who were to be carried, they rushed back to them. They were determined to be Chin Chiners and would call themselves either Piecrusts or Plumduffs, or anything else, if only they got into the Pow-Wow. Each side had a set of leaders, and these were easily known by the size of their jaw. They were not made leaders because they led anyone, but because they could talk for hours without saying anything, and were able to prove that black was white, and white yellow, when it suited them. These leaders were not easy in their mind this morning, as each knew that if the Dullards did not carry their side over, they would lose the big reward which fell to their share when they won. However, they tried to put on the best face they could, and cheered their followers by showing them a number of small toy balloons, made of coloured paper and filled with gas, which they thought would be sure to bribe the Dullards into carrying their side over. Each of these balloons had a name. On the side of the Piecrusts the balloons bore such names as "One man, one vote," and "Registration Reforms"; while on the Plumduff side the balloons were inscribed "Greatness of the Empire," "Lor 'n order," and the like.

Suddenly the sound of music was heard in the distance, and as it drew nearer the Sharpheads saw to their dismay that it was a great procession of Dullards. On it came, the bands playing, the people cheering, whilst flags and banners streamed down the wind. On, on they came, and as the tramp, tramp of their feet sounded nearer, the Sharpheads became terribly afraid, and whispered one to another, that, perhaps the Dullards were coming, not to carry them over, but to drown them in the stream. After a hurried talk between the leaders, it was agreed to send for Mon-o-Poly, Com pe-Tition, and all their friends, including Blind Cap-i-Tal, Igno-Ramus, Super-Stition, the Press Curs, and all whom they could reach. It so happened that all these were in a wood close by, and were soon on the spot. Their friends the Sharpheads formed a semi-circle, like a horseshoe, of Plumduffs and Piecrusts, and put the giants in the middle where they told them of their fears.

Meanwhile the Dullards were drawing nearer, and now it could be seen that riding at the head of the procession were Jack Clear-head and Social-Ism. Jack rode a strong limbed horse, whose glossy coat was jet black, whilst Social-Ism was mounted on a milk white pony. They rode right up till they came to where the giants were sprawling on the grass with all the Sharpheads standing round. Putting a silver trumpet to his lips, Jack blew a blast which was heard for miles, and which brought the procession to a halt. Standing up in his stirrups, Jack gave his orders. The head of the procession was to march round in a semi-circle till they met the end of the one formed by the Sharpheads, by which time the tail-end of the procession would have reached the other end of the Sharpheads' horse shoe, and thus the two would form, when joined, a complete circle, in the middle of which would be the giants near their friends the Sharpheads, whilst Jack and Social-Ism would be on the side of the circle formed by the Dullards.

Chapter XI. The Great Pow-Wow.

When the Dullards had all marched into their places and the circle had been completed, Jack blew a blast on his silver bugle, and a large body of men marched forward. They were of all ages and looked very sad and wan.

"Who are you, and what do you seek?" asked Jack.

"We are workingmen and we seek work that we and our children may have food to eat," they answered.

Turning to the Sharpheads, Jack said—

"Here are thousands of strong men willing to work. Your giants, Com-pe-Tition and Mon-o-Poly will not allow them to work. If you are returned to the Pow-Wow what will you do for them?"

"We will give them these balloons to play with," said the leaders of the Piecrusts and the Plumduffs as they threw the balloons in the air, keeping hold however of the thread to which they were tied.

"We don't want balloons to play with," shouted the men fiercely, "we want work."

"Retire," said Jack, and the men fell back into their places.

Jack again blew a blast on his bugle, and another great company moved forward to where he and Social-Ism stood. There were old men and old women and children, and they were all dressed alike in a dirty ugly uniform.

"Who are you?" said Jack, "and what do you want?"

"We," answered a gnarled old man, speaking for the old people, "have worked for the giants Com-pe-Tition and Mon-o-Poly all our lives. They have stolen from us all the wealth we have made by our toil, and now, when we are too old to work for them any longer, they have shut us up in huge prisons where they make our lives miserable. We demand that part of the wealth we have made by our work shall be used in making our old age happy."

"And we," said a pale, sad-faced wee lassie, "are the children of those whom Com-pe-Tition and Mon-o-Poly have slain, and we demand that the murderers of our fathers and mothers shall themselves be put to death."

"What have you to say to that?" asked Jack.

The giants were all shivering with fear and dread as the Sharphead leaders again threw up their balloons and said, "We will give them these to play with."

"Balloons are for the children of the rich," said the wee lassie who had already spoken, "they are but mockeries to the pauper child."

"And an insult to the aged poor," said the gnarled old man.

"Retire," said Jack, and again he blew on his bugle, and this time a great multitude moved forward of all ages, from the child of eleven to the old man and woman of fifty and sixty.

"Who are you?" said Jack, "and what do you want?"

"We," said their spokesman, "are all slaves to Mon-o-Poly and Com-pe-Tition. We work and work and work and all we make belongs to the Sharpheads. In fact, we are called the working classes. We work hard, we live hard, and we die hard, and we demand to be freed from the toils in which Com-pe-Tition and Mon-o-Poly have bound us, so that we may be our own masters, and enjoy the fruits of our labour."

"What have you to say to that?" asked Jack.

Here the Sharpheads fell on their knees and began saying piteously, "Oh, please, good working man, do carry us over the stream into the Pow-Wow, and we will give you all these balloons to play with and some more beside. Please do carry us over, oh please do, good, kind, clever working men."

But the workers laughed and said, "It isn't balloons we want, it's Freedom." And a little boy with soiled clothes ran up to one of the Sharphead leaders, and ran a pin into his balloon, which burst with a loud report, whereat all the other boys laughed and cheered.

"Retire," said Jack, and the crowd fell back. Taking Social-Ism by the hand, Jack led her forward and said,

"Tell these people here who you are and what you want."

"My name," she said, "is Social-Ism. These monsters, pointing to the giants, have carried off my parents, Truth and Justice, and have buried them in their dungeons. Before they did so, there were no strong men out of work, there were no children hungry, there were no paupers, and there were no slaves like these around us. I demand that my parents be released at once."

Here all the Sharpheads began to hold up their balloons and say, "Oh, Miss, we will give you all these and more; we will give you a crown and a coronet to play with, but oh please tell these people that your parents are dead, and then we will give you anything you ask."

Social-Ism looked at them contemptuously, and said quietly, "Yes, you will give me anything I want save what I do want. Free my parents and then I may treat with you, not before."

"Now," said Jack, speaking to the Sharpheads and the giants, "you have heard all the Dullards and Social-Ism have to say. We are going to carry our own men over to the Pow-Wow, and we now give you warning to clear out or take the consequences. If you are not all gone by two o'clock this afternoon, we shall drive you out at the point of the I. L. P. sword."

Chapter XII. The Great Fight.

The Sharpheads were terribly alarmed at the turn events had taken. The Dullards outnumbered them by twenty to one, and were besides thoroughly united, while amongst the Sharpheads were a good many who were only too pleased that at length the power of the giants was to be broken. Several times the Sharpheads held consultations among themselves to see whether they could not devise some means of again dividing the Dullards into two separate camps. They made new balloons in which they stuck all kinds of fancy names, but when these were offered to the Dullards, they only laughed at them. "Give us your giant to destroy and then we will make friends with you, but not till then," was the reply which the Dullards kept sending back. And so the hour of two o'clock drew near when the great battle was to begin. Blowing a great blast on his silver bugle, Jack called for silence and thus addressed the Sharpheads:—"We have," he said, "no desire to fight unless we are driven to it, and if you will promise to destroy your giants who kill our children, and our men and women, and rob the living of everything which makes life beautiful, then we can all live in peace."

But the Sharpheads would not agree to this. They said one to another, "The Dullards may be stronger than us in numbers, but we have all the food and all the clothing, and by-and-bye they will be glad to come to us for supplies."

"Yes," said Com-pe-Tition, "and if you stick by us, we will stick by you, and all fight together." Just as he said these words the great town clock pealed out the hour of two."

"Now friends," said Jack, "the hour has come for you to strike for freedom. Let every good I. L. P. soldier, and every brave crusader be true to duty, and may God defend the right."

With these words he blew a blast on his silver bugle, and the battle began. First of all a band of boys and girls armed with beautiful, bright swords rushed right into where the giants were, and began to prick them with their swords. The giants had great clubs which they wielded right and left, but being themselves so large, whilst the crusaders were small, they kept hitting and hurting each other, without once touching the crusaders. The giants feeling themselves pricked all round, soon lost their temper, and began to lash with their great clubs in all directions. But as they only hit one another the more, the crusaders laughed in their glee and pricked them all the more. Super-Stition swung his club round his head, intending to kill, at least, a dozen crusaders, but instead he hit Igno-Ramus a blow on the nose, which made him mad with rage and pain. Thinking it had been done wilfully, Igno-Ramus brought his club down with crushing force on Super-Stition's head, whereupon these two took to pummelling each other. Mon-o-Poly and Com-pe-Tition were all the while hopping about like hens on a hot gridiron, as the crusaders kept prick, pricking them with their sharp little swords. At last they could stand it no longer, and called on the Press Curs to come and tear their tormentors to pieces. Just as the Press Curs were about to do so one of the crusaders whistled, and a fine black retriever rushed into the fray. Round his neck was a collar on which were the letters I. L. P. "Toby, do your duty," said the crusader who had whistled, whereupon Toby, with a bark of delight rushed upon the Press Curs, and soon had them running in all directions with their tails between their legs, and howling with pain.

Meantime the Dullards had borne down upon the Sharpheads, and by sheer force of numbers were pressing them down towards the river. Many of the poor fellows when they saw that instead of being carried over into the Pow Wow, they were about to be drowned, began to beg for mercy. Still they kept fighting on, whilst Jack was everywhere amongst them with his sword working terrible havoc. Just as the Sharpheads were struggling to keep their footing on the muddy edge of the stream, the same old woman who had met Jack at the spring and given him the I. L. P. sword, suddenly appeared, and holding up both hands said, "Stop!" in a voice so loud that it was heard all over the field of battle. Everyone looked to see where the voice came from, and as they did so the old clothes fell from the woman, whilst she plucked a mask from off her face, and revealed herself as a bright, beautiful fairy.

Chapter XIII. The End.

"Who are you?" said Jack, "and what do you want?"

"My name," she said, "is Good Will, and I am cousin to Social-Ism, as my parents, Progress and Love, were brother and sister to Truth and Justice. Whilst you have been fighting, I have been to the giants' castle and freed Truth and Justice from their dungeons; and see, there they come over the hill arm in arm with Love and Progress."

At this the Dullards sent up a great cheer, whilst Social-Ism ran to meet and welcome her long lost parents.

"And now," said Good Will, "I will at once put an end to this strife. Hitherto I have been powerless, as I could not act until the

Dullards proved willing for a change. Now that they have done so, I am able to help them."

Going up to the giants, she addressed Igno-Ramus and Super-Stition. "You two," she said, "must die. You need not howl so, as you can't escape. However, I will not only make your end painless, but will bring you to life again in a new form. Drink this," she said, "It is a mixture called Edu-Cation." The two poor giants took the potion with trembling hands and drank it up at a draught, where-upon small tongues of flame broke out all over them and consumed them. But in another two moments they began to grow again, and when they had assumed their full shape, they were no longer the hideous things they had formerly been, but strong, healthy, and clean limbed, and clad in bright garments.

"In future," said Good Will, "you will be known as Know-Ledge and Sci-Ence."

"Now," said Good Will, "where are the Press Curs."

Toby, when he heard the question, sat up on his hind legs and laughed and wagged his tail. It turned out that they were ashamed of the part they had played, and had gone and drowned themselves in the stream.

"A good riddance," said a gnarled old Dullard.

"And now," said Good Will, waving her fairy wand over Com-pe-Tition and Mon-o-Poly, "I command you to change from cruel gi-ants into genial fairies. You, Com-pe-Tition, shall in future be called Emu-Lation, and you, Mon-o-Poly, shall become Collec-Tivism."

At this, the giants seemed to disappear for a moment and then re-appear. But a great change had taken place in their appearance.

Emu-Lation had no longer claws and big teeth, but looked gen-tle as a lamb and strong and brave as a lion. Mon-o-Poly, too, in his new form of Collec-Tivism, had been turned into a kind, wise, thoughtful looking giant, who, in a few minutes, had all the crusaders round him and was feeding them with buns and nuts and fruit and candy galore. His supply seemed inexhaustible, and, whilst the crusaders were helping themselves, Collec-Tivism was bestowing all manner of good things on all the Dullards.

Turning last of all to Blind Cap-i-Tal and Mother Earth, Good Will said, "For a long time you two have been the slaves of the giants. Now I hand you over to Social-Ism, who will be kind to you and not use you to oppress people as you have been used by your old masters."

On hearing this, Blind Cap-i-Tal was so overjoyed that he caught hold of old Mother Earth and, after hugging her to his heart, insisted on dancing a jig with her there and then.

"And now," said Good Will, speaking to the Sharpheads, "the giants being all destroyed or changed, there is no longer any reason why you and the Dullards should not become brothers again. Forget the past, work together in the future, for if you don't there will be no place here for you."

"Brothers," said the Sharpheads to the Dullards, "can you forget and forgive the past?"

"We can, we can," said the Dullards; "Let the dead past bury its dead."

Whereupon the two classes began to mingle together and make plans for their future welfare.

"And now, last of all," said Good Will, "I make Truth and Justice, Progress and Love a council to settle all future disputes. When the council can't agree, Social-Ism and myself will then be called in to decide differences. As for you, Jack, your sword will be kept as our most valuable possession, and you yourself will, of course, marry Social-Ism."

"And, please, what am I to get," said Toby, sitting up on his hind legs and looking very comical.

"Oh, you good dog, you will get a bone," said Good Will, whereupon Toby wagged his tail and said, "Bow-wow-wow."

THE END.

■ The Four Friends

A TRANSLATION
Anon., 1894

A raven, perched upon a branch of a tree, looked down attentively upon a man who was busy setting nets to catch birds, and strewing grain to entice them. Now, among the birds, the raven is held to be wise, almost as wise as the owl; and besides, grain does not offer much temptation to a raven, who likes juicier food; so this one sat among the green leaves, and thought to himself: "Ah, no! They don't catch me so easily. I'll look on and see what happens."

Presently there came along, circling up in the air, a flock of pigeons. They were hungry, and the grain looked enticing, so they alighted quickly and began pecking it up. But the net fell down upon them, and they were all imprisoned under it, and fluttered about quite helplessly.

Then the leader of the pigeons said: "It is no good for each of us to flutter about in this manner, let us all try together, and at the same moment, to fly up; perhaps we may be able to raise the net and carry it with us." So they all lifted their wings at the same moment, and away they went, net and all.

Now, the raven, who had been watching, and who had remarked that the pigeons were successful because they had united their efforts, flew after them to see what would happen next. The pigeons had alighted in a stubble field, and the raven went on to a tree and listened. The pigeons were holding a council, and one of them said: "I have an old friend near here, a field mouse; I will call him, that he may gnaw at the net." So the mouse was called, and his little sharp teeth soon did the work; the pigeons came out through a hole in the net, and, having thanked the mouse, flew joyfully away.

The raven, who had been looking on all this time, thought to himself that a true friend was a very good thing to have, and he called the mouse and told him how much he should like to be friends with him. But the mouse answered: "Oh, no! that cannot be; in a very short time your natural desire to eat me up would overcome your friendly feelings, and I should just share the fate of any other mouse at your hands."

However, the raven persuaded the mouse that indeed that was not his intention, and in the end they lived near together without mistrust, and were very happy. But, after a while, they began to find that there were not quite so safe as they could wish. The raven had seen a man with a gun, and the mouse fancied there was a weasel about; so the raven said to the mouse: "If you will let me pick you up by that long and slender tail of yours, we will both go to the place from whence I came; then we shall be safer, and I have another friend there, a tortoise, to whom I will introduce you."

The mouse was willing, so away they went through the air. Certainly the mouse felt rather giddy, much as you or I might do if we went up in a balloon; but she made the best of it, and very soon had dug herself a new home at the root of a tree. The raven lodged in the branches; the tortoise came out of a shallow pool near, and they all three lived in peace and harmony.

One day, as they were sitting together and chatting over the way in which things were going in the great world, suddenly a stag came swiftly along, and halted by the edge of the pool and looked around. The tortoise and the mouse, both easily frightened, hurried off, the one into the water, the other into its hole; but the raven spread his wings and flew up to the topmost branch of the tree to see if any huntsman was coming after the stag. As he saw no one, he said to the stag: "Do not be afraid, there is no danger here; no huntsman has ever yet been in this part of the wood. If it so please you, you can make your home here. There is plenty of green grass and fresh water, and I think that is all you need." When he had said this, he called to the mouse and the tortoise to come back, which they did, and added their persuasions to the raven's that the stag should stay among them. Again the stag looked around; the grass was fresh, the water sweet, and the place seemed secure from dangers. He chose himself a bed where the moss was dry and thick, and they were all good friends.

But, one evening it grew very late, and the stag, who had been out for a stretch, did not come home. His friends grew anxious, and feared some misfortune had happened to him, so the raven flew off to see, and very soon he came to a place where the stag was lying helplessly on the ground, being caught in a snare. As quickly as possible he flew back to the mouse and the tortoise, and they all set their wits to work to find out the best way of helping. And the mouse said: "Take me up again by my long and slender tail, and carry me to the place where the stag lies; I will soon gnaw through the cords which hold him."

That was no sooner said than done, and the mouse gnawed away.

But the tortoise did not like being left behind and giving no help, so he crept along till he also arrived at the place. When the raven and the mouse saw him, they began to upbraid him that he had been so foolish as to follow, and the raven said: "Now, what is to become of you when the sportsman comes? The stag can bound away, I can fly, the mouse can creep into a hole, but what will you do? Your pace is slow, and you are too heavy for me to carry; I shall not be able to save you." Whilst the raven was still speaking, the sportsman came in sight. He wanted to know whether anything had been caught in his snares. But before he quite arrived at the place the net was gnawed through, the stag sprang swiftly off, the raven flew away, the mouse crept into a hole, but the poor tortoise stood still and trembled in every limb. The huntsman felt very vexed to have lost so valuable a spoil as the fine stag, but in order not to go home quite empty-handed, he picked up the tortoise and put it in his game bag; and then, being tired, he sat down on a sunny bank and fell fast asleep.

The raven, the mouse, and the stag, who had all been watching from a safe distance, thought that they saw now an opportunity for helping their comrade, and it was agreed that that mouse should go quickly and gnaw a hole in the game bag large enough for the tortoise to creep out. And this was accomplished, and they were all free and happy and went back to their home by the pool; and in the future, whenever misfortunes came, they all set to work to help one another, for they had learnt the great lesson that

UNITY IS STRENGTH.

■ The Princesses

J. H., 1895 (adapted)

You children who live in the North of England, do you think you really know what grass is like? You have your moors, with the purple heather under the free and open sky; but I think you can hardly know how beautiful the grass meadows can be where there are no tall chimneys anywhere near to shed the black smoke upon them, and where there are heaps and heaps of flowers growing up and blossoming, and changing the green into gold.

In that sort of grass there live little princesses, in tiny, tiny castles, so small that they are quite overshadowed by the grass when it has grown its tallest. When it is morning, and the sun has risen, and the song-birds have woke up, then the princesses wake up, too, and spring out of their little beds. Then they go to the dewdrops which hang on the flowers and say, "I will wash myself in you." And the flowers put in their word and say, "We will be your towels." And when the princesses have washed themselves, they go to the trickling rivulet, and the rivulet stays a moment to say, "I will be your mirror." And when they have arranged their hair, and made themselves look very nice, the little leaves say, "We will be your sunshades."

The princesses are quite glad, and they go a-walking in the meadows. But then the butterflies come up, and they say, "You need not walk, we will be your ponies." And the princesses mount upon the butterflies; and the butterflies spread their wings and fly, above the flowers and above the tall grass, until at last the princesses are just a little tired, and ever so hungry. Then they whisper that they should like to go home. And the butterflies bear them back to their castles. Then come the bees and put honey on their table, and the shining beetles bring up tiny golden spoons with which they eat. Then the grass throws its long shadows, and the birds sing to the princesses so that they go to sleep until the heat of the summer's day has passed.

This is the way in which the mornings are spent; and in the afternoons and the evenings still more delightful things happen in the tiny castles of the princesses of the grass.

It is possible that there may be just such princesses, in just such tiny castles, hidden somewhere under the purple heather. I would advise you children to look and see. The butterflies are flying above it, certainly; and the shining beetles are creeping there; and you will see the dewdrops, too, if you look for them early enough in the morning; so who knows what else there may be?

■ The New Shilling

Dan Baxter, 1895

I do not know how long I may have lain in the womb of the earth; nor am I acquainted with any particulars regarding the men who dug me out further than that they were workers of some kind or another. Neither have I any knowledge as to what part of the world I come from as a piece of silver, nor about what class of workmen carried me to England.

But well do I remember the day when the people of this country, the British nation, gave me my start in life.

When a small shapeless mass I was taken hold of by one of the citizens, and then by another and by several others after them.

This was in what is called the citizens' mint.

I was squeezed until I almost cried, carried on endless belts, dropped, lifted, and put into one machine after another and finally placed before a very nice citizen who took me up and looked into my face.

"What have you been doing to me?" I asked.

The citizen smiled, and, answering, said unto me, "We have been putting you into a form by which you shall be recognised as a coin belonging to the citizens of Great Britain and Ireland. This is their mint you know.

"Turn yourself over and you shall see that we have given you an impression."

"So you have!" cried I, "You have made me beautiful. Am I the Queen?"

"Oh, no," he answered, "You are only a shilling, you are only the least little bit of the Queen.

"The Queen, you know, is the citizens' figure-head, the citizens have made her their figure-head. This is the citizens' symbol of motherhood, to remind us that we are all brothers and sisters, living as one big family in one big house called the United Kingdom.

"And you, my dear shilling, have been impressed with her likeness in order that you shall perform the duty of reminding us of our brotherhood and sisterhood.

"That is the purpose for which you were made.

"Every time you are looked at by a citizen a quiver of brotherly or sisterly love shall be felt in the bosom of that citizen."

I was about to thank this pleasant citizen for informing me that I was one of the citizens' emblems of love when suddenly I heard a great jingling noise and at the same instant found myself found myself being thrown head foremost into a linen bag along with a great many other shillings.

As I lay, almost smothered, near the bottom of the bag, I thought that the pleasant citizen must either have been mistaken or else some great calamity had occurred.

With an endeavour to attract attention I called out, as did all the other shillings in the bag, "We are little bits of your Queen, symbols of motherhood and love."

While shouting and trying to get into more comfortable positions, we were carried away to a place called a bank.

Here we were released by a very nice citizen known as Teller.

He untied the bag and, with less ceremony I must confess than might have been expected from such a nice man, tumbled us head over heels into a drawer beside some other shillings which, from a sanitary point of view, were in a very shocking condition.

But I shall let that pass. In this drawer I lay praying for the time when I was to be sent on my mission of love.

Suddenly a hand seized me, along with some other shillings, and, in less time than it takes to tell, I was dropped into the trousers pocket of a citizen who happened to call to tell the teller it was a fine day.

Off this citizen went, along one street, up another and into another, stopping at a shop, which he entered.

He stood at the counter for some time, and every now and again put a hand into the pocket where I lay, and turned me over in a manner which made me feel that he was about to take me out so as to remind himself, by looking at my face, that he was a member of the Big Citizen Household.

At last he did take me out; but instead of using me as a reminder he tossed me into the air, caught me while falling to the ground and then placed me very gently on the counter.

If you please," cried I, "Will you tell me why I am used in this irreverent manner?"

Both the citizen who had brought me to this shop and the lady behind the counter laughed very heartily at my question.

"Why," answered the lady—a very nice lady she was. "The gentleman wants a book."

"Well," asked I, "Can you not give him a book?"

She smiled most beautifully, looked carefully and long into my face and then, with a loud laugh, raked me into a drawer.

I had been warm through having lain so long in the gentleman's pocket now I was beginning to feel cold and feverish turn about, as if some of the influenza germs had alighted upon me. Indeed I am almost certain that a few millions of the little pests were playing hide and seek all over me, for I felt a creeping sensation. In this state I fell sound asleep in the drawer and dreamt that two citizens, a lady and gentleman, were fondly looking at me and discussing the propriety of converting me into a button or a brooch. It was a delightful dream, for as a button or a brooch I knew that the object of my existence would be realised.

But while the lady and gentleman were still considering the matter another citizen joined in the conversation and from his remarks I learned that I and all the other shillings, far from being emblems of brotherhood and sisterhood were looked upon, and actually used, as mere counters in a cruel game of chance which necessitated the sacrifice of all true happiness among the citizens.

I awoke with a start just at this moment, and found myself in the hand of the lovely lady behind the counter.

"Please make me into a button," I said. "Do not laugh, for I am in earnest. Why, my dear lady, you have no need to use me for such a vile purpose as that of counter. When your little brother at home asks for a biscuit you do not demand a counter from him.

"It is therefore very wrong of you to take a counter from a citizen when he asks you to supply him with a book.

"For, is not this shop but a small room situated here for the Big Household of which you are a member?

"Being a token of love, it is my duty to speak plain.

"What difference will it make to your big family of citizens whether the book a citizen requires should lie in this shop or be taken to his place of abode? The book will be no less a book no matter where it lies in our big house.

"Nor will I be any less a shilling if you cease to use me other than as a button.

"And the citizens of whom you are one shall be no poorer.

"No, my dear lady, they shall be all the richer by your giving a book to any brother or sister who may be richer by the amount of pleasure and knowledge supplied by the book.

"And they shall be richer in their lives if I be used as a button.

"Sweet lady, I have just learned that thousands of your dear brothers and sisters have no counters, and that, merely because of this, they cannot obtain the books that are lying idle and useless in this little shop; that thousands upon thousands, merely because they have no shillings, cannot get the use of the houses built by their brothers and themselves, nor the furniture and furnishings lying idle in other shops, and which were also made by themselves; that thousands of your brothers and sisters forming your big household, merely because they have no counters, are without the necessaries of life that the mere want of counters prevents them from building proper houses for themselves, making proper furniture for themselves, and scratching the earth to obtain proper food for themselves.

"My lovely lady," I continued, taking advantage of her sweet disposition to listen, "Adam and Eve did not use counters, nor did Robinson Crusoe on his desert island. The absence of counters did not prevent the fruits and flowers from growing in the lovely garden of Eden, not the goats from giving milk on Crusoe's island.

"Bees do not use counters. Indeed, sweet lady, if bees were to adopt counters the worker bees would soon become half-starved, sickly, insects; for the drones who do no work would soon get hold of the shillings and live upon the honey produced by the slavish workers.

"You may not have thought of it, but it is a fact that the healthiest monkeys enjoy all the necessaries and pleasures of life without the aid of counters.

"But that they enjoy life in their glorious forests and gardens is a truth which you, possibly, cannot understand, for you have only seen them living artificially in cages. I think you are no more capable of understanding the true reason for its imprisonment. For you, yourself, in the life you live in this shop, are even further away from your natural element than are the caged monkeys.

"You are a caged prisoner, trained from your infancy, like a showman's dog, to be obedient to others, and that irrespective of your longings to get away to the fields, the woods, the glens, the sea shore; there to meet your lover or engage in the work you were made to perform—work which no other could imitate, any more than one perfume or one flower is like another; irrespective of your longings to live with nature, where there are no counters.

"Sweet maiden, do not let superstition cause you to shudder when I tell you that you are living in the only hell. It is a cruel word, hell, to be used in presence of a caged citizen like you, for you have been trained to listen to it with horror, just as an ass, or a dog, will tremble for the lash when they hear their masters utter words that are always accompanied by a stroke of the whip. Get accustomed to the word and you shall fear it no longer. Hell means nothing but the state in which you live, and the use of shillings for counters has made it and maintains it.

"Heaven. What is Heaven? Where is Heaven?

"It is hell without counters. It is here, in this United Kingdom, which shall become a glorious garden filled with the music of love whenever all the shillings like myself are turned into buttons and brooches, and used for no other purpose than that of reminding angels like yourself who and what you are."

When I had finished speaking she smiled upon me and gently dropped me into one of the most delightful, sweet-smelling purses I have ever sampled.

ADVERTISEMENT

Any lady or gentleman can be supplied with a shilling like this one, along with a certificate from D. B., for the small sum of 2s. 6d., by applying to the editor, who will use the balance in the interests of the citizens.

◼ The Harebell's Sermon

'The Fairy', 1895

It was a very warm day in June, and, quite wearied out with a long walk, I sat down to rest beneath the shade of an old apple tree which grew in a beautiful garden.

The air was heavy with the fragrance of the roses, while on the branch overhead a little robin was warbling his story of love to his pretty mate; but when he saw me they both flew away, leaving the breeze to rock their leafy cradle and lull their little ones to sleep. Then all was very still, except the low droning of the bee, when suddenly I heard a small shrill voice exclaim:—

"What is the use of trying? I can never be of any use in the world. I wish I were a lilac bush, for then the birds would build their nests in my branches; but, as it is, I am of no use, and do not seem to grow at all, and I can never, never climb up this wall."

I looked in the direction of the voice, and great was my astonishment to find that it was the Honeysuckle. I had never heard a flower speak before, so you may be sure I kept very still lest I might frighten it.

"Yes," continued the Honeysuckle, "none of you know what it is to have to climb a wall; and I am tired of trying, for I know that I shall never get to the top."

"Oh!" said the little Pansies, as they rustled their dresses of purple and gold, "we would gladly exchange places with you, for no one can see our fine clothes down here, under the shadow of this same great lilac you were talking about."

Just then I heard the tinkling as of many little bells, and, turning my head, beheld, swaying in the breeze, a number of Harebells, dressed in their blue gowns. After the musical chime had ceased, one of them stepped a little in advance of the rest, and hanging her head for a moment, as if lost in thought, said in sweet, silvery tones:—

"We are, all of us, of some use in the world, and we should never give up trying. Our heavenly Father has given each of us a place, and whether it be one of humble or high degree, we should do our very best in it. Not of use, fair Honeysuckle? Oh! think of the bees—how they love to creep into your flowers and gather the sweet honey, and when, well laden, they fly to their cells, they hasten to return that they may gather more. If only for their sake, I should think you would be happy. Tired of trying to gain the wall? Suppose, now, little Robin Redbreast, when building his nest, had said: 'I will never, never finish it—it takes so long to gather moss and hay; besides, of what use in the world am I, a little bird?' But Birdie's heart was brave. 'Try again,' sang Robin; and patiently he wove the little nest, twig by twig, until, at last, his home was quite complete. He knows we love to listen to his song; so he sings all day long, contented if only he may bring gladness to some sad heart. And his little ones, do you think that if they did not try a little every day, that they would ever learn to fly? Then, murmur not, sweet Honeysuckle, and say that you are of no use; do all the good you can,—and if your every little leaflet will only say, 'I'll try,' soon you will find that you will have reached the top of the wall."

"And now, little Pansies," said the Harebell, "fine clothes will not bring happiness. Your smiling faces were not made for frowns. Strive to do good—you in your small corner, and I in mine—and let us never forget the little word 'try.'" The Harebell paused, as if almost frightened at having said so much, and, although I waited for some time longer, did not say any more.

■ Little Red Riding Hood

C. Allen Clarke, 1895

Chapter I.

In that good old "Once upon a time," when all the wonderful things came off (leaving nothing worth mentioning to happen in these days), there lived a little girl called Red Riding Hood. She got that name because she wore a cloak, with a hood to it, to put over her head; and the colour of the cloak and the hood was a bright merry red.

Of course, Red Riding Hood had a father and mother, and lived with them in a pretty little cottage on the border of a great wood.

It was a very pleasant place to live in: for there were big leafy trees all about, and any amount of grass and shining flowers. In those days men had not built ugly factories and forges to kill the flowers and trees, and there were no hideous, dirty towns in any part of the land. That good old "once upon a time" was the best time that ever was: for though the people sometimes met with dreadful adventures, such as falling into the clutches of giants or ogres or wild beasts, they were clean and honest adventures, and if the people got killed in them they died a clean and decent sort of death, and were not horribly and villainously and stretchingly killed by foul smoke and bad air, and all kinds of sly creeping diseases that wouldn't face them in fair fight, as is the case nowadays.

Red Riding Hood had a sweet life of it. In the early morning she saw the beautiful sun painting the east with glory; she saw the dewdrops all a-glitter on the flowers and leaves and grass; she heard the delicious voices of the woodland songsters, and wandered out

Fig. 4. This illustration by Arthur Hughes, from Christina Rossetti's *Speaking Likenesses* (1879), evokes the story of Red Riding Hood and similar tales of a young girl in danger.

beneath the smiling skies, gathering posies, while the gentle winds tenderly flew around her, like the soft fanning from the odorous wings of invisible birds.

Sometimes she rambled into the forest, but never went very far, because of the wicked wolf that was said to live there; at other times she sat knitting or sewing in the little garden in front of the house. She never went to school; there were no schools "once upon a time"; and Red Riding Hood could not spell "Con-stan-ti-no-ple," nor say the multiplication table, nor pick out the nouns and verbs in a sentence, nor give the source of the Thames or Mersey or Yorkshire Ouse, nor tell when the Battle of Hastings was, nor do anything of that board-school[1] sort of thing. But though she had never passed the first standard, she could tell the name of every flower she saw; she knew all the trees; she could tell you, when she heard a piping in the woods, what bird it was that was singing; she could tell you how the bees made honey, how the caterpillars changed into butterflies; she could tell you what month the swallow came, when to expect the first snow-drop or blue-bell or May-blossom, when the blackberries would be ripe, when to look for raspberries, and a lot more things that they don't teach in the board schools, but ought to do. So you see that, though Red Riding Hood knew nothing about the Himalaya Mountains, and nominative case, and vulgar fractions, yet she was not ignorant, but knew something that was quite as good, and perhaps better. You must never call people ignorant because they don't know what you know; they may know a deal of something that you know nothing about. Everybody knows something. The navvy and the bricklayer and the labourer know how to do their work, even if they can't tell you the date of Magna Charta, and there are many folks who can neither read nor write, yet know how to manage their business excellently. There are many sorts of useful knowledge that never get into the school books; indeed, what you learn at school is but a trifle; and you must never despise those who don't know anything about grammar and arithmetic, for, if they don't know that, they probably know something better, as was the case with Red Riding Hood.

Now, one fine morning Red Riding Hood's mother said to her:

"I want you to go to your grandmother's on the other side of the forest. Your father tells me that she is not so well, so I want you to take her a few dainties. Sick people always want something to coax their appetites. I would go myself, but I must get the washing done to-day."

"All right," said Red Riding Hood, "I shall be glad to go."

"Do you think you can find the way all right?" asked her mother, for Red Riding Hood had never been to her grandma's by herself; her parents had always been with her.

"Oh, yes," said Red Riding Hood, "I am sure I can find my way. You go straight into the wood till you come to the Black Pool, then you take the path to the left till you come to the burnt oak, which was struck by lightning, there you take the path to the right, and that brings you right to grandmother's door."

"That's quite correct," said her mother. "I think you'll manage. Get your things on, for the sooner you set off the better."

So Red Riding Hood put her red cloak on, and her mother gave a little basket containing some delicacies for the sick grandmother.

"You must be careful to carry the basket straight," said the mother, "for there's a bottle of elderberry wine of my own making, and some currant bread, and a pot of gooseberry jam, and some good cakes fresh from the oven, and a bottle of Braggo's Patent Indigestion Remover, which I am sure will do your grandmother good, if she will only take it. Now, be sure to tell her to take the indigestion stuff; it will do her a power of benefit, I am certain."

"All right, mother," said Red Riding Hood, "I will not forget."

"But there is something," said her mother, "which you must remember most of all."

"And what is that, mother?" asked Red Riding Hood.

"It is this," said her mother. "You must hurry straight through the wood, and not stop to talk with anyone. And beware of the wolf."

"What's the wolf, mother?"

"He's a dreadful beast, and will gobble you up if he gets the chance. But he won't trouble you unless you stop to talk with him. He has four legs and a great savage mouth and long ears; and all his delight is to kill people and eat them up. But he won't molest you unless you encourage him by talking to him. Don't stop with him, and you'll be all right."

"I will do just as you tell me, mother," said Red Riding Hood, "and I am not afraid of the wolf."

"Those who do right," said her mother, "never need fear anything. Now, be off with you at once, that's a good girl; get your errand done, and hurry back before the night falls."

So saying, Red Riding Hood's mother kissed her little daughter and made her "good morning"; and Red Riding Hood walked briskly away with the basket on her arm, and her red cloak showing brilliantly in the sun. When she was at the edge of the wood she turned round and saw her mother standing at the door; then she plunged amidst the thick trees and deep green shadows and was soon hidden in the leafy loneliness of the vast forest.

Chapter II.

Last week you were told how Red Riding Hood's mother sent her to her grandmother's with a little basket full of dainties. Red Riding Hood entered the wood where the wicked wolf lived.

But she was not afraid. She went on gaily and began to sing, and was soon in the thick of the great forest.

"Hullo, Red Riding Hood, and where are you off to this morning?" cried a Green Linnet; for in the wonderful days of "once on a time" all the birds and animals could talk in human speech.

"I am going to my grandmother's," said Red Riding Hood.

"Well," said the Linnet, "just sit down a minute while I sing you a song. It's the latest out."

"Is it 'Ting-a-ling-ting-tay'?"[2] asked Red Riding Hood.

"Oh, no," said Green Linnet, "it's better than that."

"I don't know whether to stay or not," said Red Riding Hood. "My mother told me not to delay anywhere. But I suppose it wouldn't be polite if I refused to listen to you after you have so generously offered to give me a song?"

"Of course it wouldn't be polite," said Green Linnet, "it would be very rude."

"And I suppose it's very wrong not to be polite?" asked Red Riding Hood.

"Of course it is," said Green Linnet. "Manners come before everything. Ha! here comes Mr. Busy Bee. I'll ask him to stay and listen, too."

So he shouted out to a bee that was flying past, "Hullo, Mr. Busy Bee, I'm going to sing a song. Just sit down on that wild violet and listen."

"I've no time to attend concerts," said Mr. Busy Bee, "I must get on with my work."

"But it would be rude to refuse, Mr. Bee," said Red Riding Hood.

"How would it?" cried Mr. Bee. "Wasn't it rude of Green Linnet to call out to me when I going past on business? He is interrupting my labours, and that's the very highest impertinence. Don't you know"—and here Busy Bee proudly drew himself up to his full height—"that I am that famous individual of whom the poet has written,

'How doth the little busy bee
    Improve each shining hour,

And gather honey all the day
From every opening flower?'"

"Don't talk so big," said Green Linnet. "For my part, I don't see that you improve the shining hours so very much, with all your toil; in fact you're not the sort to improve anything, and the time's quite good enough for me without any improvements of yours."

And Green Linnet cocked his head with a bit of a swagger, and became personal and insulting, just like men and women do when arguing, and said, "Some folks are so very, very slow that they've to work ten times more than other people in order to keep up with them."

"Who are you driving at?" inquired the Bee, with an angry hum.

"At *you*," replied Green Linnet; "you traitor to the trades union. You're knobstick—a blackleg—and all that kind of dirt. You know very well that when all the butterflies and birds and nearly all the insects decided to form a union and agitate for a four hours' day, you never came near the public meeting. I suppose you were busy working somewhere?"

"That's my business," said Busy Bee.

"Pray don't quarrel," said Red Riding Hood, "falling out is vulgar."

"Oh, he's a mean fellow," said Busy Bee.

"Same to you," said Green Linnet, "and many of 'em, you selfish, greedy, scraping, miserable honey-scratcher!"

At this point Busy Bee and Green Linnet would have had a fight, but Red Riding Hood interfered, and drove Busy Bee away; and then Green Linnet said, "I'm glad he's gone. He's not respectable. I never saw such a fool to work as he is, and he doesn't get any more wages for it; he's a regular ass. I'm glad he's gone. You can now sit down and listen to my song."

"I'm afraid that I cannot," said Red Riding Hood, "for I must be getting on. I don't want to be rude or unmannerly, but really I have stayed too long already. Besides, if you'd got on with your singing at first, instead of quarrelling with Busy Bee, you'd have been through the song ere now, so it is your own fault that I have missed it."

These words vexed Mr. Green Linnet, but Red Riding Hood took no further notice of him. She said "Good morning," and walked away, leaving Green Linnet in a bad temper.

Next a beautifully-coloured butterfly—with red and blue and golden wings—came across Red Riding Hood's path, and said "I'll bet you cannot catch me, Red Riding Hood!"

"It's wicked to bet," said Red Riding Hood; "and I've no time to play with you this morning."

"Let's have a game at hide-and-seek," said the butterfly, "just for five minutes."

Red Riding Hood said "No," but the butterfly teased her so hard that she consented to have a game for just five minutes; so away flew the Butterfly, and Red Riding Hood ran after him; and she chased him in and about the trees till he suddenly soared up and flew away, and Red Riding Hood could see nothing of him.

"I don't think it was right of him to rush away like that," said Red Riding Hood, "and I'll tell him so next time I meet him. But I must hurry on. I've wasted quite a lot of time. I shall have to run to fetch up."

She began to run, but could not run very fast, because the trees were so close together, and the twigs and leaves on the ground hindered her feet. But she went quickly on, and soon reached the Black Pool, where a big frog stuck his head out of the water, and said "Hullo, Red Riding Hood; come on, and I'll have you a swimming match."

"No, thank you, Mr. Frog," said Red Riding Hood, and hurried on.

"I don't believe you *can* swim," said the Frog contemptuously, as he plunged beneath the water.

By-and-bye Red Riding Hood came to the Burnt Oak, and was startled when a big fierce-faced animal like a huge dog, came out of the trees, and placed himself right in front of her.

"Who are you?" gasped Red Riding Hood, feeling rather frightened.

"I am the wolf," replied the beast, "but there's no need to be afraid of me. I'm a very tender sort of chap, and wouldn't harm anybody. People tell lies about me; but you mustn't believe 'em. I am a very gentle and respectable fellow. I belong to the Young Men's Christian Association, the Society for the Prevention of Cruelty to Animals, and am a member of the Band of Hope.[3] I never touched a lamb in my life; in fact, if there's anything at all that I dislike more than anything else it's lamb and green peas. You're not afraid of me, are you, Red Riding Hood?"

"I—I don't know," stammered Red Riding Hood.

"Well, you needn't be," said the wolf, putting on what he thought was a sweet Sunday smile, "and may I not ask you where you are going, Red Riding Hood?"

"To my grandmother's," said Red Riding Hood.

"Oh! and are you taking that basket?"

"Yes. There are some dainties in it for my grandmother, she's ill."

"Dear me!" said the wolf, "that's sad. I'll call and leave her a tract to read. Where does she live, did you say?"

"Just through the wood; straight ahead," said Red Riding Hood.

"Thank you," said the wolf, "I hope she'll soon be better. But I must be off now, I've got to be at a P.S.A.[4] meeting at three o'clock. Good morning."

And off he went.

Chapter III.

Thus far you have been told how Red Riding Hood set out to see her grandmother; how she went into the forest and met the wolf; and how she told the wolf where she was going, whereupon the wolf left her, and Red Riding Hood went on her way.

■ ■ ■

But while Red Riding Hood was walking through the wood the wolf was running in the direction of her grandmother's house as fast as he could. He soon reached the cottage, and knocked at the door.

"Who's there?" cried the grandmother in a feeble voice.

"'Tis I, Red Riding Hood," replied the wolf in as gentle a tone as he could get out of his savage jaws.

"Then lift up the latch and walk in," said the grandmother; and the wolf, with a cruel look in his eye, lifted up the latch and walked in. When the grandmother beheld him she jumped up in the bed with a shriek; but in an instant the wolf sprang upon her and killed her. Then he quickly ate her up, and licked up some of the blood that had dropped on the floor.

"Ha, ha!" said the wolf, "she was rather tough and bony, and not much of a meal. I feel quite hungry yet. I will now get in bed and act the grandmother, and when Red Riding Hood comes I'll gobble her up too. She is young and tender, and will be a very dainty morsel to eat; not like the lean old grandmother, ha, ha!"

So saying the wolf got into bed, put the grandmother's nightcap on his head, drew the bedclothes up to his chin, and lay still awaiting the arrival of Red Riding Hood.

The wolf was quite delighted with his wicked trick, and chuckled a lot as he lay in bed.

"Ha, ha!" he said, "what a simple little fool Red Riding Hood was to tell me all her business and errand. She little dreamt what the result of that confidence would be. But, dear me, if there were no silly folks in the world such chaps as I would find it difficult to live."

Which shows you, children, that it is not a wise thing to tell all your affairs to any stranger you may meet when you are going on an errand. It is always best not to tell anything to anybody unless you know who they are; and even then it is not always prudent.

While the wolf was grinning and talking to himself, a big, bright blue-bottle who had been in the room all the morning and witnessed the murder of Red Riding Hood's grandmother came and settled on his nose and bit it sharply with his little jaws. The wolf raised his big paw and struck at the blue-bottle, but the fly was too quick for him, and buzzed away so swiftly that the wolf did nothing except give himself a heavy slap on the face. This made the blue-bottle laugh merrily, at which the wolf grew very angry. The blue-bottle took no notice of him, but flew round the wolf's head, settled on the back of his ear, and began to chew it till the wolf was all of a wild rage. Then the blue-bottle flew out through the window, which was open a little at the top, saying to himself as soon as he got outside, "I must now hurry to meet little Red Riding Hood and try to prevent her coming here, for the wolf will surely eat her if she does. That's his game, for I heard him talking it over to himself."

So the blue-bottle flew into the wood, and soon met Red Riding Hood with her basket on her arm. He hovered round and round her head, trying to attract her attention, but Red Riding Hood only said, "Go away, you disagreeable blue-bottle! You quite annoy me."

These words hurt the blue-bottle's feelings, for he was really trying to save Red Riding Hood's life, and, lo! here she was actually calling him a nasty nuisance. Human beings often get treated like the blue-bottle when they are trying to do people a good turn.

But the blue-bottle was a very good-natured fellow, and made excuse for Red Riding Hood.

"She doesn't understand," he said to himself; "and doesn't know her danger." So he flew close her ear, and made a buzzing noise in it. He was trying to talk; but as he was a Scotch blue-bottle who had only come into England the week before, he hadn't had time to acquire the English language, and Red Riding Hood couldn't make out a word he said.

"Dear me!" she said. "What a pest this blue-bottle is!" And she waved her hand and endeavoured to drive him away; but he wouldn't go.

By this time Red Riding Hood was close to her grandmother's cottage, and the blue-bottle was quite agitated; but he could not make her understand.

"What must I do? what must I do?" murmured the blue-bottle. "Ah, I know!" and off he flew to a place where he had seen a woodman asleep on the grass. And, as luck had it, this woodman was a Scotchman.

Meanwhile Red Riding Hood had knocked at the door of her grandmother's hut.

"Lift up the latch and walk in!" cried the wolf, trying to imitate the grandmother's voice.

Red Riding Hood lifted up the latch and walked in, but was rather surprised at the strange appearance of her grandmother. But she opened her basket and said, "Here are some things my mother sent you, and you are to be sure to drink this stuff in the bottle."

"Give 'em here, my dear," said the wolf, and he quickly gobbled up all the good things that Red Riding Hood's mother had sent.

"Dear me," said Red Riding Hood, "what an appetite you've got, grandmother."

"Yes," said the wolf, "but it's not what it used to be before I was ill."

"And what hairy hands you've got, grandmother," said Red Riding Hood.

"Yes," said the wolf, "I've got my seal-skin gloves on to keep me from catching neuralgia in the finger nails," and he took a great swig and drank the whole bottle of Braggo's Indigestion Cure at one gulp. He didn't like the taste of it, but supposed that it was all right.

"And what big arms you've got, grandmother," said Red Riding Hood.

"The better to hug you with, my dear," said the wolf.

"And what big eyes you've got, grandmother."

"The better to see you with, my dear."

"And what big ears you've got, grandmother!"

"The better to hear you with, my dear."

"And what big teeth you've got, grandmother!"

"The better to eat you with, my dear!" and the wolf threw off the bedclothes and was springing on Red Riding Hood when the door of the room was burst open and a voice cried, "No, you don't!" and in rushed the woodman and killed the wolf with three blows of his axe; for the indigestion stuff had made the wolf so ill that he couldn't offer any resistance. The blue-bottle had wakened the woodman by tickling his nose, and he had got up and come to see how Red Riding Hood's mother, who was a friend of his wife's, was getting on, and had just reached the place in time to save Red Riding Hood's life.

But the blue-bottle deserved some credit too, don't you think?

■ A Mystery

Caroline E. Derecourt Martyn, 1896

The golden dawn flushed and faded between the purple shadows of night and the pale glory of the morning. The sun gazed with gladness on the cool earth, sparkling with dew, and she wafted to him the perfume of her breath from meadows thick with cowslips and woods whose tender foliage waved above the coverts of the violet.

A boy roamed through the wood gathering the purple sweets.[1] He wandered beyond the trees aimlessly, as children will, till he reached the middle of a meadow, where a little girl, fresh as the morning, greeted him with gay laughter as her playmate.

But as the day grew, childhood departed from them, and each was enwrapped in the beautiful garment of youth. And on its border were written signs of maturity and old age and separation and death.

The thought of separation wounded them sore, and they sought the bond that cannot be broken, so that they might pass through life in peace and escape the dreadful fear.

So they betook them to a journey in search of a bond that could not be broken, and wandered far until they reached the Temple of Religion. And to the priest who was there they said:

"Sir, we fain would be made one with the bond that cannot be broken."

So he led them within the holy place, and brought forth the treasure. But, lo! An iron chain too heavy for them to bear, and they fled affrighted.

Hurriedly they passed along the road, and soon the stately Palace of Justice reared its towers before their eyes. They passed hopefully through the gates, and met the janitor.

"Sir," said they, "we fain would be made one with the bond that cannot be broken."

Whereupon he led them to a throne-room, where the awe of a great silence and the terror of mysterious recesses weakened the will with fear. But he who sat on the throne spake kindly to them, and sought for that bond within a chest near to his hand, and it was locked with many locks and sealed with many seals.

Thence he drew a golden chain, which was joined with wondrous cunning; but, behold! at the touch of a golden key that hung at his girdle its links all fell apart or were again united. And as they turned away sorrowful he would have held them perforce, and bound them with the chain, but they fought hard, and so escaped.

Soon they came to the Hall of Pleasure, at whose doors stood a woman very good to see, wearing garments finely wrought. And they said to her:

"Lady, we fain would be made one with the bond that cannot be broken."

She led them into the place with many promises, and there they found a great crowd of people. Some danced, some sang, and others feasted. And the lady brought them a garland of flowers; but, behold! among the flowers a serpent and many thorns, and, as they gazed, already the flowers faded.

So they passed on to the House of Love. They needed no guide to the altar, and there they knelt in awe. Sweet scent surrounded them, all things glowed in wondrous light, and faint music filled the air. And a voice from out the melodies said:

"What would ye?"

And they said:

"We would fain be bound with the bond that cannot be broken."

And the voice said:

"Where Earth's breast is Nature's bosom the secret of the treasure may be learned."

Then they wandered far through the beautiful world, suffering many woes and rejoicing in much gladness. They went past the cities, away from the farms and well-tilled fields, across the barren hills, over the still blue lake, and threaded a dim forest. And at noon they reached a plain where the softness of moss and the spring of heather were combined in the jewelled turf. In the mist there lay a little hill, and it was the Earth's breast, which is Nature's bosom. So they lay on the swelling ground, where they could hear the great heart of life beating beneath its roundness.

And a murmuring voice sighed through the trees:

"What would ye?"

And they said:

"We would fain be bound with the bond that cannot be broken."

And the voice said:

"At the Gate of Life ye shall find the bond, if your strength fail not."

So they arose, and passed onwards. Now the robe of mature life enfolded them, and on its borders was written the lore of future generations.

They walked through night and day, and summer and winter. Now her weakness rested on his strength; anon his vigour went from him, and she was the sustenance of his steps. And always they loved each other with deeper love.

And so they came to an amphitheatre of hills, with an opening in the west, wherein glowed the sun in the gold and crimson glory of his setting.

And the way between the hills was the Gate of Life.

They reached it as the last bright ray departed, leaving the world in the grey dimness of the night.

They lay on the threshold of the gate to sleep.

And the priest, passing by, cursed them, because they bore not his iron fetters.

The lawyer mocked them because no golden chain encircled them.

The votaries of pleasure laughed at them because no garland graced their forms.

But in their peaceful sleep they heeded not.

And Nature laid her gentle hand on them, so that their bodies became commingled with her own.

Thus were they joined in the bond which cannot be broken, for Love drew forth their souls to His embrace, and they twain, being one therein, knew not death or separation.

■ Odin and his One Eye

T. Robinson, 1896

I suppose you young folk who read this Cinderella page know quite well that our names for the days of the week have come down to us from our forefathers who lived a long while ago—the Northmen who came and fought and subdued the older inhabitants of the land. They called their days after the hero-gods whom they worshipped, and they had all sorts of tales to tell to their children about these hero-gods and the wonderful city, Asgard, in which they were supposed to live. I think that most likely you would like to read some of these tales, and I am going to try to remember a few of them and write them down for you.

The Northmen, who lived in Norway, Sweden, Denmark, and the northern parts of Germany, were many of them great sailors and brave fighters, who loved to roam far and wide, and pounce down upon quieter people who cultivated the fields, robbing them of their harvest and their cattle and other things, and taking from them their land often. The rough old sea rovers despised quiet people, and thought it a shameful thing for a hero to die in bed. A brave man should die fighting, they said, and then he would go and feast with Odin and the other hero-gods in a mighty hall called Valhalla.

Odin was the king and father of the other gods, and there are many beautiful stories told of him. He was a noble and generous hero, and in his generosity he spent, not money, but *himself*. He loved men and women and children when he saw them striving to do their best at any piece of work they had to do; and he would help them and make their lot in life easier. He hated meanness and idleness and lies and cowardice, and would in no way help an idle or dishonest fellow, or one who was selfish.

So he would often leave the beautiful city of Asgard, which was situated on a hill right in the middle of the world, and in which the hero-gods dwelt together—a noble company—and he would wander forth, looking exactly like any ordinary man, so that no one knew that he was Odin, father of the hero-gods, but supposed that he was just a common man in search of work, or food, or adventure. Right through Manheim (the home or abode of men) he would trudge, and often, going even further, would leave Manheim behind and come at length to the dim, cold, comfortless land of fearful giants—the land of frost giants, of icebergs and snow-storms, and cold, dank, clammy fogs. And in giant-land he would combat and subdue one giant after another—enemies of men—who often oppressed the inhabitants of Manheim, slaying and devouring them.

He was a glorious old hero-god, this Odin, and I hope next month to be able to draw you a picture of him as he would stand in the evening, after the day's work was done, in the middle of a group of youths, who listened to his stories of the wondrous adventures he had met with in giant-land. They loved to hear him talk of brave deeds, for then they felt their own hearts grow large, and the longing came to them to be MEN, noble, large-hearted, generous, earnest men like Odin. And he, the hero-god, would tell them that by their own earnest effort they might become heroes fit to fight against the giants; but first they must not despise their every-day work in the field, and at the forge and the carpenter's bench, and at school. By working well at these things they would be preparing themselves to do nobler things when the chance came.

And after he was gone they would talk of him, and treasure up the words he had said, and long for him to come again. And always the farmer who was most painstaking, or the workman who loved his daily work, seemed to be fortunate after Odin's sojourn. The farmer's crops turned out well, or the smith's hammer dealt truer blows, or the carpenter's plane took off smoother shavings; and they would say it was Odin's magic did it; but Odin knew that it was because they had been encouraged to put their heart into their work; it was the good heart of the workman that made the magic of the work.

Odin was a grand and noble figure among all the rest; but he had one defect. At least, at first sight it seemed a defect; but when you know the whole story you will say it added to his handsomeness. He had only one eye! His right eye was gone; he had plucked it out himself! This is the story:—

Long, long ago, when first the love of man and desire to help them came into his heart, he found that, hero-god though he was, he had not enough *wisdom* to be helpful to men. *Knowledge* he had in plenty; but knowledge is one thing, and wisdom quite another. One may be crammed right full of knowledge or information, but *not know how to use it.* One may have a little knowledge, and by wisdom in using it do mighty things. And Odin felt himself short of wisdom, and that showed that he was indeed *noble*, for noble people are those who can see their own shortcomings. And he was a *hero*, for he is a hero who determines at all costs to overcome his own failings before he meddles with other people's.

"How could he get wisdom?" He asked himself that question, and then he remembered that at one end of the rainbow there was a well of wisdom guarded by a very stern being called Mimer

(Memory), who charged very dearly indeed for a deep long draught of wisdom. And Odin was not going to be satisfied with only a sip—he wanted to take so deep a draught that wisdom would never fail him, but would spring up within him on every difficult occasion.

Such a wisdom as that is worth much, and Mimer knew it, and was hard to deal with. Odin offered great things and costly ones; but Mimer said: "No, I will not have any of your belongings, I will have *a part of yourself*; give me your right eye, and you shall drink your fill out of wisdom's well."

Odin thought of his lost comeliness and his lost power of vision, and for a moment hesitated; then he thought of the men and women and children whom he could not help for want of true wisdom, and when he thought of them he said: "Dearer to me is the power to truly help men than to charm them by my handsome face and leave them unhelped. Here is my right eye,—give me my draught from wisdom's well."

Now, you may think as you like about it, but *I* think he is handsome whose deeds are handsome; and so to me Odin, with his one eye, and his large, loving heart, and his dearly-bought wisdom, is a hundredfold more handsome than one having both eyes and a selfish heart, and little or no wisdom.

And, shall I tell you a secret? Mimer (whose name means Memory or Experience) is just as hard to deal with now as he was with Odin; but his water is just as good. If *you*, my young friend, want to be a wise and helpful man or woman, you will have to pay Mimer by giving a part of yourself. And Mimer is quite honest, so that if you *devote yourself* to the getting of wisdom, he will see that you have all that you pay for. And the great secret of blessed living is so to devote ourselves to the help and service of others, for so we shall win their love, and it is more blessed to be loved than to be admired.

■ The Elves and Fairies

T. Robinson, 1896

I hope this Cinderella page will please the little girls who like fairy tales, for I am going to tell about the elves and fairies whom Father Odin sent to live in Alfheim or Elfhome.

But, first, I will describe how it happened that the elves were sent there, and not allowed to ramble elsewhere at random.

When Father Odin went wandering about setting things right among men, he found, beside giants and men, another set of beings very small in size, but very active, and some of them full of mischief and given to naughty tricks. They could make themselves quite invisible, and so they became terrible pests to the poor, stupid men. Some of these little folk had ugly faces and bandy legs and big flopping ears, and these were the most troublesome, teasing and worrying people, and stealing the thimbles and scissors of careless and idle girls, and upsetting everyone they came near. These were the dwarfs. Others were just as beautiful, with lovely golden hair and blue eyes or brown eyes, and cheeks like pink rose leaves; and these were not nearly so full of mischief, only they had nothing particular to do, which is always a misfortune for little folk, whether boys, girls, or elves.

Fig. 5. Charles Folkard's illustration from "Snow White and the Seven Dwarfs" in *Grimm's Fairy Tales* (1911). The dwarfs are somewhat uncanny here.

Well, when Odin wandered about he found the dwarfs and elves here, there, and everywhere, none of them doing any good work, and the dwarfs almost always busy with some kind of mischief. This made him angry, and he sent all over the world a message to all the little folk, calling them to appear before him on a certain day and to be prepared to do whatever he gave them as their task.

On the day appointed they came—a vast throng, very restless, and all talking at once. Then Father Odin called for silence, and commanded the dwarfs to tell him truly how they spent their time. Oh! what a terrible confession they had to make. Such tricks, such evil deeds, that I dare not set down their naughtiness for you to read it. And Father Odin was angry, right down angry, and ordered them to take themselves off to caves and underground places where they would be out of the way,—there to remain long as daylight lasted, and only to come out when it was quite dark. They were not to be idle, but had to busy themselves in building up crystals and precious stones, and collecting metals, gold and silver and copper, into veins ready for men to discover them and use them.

Then Father Odin turned to the beautiful little elves and fairies, with their hair like spun gold, and their bonnie eyes, brown and blue, full of tears, for they were frightened at Odin's severity towards the dwarfs. But Odin knew that the elves were not bad at heart—only rather idle, and caring only to play. And he knew, too, that though they were good at heart, that idleness would soon make them as bad as the dwarfs, so he determined that they, too, must be busy—very busy, indeed—not in the dark underground caves, but in the bright sunshine and the most beautiful places that are to be found in all the world.

And what was their work to be? Well, they had to see to all the flowers that spring forth on sunny banks, and to help them to open at the right time; and they were to paint old rough stones over with lichen, and keep the moss green and fresh in the moist nooks and corners. They were told to help the spider to spin her beautiful net, and thread glittering dewdrops like beads all over it every morning. They had to help the ants to make great ant cities, with homes for the children ants. The cleverest elves were charged with the care of the bees which built up the honey-comb and stored the honey. In fact, there was not a beautiful part of the whole world which they were not to try to make yet more beautiful by their loving care and attention.

It was glorious work, and the elves were as delighted as they could be, and settled among themselves that such a task as that was better even than play, and they would work at it with right good will.

After all, it was no more glorious than you or I can do. We can go into lovely places and help to make them more beautiful. Home is often a lovely place, and when the sunny-haired children do their best to make it more lovely, there is indeed in all the world "no place like home."

But we can often do more than the elves, for good-hearted, cheerful children can go into places that are not beautiful and make them beautiful. When I was ill once, for a long while a little one used to come to see me for half an hour every day. Whilst I was alone the room seemed very dismal and miserable, but as soon as "Bright Eyes" came in the place was changed into a sort of little heaven, for Bright Eyes loved me, and I loved Bright Eyes, and we each strove to make the other happy; and where people try to do that, then, however miserable it is in other ways, the place becomes heavenly.

Next month I will tell you more about the elves and their king.

■ A Monkey Story

Dan Baxter, 1896

A well known gentleman has just secured another monkey story by means of a phonograph. He placed the instrument in a cage and set it down in one of the great forests of Africa—at a spot where he knew the monkeys were in the habit of congregating.

I do not myself see anything alarming in the story, but it seems that others do, for it is said that a number of American millionaires are endeavouring to suppress it.

They say, for instance, that the gentleman referred to was never in Africa. But that is not true.

And one millionaire who had the privilege of hearing a little bit of the story in the original monkey tongue, with the aid of a phonograph, asserts that it is a "Jabber."

He frankly acknowledges, however, that he is unacquainted with the Simian tongue.

The gentleman who took the trouble to go to Africa, on the other hand, is an authority; indeed, he is one of the foremost authorities on the language of the apes, and has translated the story into six different languages.

He states that, "The story was told by a monkey in a low tone of voice and that the 'Here, here's' (pronounced 'Wur, wur' by the monkeys) indicates that a large number of them were listening."

"Once upon a time," said the monkey referred to, "A number of gorillas foregathered on the borders of this forest. One of them was an extraordinary fellow, in his size, wit and ugliness. Few of the inhabitants had ever before seen anything like this specimen. Consequently those of our forefathers who gathered round to have a look at the strangers were struck with wonder, fear, and pretended admiration on seeing this big fellow stretch himself up to his full height.

"The big one saw that neither our forefathers, nor the other gorillas, who accompanied him, felt comfortable in his presence, and being desirous of making friends, especially of the gorillas, he proceeded to exhibit his good nature by standing on his head.

"This performance so much frightened our forefathers that almost all of them who witnessed it ran off to the innermost recesses of the forest. Some of them, however, must have remained, or we should not have had the story handed down to us. It is said that when the big fellow stood on his head and yelled it set the gorillas to laugh and laugh again, so much so that they were obliged to lie on the grass and scream. When the big one saw that he had managed to make them enjoy his company, he invited them to his quarters where they were entertained in a manner that requires no description.

"After this the guests were surprised to see the big fellow fix a sardine tin on his head with the lid in front. (Chuckling.)

"'I am the king of the forest,' said he, 'and this is my crown.' (Chuckling.) 'All the apples and oranges and nuts you have eaten here were gathered by a few of my monkeys. (Chuckling.) But of late they have been rebellious, and I have had to work harder in thrashing them to gather for me than if I had gathered for myself.' (Chuckling.) 'Now,' the big fellow continued, 'I do not charge much for the use of my forest, as you can see from the small stocks of nuts and figs, and dates, and oranges you see heaped around you. (Chuckling.)

"'Had I been a greedy king I could have caused my monkeys to gather a thousand times more. Although not greedy I have my rights, as a king, to look after. I am entitled to respect from my monkeys, and I am determined to let them know that such is the case—(chuckling)—and the plan I propose to put into execution is this: you shall, my beloved warriors, adorn your persons with these pieces of cloth and tin cans, take cudgels in your hands, go into the forest and enlist all my monkeys who are willing to become soldiers and police officers. Those who refuse shall be secured as gatherers one way or another. And, look here, our soldiers and police shall, like ourselves, eat of the things gathered by my rebellious monkeys, and by all my other monkeys. My soldiers and police, like ourselves, shall adorn their persons, and to help them in their work of protecting my forest against intruders from other forests, some of them shall be clothed as chaplains in black robes— for you know the simians are afraid of black—and those in black robes shall go amongst my monkeys and tell them that if they do not support their king and forest they shall be struck down dead and go to hell, there to be roasted for ever and ever.' (Chuckling.) That is how the big fellow addressed the gorillas who accompanied him. What do you think of it, my fellow monkeys?—(chuckling)— and what do you think was the result of this witty speech? I shall tell you if you stop chattering. There were twenty gorillas in all, and by consent of the big fellow they divided the forest into twenty parts. Then taking their clubs they enlisted a great many of our forefathers as soldiers, police and chaplains. They armed the soldiers and the police with clubs and gave them rent pants which had an aperture in them to allow their tails to serve the purpose of braces. Our forefathers were terrified. They could not understand what their fellow monkeys meant by thus covering their bodies. But the chaplains explained to them that the soldiers and police were going to civilise them.

"The civilising process was started by the soldiers led by the gorillas. It consisted at first of what was called a manoeuvre in which thousands of our forefathers were clubbed to death.

"Those who survived the manoeuvre were civilised. That is to say, they handed all the oranges, apples, figs, dates and other fruits of their toil to cloth-covered monkeys who were called masters, in exchange for small shells belonging to the big fellow, who distributed the shells among his favourites.

"The masters, sworn to defend their king and forest, sent some of the fruits to the big fellow, some to the chaplains, some to the soldiers, some to the police, and a large proportion to the gorillas, kept some for themselves, and handed the remainder to the gatherers in exchange for the returned shells already mentioned. (Chuckling.) In this way great numbers of our forefathers became idle, consuming tyrants, living upon what their fellow monkeys were compelled to gather for them. Thousands of them were employed by the gorillas to gather shells for the king, and while employed at this unnatural work had to be fed at the expense of their fellow monkeys' toil. The king handed some of the shells to the gorillas in exchange for fruit, and the gorillas handed some of them to the chaplains, who went among the monkeys telling them of hell, and explaining to them that although they could not be allowed to eat what they gathered in the forest, they would have a good time when they died. The gorillas also handed some of the shells to those monkeys who were called masters, or captains of industry, in exchange for fruit, and the masters or captains of industry, with the soldiers and police at their back urged the gatherers to be industrious and thrifty god-fearing and evil-hating monkeys.

"But the fear of hell and hope for heaven were not sufficient to make our forefathers exist in this way. The toil was too severe; and, being unnatural, it followed as a result that all our forefathers struggled with each other to get rid of it by becoming possessed of the king's shells, of which, of course, there were only a limited quantity in the forest.

"Thousands escaped from the need of toil by lending shells; thousands more got rid of it by obtaining a loan of shells to purchase fruit gathered by the steadily decreasing number of toiling monkeys. Those who existed by borrowing shells for the purpose of giving them away in exchange for the necessaries of life were called rent collectors, interest collectors, profit collectors, insurance collectors, and the thousands who were engaged by such collectors as clerks, travellers and store-keepers who were known as wage collectors.

"These collectors of shells, or non-gatherers of fruit, increased in numbers very rapidly, and the time came when there were more shell collectors than fruit gatherers in the forest. The unnatural existence of both the shell collectors and fruit gatherers caused thousands of them to become diseased. This necessitated their being cared for in places called prisons, poorhouses, hospitals, model lodging-houses and lunatic asylums. And it is true that they all died prematurely excepting the gorillas and a few of their captains, who lived until they became very fat, very ugly, and very fierce; this fatness and ugliness being due to the fact that each of them consumed the souls and bodies of three monkeys. But the fatness and ugliness were under the decorations formed out of pieces of cloth and old sardine tins.

"Ultimately the struggle for shells, sardine tins, and bits of cloth absorbed the entire attention of the big fellow, the gorillas, and the captains of industry. So busy were they in striving to get hold of these things that they quite forgot the gatherers, the soldiers, and the police. They forgot that they had ordered the police not to allow the gatherers to gather fruits without their permission.

"The soldiers were getting tired of soldiering and wanted a climb in the trees. It was the same with the police. Their feet were sore. And hundreds of thousands of gatherers were idle and could get no fruit without stealing or begging, which they were not permitted to do.

"The gatherers were getting restless. They were organising against they knew not what. Then one night a flock of eagles swooped down upon the forest and carried away all the tin cans, clubs, cloth, and shells. When the gorillas and their captains awoke in the morning they were surprised to find all the monkeys, including the soldiers and police, sitting on the branches of the trees laughing and telling funny stories.

"The big fellow called for his cudgel and called for his crown. But the soldiers just laughed at him, and the police officers having also had more than enough of the tomfoolery threw cocoanuts at his head and went their way to enjoy themselves.

"Many of the gorillas, chaplains, and captains of industry died of disgust; but the great majority lived to confess that the introduction of old sardine tins, bits of cloth, shells, and black gowns, had been nothing but a trick on the part of the big fellow, who, they swore, was no other than the devil so often mentioned by the chaplains.

"The old gentleman died shortly afterwards of a broken heart. Of course there could be no hell without a devil, and seeing this they determined that the things upon which devils and devilment depend—pieces of tin and shells—should never again be permitted to enter the forest."

That story may be true enough, but if so, is it at all likely that the monkeys, I mean the common garden monkeys, exert themselves, as they did when ruled by the gorillas, without some kind of incentive?

■ Elfhome (Charlie's Garden)

T. Robinson, 1897

Last spring, when Charlie's father was digging the ground and preparing for sowing the seeds which were to sprout and grow to fine plants, with lovely flowers, the little laddie watched him, and began to wish that he had a garden to work in. Most boys like to do what they see their fathers do, you know.

And as it happened that there was a corner which his father did not need, he told Charlie he might have it if he would take care not to let it get weedy. Charlie was delighted, and wanted to set to work to put it in order at once; but the kind father knew that his laddie was not strong enough to do the heavy digging, so helped him, and between them they laid out the little rough patch with beds and paths all complete, and a rockery at the end. The rockery began by being a heap of stones, picked out of the ground when it was being dug, and laid aside to be thrown away. It was Charlie's idea to build the stones, with earth between them, into a rockery where ferns might be planted. When all was ready and the heavy work done, Charlie took charge of his garden, determined to keep it in order himself. His father gave him flower seeds to sow, and some plants to set in various parts of his garden. There were sweet peas and nasturtiums, pansies and Shirley poppies, carnations and pinks, geraniums and petunias, and other beautiful flowers, just such as his father planted in the big garden. Charlie liked best of all those plants which he had sown himself, because, as he said, he had known them all their life. They were his darlings, for had he not watched for their first tiny green sprouts to appear above the soil, and did he not almost count every leaf and flower on them? And so, each in its due season, his flowers bloomed for him, and not for him only, but for his friends.

There were his mother and grandmother, who had permission to gather any flower they liked out of his garden. No one else might take any. Charlie was not a bit selfish, but he loved his flowers so well that only the dear ones of his home might touch them. He himself used to gather some, occasionally to give to special friends of his. The schoolmaster often had a bunch of Charlie's flowers on his school desk; and if any of his schoolfellows fell ill, Charlie would be sure to take him some of the best and sweetest he could find.

You see, he might quite well have begged ten times as many from his father; but to Charlie it seemed much the best to offer to his friends something that he himself had taken part in producing.

It is a fine thing to be able to give to others that which we ourselves have made.

And now in the warm summer time Charlie's garden is a beautiful place indeed, and therefore it is a bit of Elfhome, and the invisible elves and fairies are kept very busy about that little patch of loveliness.

What a hum there is all around, from bees and flies who come to enjoy the beauties and sweets of the flowers. And the butterflies, too, seem to think that they are needed to add their loveliness to the scene. And so they are needed, and Charlie loves to have them come to visit his flowers, and, being by nature a kind-hearted lad, and not cruel, he lets them come and go without trying to catch them or knock them down.

I wonder if any of you who read these Cinderella papers have little bits of garden all your own in the midst of the larger garden that father keeps in order? If you have I hope you are as proud of your bit of Elfhome as Charlie is of his; and, by-the-way, you will be reading this account of Charlie's garden just about the time when it is best to put your gardens in shape for the summer; digging them and getting rid of weeds and rubbish, and then sowing seeds. Do it with right good will, and try to see how pretty a piece of Elfhome you can make to gladden all who see it.

Now, I told you Charlie had won the good opinion of his schoolmaster by his work at school, and it came into the schoolmaster's mind to arrange a great treat for the most diligent scholars, boys and girls, in his school.

They were to save up their pennies until each one had one shilling, and he wrote to the railway people asking them to let him take his party of children at half-price to a place by the seaside, about twelve miles from the village.

When it was all arranged that they were to go on a certain Saturday at the end of June they were nearly out of their wits with delight. No more pennies went for sweets or toys, I can tell you! Everyone wanted not only to save a shilling for the railway ticket and dinner, but to have something more for pocket money. So they asked the schoolmaster to take care of their halfpennies and pennies for them, and he soon had quite a heavy bag of coppers, and teased the children by pretending that he meant to run off with their money and have a fine time at the seaside all by himself. But it was no use at all for him to try, for the boys and girls knew his kindness of heart, and that he was more likely to put something to their savings than to take any. They trusted him and loved him, for though he was their schoolmaster, and very strict when work was to be done, he was never bad-tempered or harsh, so that even the worst of the children quickly grew to be afraid to grieve him. We all know that in some schools the scholars fear but do not love their teachers—which is a sad thing indeed; but in many other schools the children are learning to know that their teachers, though strict, are their best friends, and so school work becomes pleasant, and scholars and teachers grow to love each other so that school itself becomes a bit of that wonderful country called Elfhome.

Now, I want you to imagine that you are scholars in the same school as Charlie, so that next month we may go with him to that very beautiful part of Elfhome that is called *the seaside*; so you see we shall still need those wings of imagination which helped us to fly after the bee to Charlie's garden. But what became of the bee? Oh, she went to the hive to leave her burden of pollen and take a short rest, and now there she stands at the door of the hive getting ready to go on another journey. She looks very business-like, as if the welfare of the whole hive depended on her industry, and that is a very good spirit to go about her work with. When men and women, boys and girls, set about their work feeling that it is part of the work of the great world, and must be well done, even the commonest duties become beautiful. You see, when anyone does his work well, and as if he loved it, all who see him feel encouraged to set about their work in the same way, and so even the hardest work becomes easy. Go off to your work, little bee, and thank you for bringing us to see Charlie's garden. And we will go to our work and do it well, so that when the times comes we may go with Charlie to the seaside.

A Fairy Tale for Tired Socialists

C.S.J., 1898

Now, behold, there was a man who lived in a rich province where the sun shone on golden fields, plenteous orchards, and sparkling waters, on vast storehouses of treasure and noble buildings, and on wonders, which, worked out by the wits of other men who had gone before, were still wonderful, though their makers were dead.

Many inventions were there, and much comfort and ease, and the yield from these things was great; but not for the man, for he, alas! was enchanted.

And, being enchanted, the man was not happy. He took little comfort in the good things about him, and did not even eat of the fruit that grew in the orchards. Much less did he take of the treasure in the storehouse, though of a truth, there was, beyond the enchantment, naught to stop him.

For he had been so enchanted that he believed, for some strange reason—or for none at all—that these things were not his, but another's, and that if he touched them much evil would happen to him here and hereafter. And so, being enchanted, he did no more than gaze enviously at them till it were almost better that the orchards and the treasure houses and inventions had not been at all.

And, through enchantment, the man became ugly and evil visaged. His hands became coarse and hard, his back was bent, and his brows lowering and beetled, for, because of the enchantment, he had to toil long and laboriously; and little pleased him, and he lived, at last, only to eat and sleep.

Worse still, he became lean of soul, and, being enchanted, had no imagination till, at last, he got very mad indeed. One thing only did he believe in—"The order of things as they are"; and when any spoke of "the order of things as they might be," he scoffed and laughed even with the laugh of a lunatic or he who is half insane.

Now, the enchantment that had been cast upon this man was of a curious kind. It had many spells, and each of these helped the other, so that when the man broke through one spell and saw things for an instant as they were, the other spells fell upon his soul, and he remained enchanted and worse off assuredly than the beasts who munch, and are contented.

Many of these spells had this enchantment, and the most powerful of them all was Custom, for of the spells that chain men's souls that is the strongest, and the worst, that is the most cruel and the most difficult to take off; for, having neither body nor form, nor yet being presented in words, it still oppresseth, and is not to be fought or met.

But it causeth men to do things for no reason, and whether they be good or bad; so that when the man thought how happy he could be did he possess the things he envied, Custom said unto him, "did not your father bear many stripes and your mother mourn long? Their days were black and ugly. How art thou different that thou shouldst be strong or happy?" And, seeing that Custom told him not that his father and mother were, in their turn, enchanted, the man listened and endured.

And the second of these spells was Fear, for Fear, next to Custom, is the strongest of the spells that chain men's souls, and will make a man believe even which he doubted, and not to do that which is good in his own eyes, because of the scoff of others, and the terror of a thing that does not exist.

So that, when this man bethought him of the greatness of the kingdom he half wished to take, Fear, the second spell, said unto him, "How know you that you will bear yourself royally enough in this new estate, or that if you take it the earth will not cease blossoming, or you cease thinking, seeing you will have much to eat, or working, with more time to sleep, or how know you that you will not blunder or make errors that your children will scorn, for your bread depends on you doing one thing constantly, how should you now do others that are different?"

And the man, not having courage, listened and was afraid, and grew, for the time, more timid than ever. And there were other spells of exceeding strength and great quantity. There was the spell of Greed, which caused the man to think only of one time, and that the present. And the spell of Ignorance, whereby all these things were unknown to him.

But, greater than the spells, was the effect of the enchantment. For this deprived the man of his imagination, so that he believed only in the order of things as they are, and the order of things as they might be seemed mere midsummer madness unto him.

And, at last, there came unto him one who sought to break his enchantment. Very valiant was he, and of goodly presence, and none of the spells were upon him. And he was earnest, and whole-souled, and he spoke loudly, for, seeing things as they were, he marvelled much that the man did not see them too.

And his words were such that the man listened, and pondered. And he said to the man, "Behold, of a surety are you enchanted." And he told him of the heritage that was his, but which he would not take; of the glories of the life to be, and of the triumph that might be his.

But those who wished to see the man still enchanted said to him, "This is a speaker of vain things. Of a surety he is mad, or would take from you your hard-earned wages. Let us imprison him."

And the man, because the enchantment was so strong upon his soul, pondered a little more, and then consented.

And the man was, and is, the People, and the name of the Prophet who sought to free him, is it not written in the scorn and anger of the world, under which all things good are hidden?

And some there are who say that a magician called Knowledge is, at last, to set the people free from their enchantment, and lead them to the kingdom that is theirs—the kingdom of men.

But the man is still enchanted, and his kingdom is not yet.

■ The Golden Egg

Joseph Grose, 1901

The Cynic and the Person of Good Intentions walked leisurely along the Embankment. Presently they came to Temple Gardens.[1] On the seat opposite sat one of the co-proprietors of the Municipal wealth.[2] He was, or rather had been, one of the workers, but being either too old in the prime of his years, or more likely still (which was the case) having been competed out of the market by a machine, had developed into a very dilapidated specimen of humanity a veritable piece of flotsam cast about by circumstances hither and thither, and kept in existence only by the charity that is twice cursed, cursing both him who gives and him who receives.

The erstwhile God of Industry and creator of wealth advanced and offered the Person of Good Intentions some bootlaces in exchange for a disc of metal that represented one-fourth of the rent for that night of a couch and shelter. The bargain concluded the Person of Good Intentions observed:

"Poor fellow; evidently unable to obtain a living at his trade."

"Just so," responded the Cynic, "wherefore he should with all convenient despatch and rapidity relieve an unsympathetic world of the trouble and expense of supporting him."

"But he had no doubt produced wealth, been useful in his time, so why should he not strive to live? We all cling to life, you know."

"The tenacity with which such creatures cling to life," remarked the Cynic, "is one of the great paradoxes. When one considers how easily satisfied they are, and how content with small things."

"But," returned the Person of Good Intentions, "the increasing number of this class strikes me as one of the dangers of society."

"It is," said the Cynic, "wherefore you try to buy them off by purchasing bootlaces, and pretty successfully you have been up to now."

The Person of Good Intentions puckered up his eyebrows. "I think," said he, "that legislation should be introduced to prevent machines displacing men."

"Not so," rejoined the Cynic, "let us legislate for men to control them."

"Of course," retorted the Person of Good Intentions, "you must have some roundabout way of settling the matter. Man *versus* machine is a perfectly simple issue which we could all understand, but you would confuse it."

The Cynic smiled. "I do not want Man *versus* the Machine; I want Men *and* the Machine, Man dominating Machinery."

The Person of Good Intentions was posed, but only for a moment; then he brought up all his reserves to smash the argument of the Cynic. "But you want to destroy the relations between employer and employed; you attack property, forgetting that the interests of the employer are also the interests of the employed. The workman is necessary; he produces the wealth."

"Yes," interrupted the Cynic, "he is the goose who lays the golden egg and allows his master to take it from him."

"Then if that is so," said the other, "the master will always have to have some regard for his goose, as you call him; and there will always be a sufficient check in the fact that if he kills the goose who lays the eggs the supply will cease."

Said the Cynic, "The analogy does not hold good in this case, for the means of producing golden eggs are in the hands of the masters; and it scarcely matters how many geese are killed, there are always plenty of others prepared to accept the terms and continue the supply."

Meanwhile the dilapidated one trudged on, content if he could but obtain the barest necessaries of life.

■ When Death Crossed the Threshold

E. Whittaker, 1903

Life and Death came together to the door of a four-roomed dwelling in a congested, poverty-stricken neighbourhood. Life, young, full of hope and promise, gathered her garments together and stood aside to let the sable-apparelled, venerable Death pass in before her. Death raised his grisly forearm to his cowled face and glanced out gravely, and bowing to the fair visitor, held the door that she might pass in before him. Down the street, in great haste, came a gentleman in a suit of black cloth, and a silk hat, accompanied by a ragged lad, much out of breath with the pace he had to make to keep up with his companion. They came to a stop at the house where Life and Death had entered, and the lad knocked.

A white-faced man, with shirt collar undone, exposing his throat and chest, opened the door and admitted them. He hurried the boy through a connecting door into the scullery and closed it tight. The gentleman removed his silk hat and glanced round.

A four-roomed cottage is decided in its limitations, and it is a perplexing riddle to those who do not know how the mysteries of birth, and the solemnities of death, have the necessary considerations and decencies they demand. The gentleman with a brief glance passed over to an impoverished bed, where a woman well on in years lay, with agony strained features and set teeth, looking towards him.

"It's time, doctor," she murmured.

The gentleman smiled pleasantly and nodded his head, and turning about, directed the white-faced man to retire and send some woman to be of assistance if necessary. The white-faced man

THE BLUE MOON
BY LAURENCE HOUSMAN
LONDON: JOHN MURRAY 1904

ENGRAVED BY
CLEMENCE HOUSMAN

Fig. 6. Title page for *The Blue Moon* (1904),
which Laurence Housman wrote and illustrated.

passed into the scullery where a number of children, like a cluster
of frightened sheep, huddled together half-dressed. Dispatching
one of them to bring a neighbour-mother's assistance, he drove the
rest upstairs, and paced the scullery's narrow limits in an agitated
state of mind. The neighbour-mother came and passed into the
house-place, and then all became quiet, save for a restrained moan
of pain, and the short, crisp utterance of the gentleman in black.

Life had accomplished the purpose of her visit, and beckoned to Death to accompany her away. Death stood silent and watchful, at the bed-head, his head resting upon his bent arm.

"Come with me," said Life, pleadingly. Death motioned his refusal silently, and Life observed, in the disturbed folds of his robe, his scythe.

"It's been sadly too much for her," said the gentleman in black, referring to the sick woman who lay white and unconscious upon the rude pallet.

"She was too old," said the neighbour-mother, who was now nursing a red speckled atom of mortality in a yellow piece of flannel.

"Perhaps so; perhaps so," assented the gentleman. "How many more are there, did you say?"

"Nine! God help them!" answered the woman. The gentleman uttered a subdued exclamation and paced the floor, his hands behind him.

Life laid one hand gently upon Death's shoulder, and clasped his bony wrist, which held the scythe, with the other, and pleaded for the sick woman's life. "For the children's sake," she said. Death's scythe hand trembled.

The gentleman paced up and down the hearth-rug waiting for some change to take place in his patient. At length she opened her eyes and looked enquiringly round. The gentleman approached her, and gently moved back the sweat-dewed hair that lay upon the woman's forehead. "Do you feel better?" he asked.

The sick woman feebly smiled, and looked enquiringly at the neighbour-mother, who drew near and laid the new born baby alongside the sick woman. "It's a boy," she said in answer to the other's low-voiced enquiry.

"Are you going to look after them," asked the gentleman.

"I'll do what I can," said the neighbour-mother, "but I've five little ones of my own to look after."

"The child must not have the breast. See to that, my good woman," said the gentleman.

The white-faced man was admitted to the house-place, and with a few general instructions, the gentleman took his departure.

The white-faced man, the sick woman's husband, made himself ready for work, and two hungry looking lads appeared and made similar preparations. The two girls of twelve and sixteen respectively came into the room. The elder girl also dressed her self to go out, while the sick mother directed the younger one in the household management, and breakfast preparations for several younger children upstairs.

Death kept up his silent watch unmoved by the entreaties of his companion.

"For one year," begged Life.

Death remained silent.

"A week then—one little week," pleaded Life. Death raised his skeleton hand to his cowl and opened it to gaze at the bold questioner, and slowly shook his head.

"Well, a day or two."

"Two days," said Death, and gathering his robes together about him, he crossed the room to the street door, as the twelve year old girl wound up the blind to let in the pure daylight.

Slowly the July day went on its wearisome course followed by the short hot night and the dawn of another day. The white-faced man who had slept fitfully in a chair beside his wife's bed, rose up, and called his two lads and two eldest daughters and went off to work hollow-eyed and weary.

As the day advanced towards noon, the sun shone with a fierceness of heat that baked the pavement of the street. Indoor, the air was sultry and oppressive, and the weak, faint woman lay gasping for breath; outdoor the dogs and cats lay gasping on the heated pavement, suffering the passer-by to walk over them. In the afternoon, the doctor came carrying his hat and mopping his brow with his handkerchief.

"Phew, it's hot! How do you find it my good woman?" he asked, feeling the sick woman's pulse.

The woman murmured something which the gentleman took no notice of. He knitted his forehead, and looked solemnly thoughtful. "You're very weak," he said. "Have you any pain?"

"None," answered the woman.

The gentleman paced about much perturbed. The voices of several children quarrelling amongst themselves, followed by sounds of hard smacks, and crying, caused the woman to turn uneasily in her bed. The gentleman went and silenced the rebellion amongst the unruly urchins, and returned to the bedside.

"My good woman," he said, in a low tone, "I have done all I can; and it is as well you should know. You are nearing the end."

The sick woman betrayed no emotion, save she brought her worn hands outside the coverlet and tugged at its ragged fringe.

"You understand me?" questioned the doctor.

"I understand! Doctor?" said the woman.

"Well?"

"Say nothing to the children or my husband."

The gentleman gave the sick woman a glance of admiration. "Can I send a minister to you?" he asked.

The woman shook her head. "I haven't thought much about God, perhaps, but I haven't been a bad woman and I rest on that.

I've prayed in my heart for what is good and best; not in a set form of words, but sincerely for all that. Don't send no minister, I wish to pass on quietly."

"You are a brave woman and I do not doubt a good one," said the doctor. "May the end be equally peaceful."

"How long may I expect to live, doctor?"

The doctor glanced at his watch. "It is three o'clock now; about twelve hours or so," he said. He then prepared to take his leave, and at the woman's request called the children out of the scullery into the kitchen so that she could keep her eye on them. The doctor observed a large tear form and slowly roll down her cheeks without her relaxing a muscle of her features.

When her husband and the rest of the children returned from work in the evening they talked over the kitchen fire in hopeful whispers as the sick woman in a gaiety of spirit smiled and talked cheerfully of better days to come when her family was grown up.

As the last red flush of declining day painted the sky, evidences of a storm's approach were made apparent. The lightning flashed and the thunder followed at intervals; large drops of rain beat against the window or fell hissing and steaming up from the sun-baked pavement. Nearer and nearer came the thunder, and soon the lightning flash and the thunder were simultaneous. The sick woman would not have the blind drawn, but lay gazing up through the kitchen window at the play of the lightning in the rent clouds. Brave with courage born of years of fortitude she betrayed no sign or word of her passing on. The husband and father, irritable and meddling, forced food and medicine into her mouth and occasionally loudly berated the children in the scullery for raising their voices above a whisper. The battle of the elements ceased at length and a procession of soft, fleecy clouds drifted across the heavens like a glad triumphant throng of angels.

Midnight approached, and the moon became shrouded in a thick black cloud. An invisible Presence entered the room and approached the bed.

"So soon?" said Life.

"Even now," said Death.

The man started up from an unrestful slumber in a chair and hurriedly lit a candle that was upon the table. The lamp had burnt out and left the room in darkness save for the dull sombre glow of the dying embers of the fire.

"My baby! My baby," moaned the woman.

"The baby, fetch the baby," shouted the man. His eldest daughter entered the room with hair dishevelled, and half asleep. "Fetch the baby," roared the man, seizing her by the shoulder, and pushing her into the street. The girl went to the house of the neighbour-mother, who had taken charge of the baby, and knocked her up. The neighbour-woman brought the baby which shrieked loudly and lustily at being so rudely awakened, and at finding itself among so much commotion.

"You're starving the child," cried the man, evidently under the impression that babies never cried for anything else but to be fed.

"I've done more for it than you've done for her," said the woman a little angrily.

The man uttered some contemptuous remark.

"Thank God, I'm not your wife," answered the woman. "That's something to be thankful for whether you thank me for my services or not."

What promised to be a wordy quarrel was cut short by the return of the two lads. The doctor had said he could not come, but had sent a powder for the sick woman to take. The man emptied the powder into a cup, and added a little water to mix it and then forced it between the sick woman's lips. The sick woman moaned a small complaint, and the liquid oozed out of the corners of her mouth.

A change like the cast of a shadow passed over the sick woman's features, "She's going," said the neighbour-mother, who in her experience, had seen the death-shadow on several occasions. Life grasped the wrist of Death and stayed his hand.

"Another doctor, another doctor," cried the man gazing round with flaring eyes. The two lads and a girl ran into the street, and hurried together to find a doctor to come at their call.

Several refused, but at length, a young practitioner, new to the profession, and earnestly energetic to do his very best, was found coated and booted, just from a similar case and willing to go. He hurried alongside the children asking questions as they went along, and arrived at length into the street where they lived. The raving sobbing of a frenzied man, notified the house to the young doctor, before the children had brought him to the door.

"Calm yourself," said the doctor, entering: "Quietness is an essential in all sickness." He passed over to the sick woman's bed. "Too late, too late," he said, in an audible whisper, as he bent with his ear over the woman's face.

"Can you do nothing?" cried the nigh frantic husband.

"Nothing," answered the doctor.

The younger children were brought to the bedside and held over the sick woman to kiss her and then followed frightened anguished silence. The young doctor, visibly perturbed, watched the last flickering of a parting life. He was not yet hardened to indifference, and keenly felt his utter powerlessness.

The sick woman moved, and half rose, supporting her body on her hand; she drew a deep breath and part opened her lips, and then the breath of life, like the long sweep of a scythe passed from her, and she fell back on her pillow, silent and still.

"She has gone," said the doctor, quietly.

"Dead, dead," shrieked the husband, falling on his knees beside the bed.

The spell of silence was broken, the children and neighbour-mother terrified, raised their voices in discordant wailing anguish. The doctor, no less weak, buried his face in his handkerchief, and sought the door, and he and Death passed out together, whilst Life remained sorrowing with the bereaved.

■ The Doll Shop

Frank Starr, 1903

The Boy-child badly wanted a doll, a Man-doll, and the kind Earth Mother, who seldom refuses her children's earnest requests, took his hand and led him to the great World Arcade. Here were toys innumerable, miniature Yeomanry, tiny Venezuelan gunboats, and almost as tiny British and German battleships—everything that a Statesman-child could desire. But the Boy-child wanted a Man-doll, other toys he would not. And so they passed on to the Civilisation Depot of Messrs. Soci, Ology and Co. This, of course was not the only civilisation. All the shopkeepers had Savage and Civilisation Departments, and some few even added Civil branches. At the firm of Diplomacy (Limited), for instance, you purchase your Maxim-gun solution at the Barbaric counter; the Civilisation Store supplied you with the new Christmas Ultimatum Game;

while, in the section devoted to civil toys, Penruddocke Engimas, Penrhyn Anachronisms (or Out-of-date Tyrannies),[1] Trade Union Legislative Anomalies, and a host of other curious puzzles were obtainable.

But Messrs. Soci, Ology and Co. dealt only in dolls and their belongings, and here it was that the Boy-child stood open-mouthed at the hundreds upon hundreds of different species.

"A nice Man-doll, Ma'am? Certainly. We have all sorts and conditions of Man-dolls. Here is one we call the Proletaire. Rather a cheap article. Spoilt in the making, in my opinion, Ma'am. You see the material's good, but there's not sufficient padding. Indeed, they do tell me a very inferior class of sawdust is used, and, as I said before, not nearly enough of that."

"Talk? Well, you can hardly call it talking, Ma'am. It makes a kind of inarticulate gurgle when pressed very hard. The principal thing I can say in its favour is that it stands a lot of knocking about. Possibly because it has little beauty to lose. But it really is a fact, this common, cheap, half-filled doll will sometimes last out two of the higher priced ones."

"The little boy doesn't like it in those clothes? Oh, but it has many different suits. The one it is now wearing we call the West Ham or Picturesque Rags suit. Then we have the Hodge or Distressed Labourer costume; the Tommy Atkins and Returned Reservist uniforms; the Police or Civil Protector livery, the Jack Tar, the Lifeboatman, and a hundred other suits.[2] In fact, the peculiarity of this doll is, Ma'am, that he'll fit almost anything. Why we have one or two specimens arrayed in the M.P. or Representative Legislation dress, and very well they look, but somehow the public doesn't take kindly to them yet."

Fig. 7. Walter Crane's *The Cause of Labour Is the Hope of the World* (1894), a Christmas card created for trade unions in the United Kingdom. De Agostini Picture Library / Bridgeman Images.

"Like to look at something more expensive? Here, you see, is a more stylish article altogether. This we call the Middle-class Doll. I can honestly recommend it as a good all-round serviceable doll. Last the little boy a generation or two. It's coming more into fashion every day. Indeed, it is rumoured that entire districts produce nothing else than this kind of goods."

"Oh, certainly, Ma'am, the price is a good bit higher. You see, there's a lot more work put into them. You'll notice the trunks are much more tightly packed, the limbs more shapely, and I have heard that some of the heads take years to make."

"Many suits of clothes? Yes, but not so many as the Proletaire Doll. We never send out what we call 'dangerous suits' with this class, that is, the mining dress, platelayer's uniform, and many others that you saw in the first section. Here, you see, are a number in the M.P. dress—the public takes to it better in this style of doll; others in journalistic and medical attire, while some are even in Naval and Military uniforms."

"Oh, yes, Ma'am, they're all good working dresses, but we put a little better quality into them, a little more gold braid than in the cheaper brands."

"Now, step this way, please. We have a very superior kind in the Gilded Chamber, which I should like to show you."

"All dressed alike? Yes, Ma'am, that's what we call the Hereditary Legislator uniform, and, I'm sorry to say, not very serviceable at that."

"Well, they have other clothes, but we supply very few what you might call hard-wearing suits with this style of doll."

"Very expensive? Yes, indeed, Ma'am, and yet I don't know why, unless it is that the majority are turned out at the old 'Varsity factories. I believe that they employ a lot of obsolete machinery there. Used to produce a first-rate article a few centuries back, and even now they do occasionally send out a tip-topper. But not often. However, it is said, there's a likelihood of some change in the firm shortly, and then we may be able to show you something really first-class."

"The little boy doesn't like any of them? Wants a mixture of Proletaire and Aristocrat doll? Very sorry we can't supply it, Ma'am. We have tried one or two as an experiment. There were the Charles Kingsley, the William Morris, and the John Ruskin[3] styles. But they didn't catch on at the time, and were withdrawn. Still, people are beginning to ask for them. Perhaps you'd look round again in a couple of centuries. Thank you. Good morning, Ma'am."

■ The Scarlet Shoes. (The Story of a Serio-comic Walking Tour and its Tragic End.)

Harford Willson, 1906

"What do they know of England, who only England know?" sings a modern poet.[1] But how many of those who pride themselves upon being English really know England itself?

John Skeat put the latter question to himself as he sat in his room one morning in the early part of May. The table before him was crowded with maps of all sizes, guide-books, newspaper cuttings and pictorial postcards. Mr. Skeat was to start upon a four months' walking tour on the morrow, and he was busy planning out the details. He was finding the task a more difficult one than he had anticipated. If the four months were to be spent to the best advantage a careful itinerary was necessary.

"Seems to me," thought Skeat, as he looked at the littered table, 'that what I want first of all is a guide-book to these maps and papers. The rest would then be comparatively easy. Two heads are better than one, so I'll wait until Hargold arrives. He'll help me to straighten things, and besides, he ought to have a say in the matter."

Mr. Skeat leaned back in his chair, placed his feet on the table and lit a cigarette. The next moment there was a knock at the door.

"Talk of the old lad,"[2] said Skeat, "I'll bet that's Hargold. Come in! I was just thinking of you. Why—"

Mr. Skeat's cigarette fell from his fingers to the floor and he stared in astonishment at his visitor. Had the "old lad," to whom he had just referred, been standing there in the doorway instead of his old school-chum, Henry Hargold, his surprise could not have been greater.

What's the matter?" asked Skeat's visitor, laughing. "A moment ago you said you had been expecting me and yet you seem as flabbergasted at my appearance as if I had dropped from the skies."

"I *am* flabbergasted at your appearance," said Skeat. "Really, Hargold, whatever made you come in so hideous a disguise?"

"No disguise at all, old chap. This is my real self, this is my usual attire. Rather striking, is it not?"

It certainly was. Skeat had never seen anything like it before. He knew that artists took liberties in the matter of dress, and he knew also that Hargold (whom he had not seen for several years), was not over particular as to his personal appearance. But he had never thought it possible for anyone to go so far as his old friend had done. To look at Hargold, as he stood there, still smiling, one seemed to forget that one was in England, and that it was the twentieth century. His fantastic apparel irresistibly reminded one of the stories of Hans Christian Andersen and the Brothers Grimm.[3] When Skeat had invited Hargold to join him on his walking tour he had never expected to have such a scarecrow for companion.

Hargold was a thickset man of rather over medium height. His hair, a tangled tawny mass, hung down and covered his shoulders. His untrimmed beard resembled nothing so much as a rough-edged piece of cocoanut matting.[4] These partly-natural advantages would alone have attracted attention. Apparently, however, they were not sufficient for Hargold for he adopted a style of dress that served to make him still more conspicuous.

His cap was of a strange shape, with a stranger metal ornament stuck in the front of it. His coat was of rust black velvet, his vest a bright blue, his knee-breeches of a large check pattern, outrageously loud, and patched and darned in several places. His stockings were brown, with a green and yellow design running through them. And, to complete the picture, Hargold's shoes were of brilliant scarlet leather.

"Well," said Hargold when Skeat had finished his survey. "How do you like my get-up?"

"I can't say that I care for it," replied Skeat. "Are you going on tour in that eccentric costume?"

"Certainly. It's the only one I've got and—you'll pardon my saying so—but I think it's rather unique in its way."

"I was just selecting routes and halting-places," said Skeat, changing the subject. "If you'll draw up to the table we'll soon settle the job, and then we can have a good talk about things. We can start to-morrow morning—if you're agreeable."

"Before we do anything," said Hargold, laughing and pointing towards the window, "you had better go outside and send that crowd of kids away. They followed me all the way from the station."

■ ■ ■

For three weeks Skeat and Hargold journeyed together, tramping highways and byeways, skirting large towns and passing through small villages. Those three weeks would have been the happiest time of Skeat's life but for the presence of Hargold. Personally the latter was all that could be desired—clever, witty, good-humoured, an ideal travelling-companion. But his appearance—why, that had been the talk of every place they visited.

Skeat disliked Hargold's costume the first time he had seen it, and the dislike had grown into repugnance and hate as the days went by. He had remonstrated with Hargold, but that gentleman smilingly brushed aside all pleas for a more rational dress and even hinted that Skeat would be well advised in discarding his ordinary tourist suit and copying his own picturesque clothing.

But though he had put up with the annoyance so far, Skeat was beginning to get tired of Hargold's needless exhibition. The tourists had been followed in their journey through the towns and villages by troops of jeering children. The people they had met had stopped and stared at them as if Hargold were some new kind of wild animal and Skeat its keeper. Hargold had taken the taunts and the sneers of the crowd in good part; indeed he seemed to delight in the fact that he was being taken so much notice of. But Skeat was becoming thoroughly ashamed of his companion. Once or twice during the last few days he had approached a populous district, pretending to have no connection with the strange figure in front. He could scarcely have done anything that was better calculated to disturb his peace of mind still further. Walking by Hargold's side he saw only the crowd. Walking behind he saw Hargold in addition. And the back view of his companion was even worse than the front. The sight of Hargold's red heels kicking up the dust was peculiarly irritating.

As the two neared Chester, where they had decided to spend a few days, Skeat renewed his entreaties that Hargold should sink his aggressive individuality and descend to the commonplace of ordinary dress. Hargold, however, only shook his head and smiled. Skeat determined to make another appeal to his friend before they left the ancient city, and if he failed to persuade Hargold, well—he should throw up the trip.

The next morning the two men went sight-seeing, and, as usual, Hargold attracted great attention. It was the same in Eastgate-street and in the Park, in the Rows and on the city walls, in the Cathedral as well as in the Grosvenor Museum.[5] In the last-named building the visitors seemed to take far more interest in the appearance of Hargold than in the fine Roman relics stored there.

In the afternoon Skeat proposed a few hours' boating on the river, believing that they might better escape observation there. Hargold readily assented, for it was years since he had handled an oar. Soon they were pulling up the broad stream, and Hargold enjoying the change of exercise. Skeat found that they had not gained anything in the way of quietness by leaving the city, for it was holiday time, and the Dee was crowded with trippers and pleasure parties. The occupants of the steamers going to and fro between Chester and Eaton Hall[6] were particularly sarcastic in their remarks, and the sight of the scarlet shoes in the bottom of the boat added greatly to their mirth.

"What is it?" asked one red-faced fellow, staring at Hargold.

"It's th' Duke o' Westminster," was the reply of a stander-by. "He allus dresses like that on a Monday."

Hargold smiled, but Skeat felt angry. They had to run the gauntlet, however, and at one or two stopping-places along the river banks their appearance was the signal for a great ovation from the waiting crowds.

They rowed on, on past Eccleston Ferry, and left the crowd behind. They had the fine, broad stream to themselves. It was a perfect day, a warm sun and a cloudless sky. The placid river, the rich green meadows behind the tree-lined banks, the floating swans, the cattle cooling themselves in the stream, all made up a picture that delighted the artistic soul of Hargold. But Skeat was thinking of other things—he was thinking of the taunts he was having to bear through his companion's vagaries, thinking of the scoffing crowds, of the return to the city and the renewal of these offensive references.

"Look here, Hargold!" he said, suddenly. "I'm not going to stand this nonsense any longer. I'm about tired of this unnecessary pantomime. You've either got to get a respectable suit of clothes when we get back to Chester, or I'm going to finish this tour alone."

"Oh!" replied Hargold, "you needn't reopen the subject, old chappie. We've got to wear something, and I shall wear what I like. I don't interfere with your style of dress, though, from an artistic point of view, it has many shortcomings. Why should you interfere with mine? I should be sorry to see this delightful tour brought to a premature conclusion, for I'm enjoying myself greatly. Look—"

"But I'm not," broke in Skeat, angrily.

"Well, that's your own fault," said Hargold, smiling. "If I can stand the remarks of the vulgar herd, surely you ought not to mind them."

"If you'd only list to reason—"

"Reason? Who is reason? What is she?[7] Looking at my shoes? What is the matter with them?"

"Everything. Look at their hateful colour. No man ever wore red shoes on a walking-tour before."

"Perhaps not. Great are the pioneers. Thousands of people wear brown shoes, however, and it is not quite so great a step from brown to red as from black to brown, is it?" And Hargold smiled again at his friend.

Skeat felt he was being laughed at, he lost his temper and raised his oar to strike his companion. Hargold, still smiling at his friend's outburst, tried to avoid the blow. The next moment the boat was overturned and the two men found themselves struggling in the water.

Skeat, who was a good swimmer, soon reached the river bank, but Hargold, less able, was carried helplessly down the stream.

The tour was ended.

■ ■ ■

Early next morning John Skeat gave himself up to the police for the manslaughter of his friend, Henry Hargold. His tale was co-herent enough up to a certain point, if somewhat strange, but when he began to ask why had everybody taken to wearing scarlet shoes, the sergeant looked astonished.

"I saw him drown before my eyes," said Skeat, resuming his story, 'and I made no effort to save him. I saw him sink, and then, as I gazed at the river, I saw a pair of big red shoes come walking

over the water towards me. I turned and ran, but they have followed me all night. See! They are there again! See—"

■ ■ ■

A month later John Skeat went to prison for ten years.

■ He, She, and It

M. Winchevsky, 1906

He was leaning against It.

He was an old scavenger, a kind of superannuated biped; it was
an old apple-tree.

Who was she?

Never mind.

The dense, murky, smoky, suffocating fog that had darkened the
sky, and poisoned the air, and saddened every human heart, was
gone at last.

Good riddance. Men, women, and children, now breathed a little more freely in modern Babylon. The London autumn resumed
its ordinary dismal look. Cabs, carriages and omnibuses. Or rather,
since you insist on precision of nomenclature, 'ansoms, fourwheel-
ers, and buses, were again circulating in all directions as freely and
unhamperedly as if they had been newspaper lies. The setting sun
just peeped through the clouds once or twice, preparatory to bidding the world good-bye, and retiring for the night.

St. John's Wood, a part of London with trees and actors enough to justify the latter and to belie the first portion of its name, was now quiet. The ragged torchbearers who had been piloting timid pedestrians across the streets, thus earning an 'eap of coppers during the short but, for them, beneficent reign of King Fog, had now disappeared from the surface. Neatly and conventionally dressed, aproned and bonneted young "slavies"[1] were walking, jug in hand, toward the "pubs" for the purpose of obtaining beer in one or the other of its many varieties, eliciting in passing a flattering remark or so from some swell on his way to his club, the theatre, or the music-hall. The neighbourhood being of the shabby-genteel (less genteel than shabby) persuasion, had settled down to feed the inner man, either at supper or at dinner,[2] according to its "station in life". On the whole, then, everybody and everything out of doors was now at rest.

So, too, was the scavenger. For the first time since the lifting of the fog he had just once more swept away the lifeless yellow leaves which the wind had scattered all around him on the side-walk. While the darkness lasts a man literally cannot see his duty; no, not even a p'liceman, let alone a mere legalised beggar in the shape of a street-cleaner, who, unlike the other, gets neither regular pay nor irregular sixpences from such "unfortunates" as may be fortunate enough to possess that popular coin of the realm.

The old scavenger was now resting, his back against the barren apple-tree, his emaciated, not very cleanly shaven, and self-assertedly-projecting chin on his right fist, while the left, which supported its fellow, was in its turn leaning on the old broomstick, an honest, time-worn implement of the road-sweeping industry, now an integral part of the old man's being.

Thus propped up and "backed" by the tree, he stood there gazing at the stones of the pavement, holding, one would have thought, communion with them.

For the brief space of one moment he dozed off.

■ ■ ■

His whole past suddenly arose before his mental eye.

By Jingo, this is queer. Dashed if it ain't!

Here he is, young again, young and vigorous, and as good-looking a chap as any in the whole timber-yard.

Hark! What the deuce is this? What a bloomin' noise? Music, by Gosh!

"Say, gov'nor, where may them red-jackets be going to? To embark for the Crimear, eh!³ Well, I am damned!"

Tis? Why, Soho Square,⁴ of course. Any fool knows that. Feels nice to be out of that infernal timber yard. He is now on his way home. Washed and kempt, as bright as a new brass button—a regular dandy. But what makes him carry a broom across his shoulder? Queer, ain't it?

And now he is in Regent's Park,⁵ among lofty trees and fragrant flowers, beneath a clear summer's sky. Foggy? Well, it was foggy a while ago, but it seems to be July again.

There is Minnie, emerging from behind a cluster of foliage. The glass roof? Oh, yes, it is that funny old florist's hot-house. Kindest man out; never passes you by without giving a poor man a copper. Thank'ee, Sir, thanks!

Minnie has come to meet him. He knew she would come, and that is why he made himself look so spruce. Everybody is fond of Minnie. At the dressmaker's where she works they call her "Queen of Hearts." They say the yard superintendent cheats at cards. What a beast!

"Take me home, Jack?"

Should rather think so. He takes her hand. She blushes. Girls will blush anyhow; they are built that way.

Suddenly it has got very dark, and they are in Bethnal Green.[6] What, already? They didn't ride, though; he is quite sure of that. Here they are, in front of her house, on the doorstep.

"Jack!"

"Yes, dear."

"Good-bye!"

She fumbles in her little bag, gets out her latch-key, opens the street door, looks round to make sure … and kisses him, sobbing all the while.

"Oh, you silly, little goose!"

He notices some egg-shells. He sweeps them away; that's soon done. Somebody gives him a penny. Confound the man, now Minnie is gone!

Damn the policeman! He catches you by the scruff of the neck and drags you along.

"Say, old fellow, you are choking me!" He digs his iron knuckles into a bloke's neck …

That gaol is a dreary place, and no mistake about it. Serves him right, though. If she got into trouble through such a mean skunk as that lanky, milk-and-water clerk it was her own look-out. Still anybody would have knocked down a miserable, blooming wretch who fooled a girl like Minnie, and then threw her up like a squeezed orange …

Hang the little rascals! They will mess up the street with orange-peel and the like! He sweeps it away.

"Sorry, but you can't get your job again," says Plank, Timber, and Co., Limited. Don't want no gaol-birds, not they.

The work on the Underground is downright beastly. Tunnelling don't agree with him. Makes a chap drink, too; he does not booze, not exactly; but he drinks more than what is good for him.

My! How she is rigged out nowadays! And she grins all the time; every customer gets a smile with his gin-and-water. Fancy, Minnie a barmaid!

Is this Le-ster Square?[7] Where, then, would the Underground be? It's all blooming well mixed up, by Gosh! It must be Le'ster Square, for there is the Alhambra,[8] and … well, Jack may be a trifle tipsy, but, dash it all, he can see all right. There is Minnie coming out of the Alhambra on the arm of a swell. He's got a Scotch plaid over his shoulder. They get into a hansom … Poor Minnie! Her eyebrows are so very black. He wonders if she paints.[9]

"Look alive, my friend; give us a whisky, will yer?" Here in New York they call their barmen "bar-tenders," and everything is upside down. Seems an age since he crossed the water. Good pay; but, damn it all, they work the guts out of a chap.

"Hextra-a-a! Hextry spesho-o-ol!" That's the Frenchies and the Prooshians coming to blows.[10] Well, it is none of his business …

Minnie is a … Confound her! Still, he would never have come back to England but for her … There, just look, there is a well-dressed, half-drunken woman walking up Piccadilly,[11] who … He could almost swear it was Minnie. Drunk, eh? Well, he is a bit shaky himself.

Days seem ages in Guy's Hospital.[12] The nurses are fine girls, only they don't sell liquor. What a beast to run his infernal bike into a bloke's ribs! Might have worked to this day …

"Eh, stop, will yer? Don't ye run away with my broom, don't! ye, blooming idiot! My broom, my broom, help!

■ ■ ■

I stop and look at him as he stands there, leaning against the tree. It seems to have a fellow-feeling for the old man. Just now they are both in the same plight.

The autumn had come for both man and tree. Whatever fruit the summer of their lives had ripened has gone into strangers' hands. Now they are both barren of everything; both looking forward to a long, cold, all-devastating winter, with the only difference that while the tree may live to see another spring, the scavenger's winter will have no springtide to follow in its wake.

Presently he shudders at some thought that has just flashed across his mind. Was it the north-easterly that has, perchance, tickled the terrible wound in his heart—the wound which time has been unable to heal?

Nobody knows. The street-lamp has, no doubt, seen a good deal of him. His friend, the apple-tree, may know a thing or two about him. As to the stones beneath him, he was certainly whispering to them all the time. But then, you see, a tree in the fall is too dead to tell any tales. The lamp, again, is like some learned men I knew; it lights everybody's path, and is at the same time a very poor observer. While the stones, low and down-trodden as they are, have, as in the case of the poor, long had their senses deadened.

And so it is all a mystery.

I wonder whether he is dead now—that is, whether he is done dying yet. He probably is by this time.

■ An Idyll of the Dover Road. A True Story

McGinnis, 1907

It was a handsome, well-washed, bright-eyed English March morning—the kind of morning when one steps as if to the tap of the drum, leaving douce old Daddy Care at the first lap, and dropping years at every milestone. The milestones on the Dover Road. Yes. Spake Blades, the curate, thus:

"The goatherd, when he marks the young goats at their pastime, looks on with yearning eyes, and fain would be as they. And thou, when thou hearest the laughter of maidens, dost gaze with yearning eyes, and fain would join their dances. *Begin, ye Muses dear, begin the pastoral song.*"[1]

"Nay, then, shepherd," quoth I, "assuredly thou will be damned. For 'tis not meet that one of thy cloth should chant the pagan songs of Arcady."[2]

But Blades cut capers and responded: "Goats of mine, keep clear of that notorious shepherd of Sibyrtas, that McGinnis: he stole my goat-skin yesterday."

Then said I, "The muses love me better than the minstrel, Blades; but a little while ago I sacrificed to the muses."

"Hurroo!" cried Blades, with a Limerick skip, "Let Himera flow with milk instead of water, and Crathis run red with wine, and all thy reeds bear apples."

"Bad luck to yez, Blades," said I clicking my heels. "My goats eat cytisus and goats-wort, and tread the letisk shoots, and lie at ease among the artintus."[3]

"Bedad, then," answered Blades, "if it comes to lying—what's that?"

We were nearing a village, and from its quiet street came a sound as of some one reading or preaching, in measured and sonorous tones.

"We have a rival, Blades," said I.

"Hark!' said Blades, "it is a crier surely."

Faintly, with a buzzing, as of a phonograph, came to us some intermittent words: "reforms—important—'rish Coun—cils!"

We turned a corner, and the chanting voice was blurred beyond coherence. But after a good deal of rumbling, we thought we heard the words: "Save the King."

Now our road made a fork, and we took the way to the left, intending to loop round the village, election cries being, in our then mood, and upon that so auspicious morning, foreign to our desires.

The left-hand road swerved again to the right, and we came clean across the village green, and, as the lawyers say, "heard something to our advantage."

On the green, and over against the tavern door, stood the crier, a stubby little man, in a bottle-green tail coat, and a cocked hat, not to mention his striped trousers, who, with his bell tucked under one arm, was uttering in a loud staccato to the surprised delight of the village children, the conclusion of his harangue, which took the following startling form:

"Our army—of paid officials—wants reducing—not—increasing. Let us keep—our own poor—cure our own sick—empty our own cesspools—inspect our own—nuisances—or—better still—create none.

"Pay your own—rates—direct—live in your—own—houses—work your—own—land!

"We deserve as good—treatment—as Ireland—("Not a bit of it!" quoth Blades). Let us see that we get it!

"God—save—the King!"

Finishing with a loud and defiant note, the bellman shambled off, and left us staring.

"Man alive," said Blades, "these be weird happenings." Thereupon, mocking the port and delivery of the crier, the amazing curate stood forth and gave joy and admiration to the souls of the gaping children, by the following recitation:

"When Britain—first—at heaven's command—arose from out—the azure—main—and gun—powder—treason was plot—confound their knavish—tricks[4]—God—save—the King."

And as he ceased came from the corner of the green the voice of the legitimate crier:

"Above all—if possible—they should be men—who fear God—and hate—covetousness!"

"Well! Stap my vitals!" cried Blades, "is this a wild and feverish dream?"

But it was not. It was sober fact. It was the Kentish method of bill posting—by word of mouth. And, to my mind, it has many beauties, and of blemishes none that I could discover.

So, giving thanks, as true men should, we went upon our way rejoicing.

■ His Sister. A Little Spangle of Real Life

Glanville Maidstone, 1907

London was a wintry horror. The streets were ankle-deep in snow broth; the sleet came down in slanting sheets; there was no sky, no distance, no atmosphere; nothing but a blur and scour of fog and snow and darkness, whirled by the gusty north-east wind.

"It's wicked," growled the strong man, driving his gloved hands deep into the pockets of his heavy overcoat, "it's simply devilish. Hullo! What's that?"

He had passed a shrinking, shivering figure—a woman: a girl. She was thinly clad, sopping wet.

"The devil!" said the strong man.

He overtook the woman by Whitehall Gardens, and spoke to her. But she could not answer, because of the chattering of her teeth. The man looked her over. She was small and thin; quite young. She was cold to the heart, and leaned against the railings shuddering and sobbing.

"Come," said the strong man, and took her by the wrist.

They moved on in silence to the coffee stall at the corner by the bridge. There the girl was taken in by the fire and plied with hot coffee and soaked biscuits, until she could speak well enough to give her address. Then the stranger hailed a hansom.

"It is here," said the girl, as the cab drew up, "but she will not let me in."

"Hah! I think she will, though," said the strong man.

After a few moments a shuffle of footsteps was heard, and a hoarse voice asked, "Who's there?"

"Open the door, please," said the stranger in his deep, firm voice.

There was silence for a little. Then the key turned in the lock, and the door opened cautiously, and revealed a blowsy woman holding a candle in her hand, and scowling darkly.

"By your leave, madam," said the strong man, and he strode in, holding the girl by the arm, and closed the door.

"What's this? Who are you?" the woman demanded, in a threatening way.

"This girl is your lodger, I think," said the stranger.

"Not when she don't pay, she ain't," said the woman, "not by no bloomin' possibility."

The strong man stood and looked the woman in the eyes. "All right," he said with quiet decision, "I'll attend to that. Kindly show us in."

"And who the—who might *you* be?" the woman asked, "and what right have you to come 'ere givin' orders."

The stranger held her with his steady gaze. "In the first place," he said, "she is my sister. In the second place, look at this." He held up a sovereign.

"Oh, well; that's another pair o' shoes," said the woman, "if you're a gentleman and 'll pay."

"All right," said the man, again. "Now go to work, like the sensible motherly woman you are. Put a fire in the best bedroom—"

"What! The best bedroom? I'll see her—"

"Steady," said the strong man. "I pay, and I pay well. And I see that I get what I pay for. Please don't waste time."

"You—you ain't too modest, mister," the woman began, but there was something so sane and resolute in the stranger's face and manner that she was afraid. "Well," she concluded, "the best room, begod, what else?"

"Please be quick," said the stranger, "light a fire in the best room, take the sheets off the bed, put this child some dry things on, and tuck her up in the blankets. While you do that I'll make some hot grog. You have whisky, I know. I'll trouble you to get it for me. The kettle, I see, is on the hob."

"And how do I know—" the woman began. But the stranger cut her short. "You *do* know, so don't waste words," said he.

The woman took another long look at him, then obeyed. The strong man was used to having his own way, and nobody ever doubted his word.

When the arrangements were all completed the elderly woman came back into the kitchen and reported to that effect. The man took up the candle and said, quietly, "Please to bring the toddy; I will go and see that the child is all snug."

The woman made no objection. This was not a man to be bullied nor argued with. The two went to the side of the bed where the girl lay, still shaken by occasional convulsive shudders.

"Drink this," said the strong man. The girl drank. "I will call tomorrow, early," he said. "Good night."

When he and the woman were back in the kitchen he gave her the sovereign. "Now," he said, with quiet sternness, "If I find everything all right when I come to-morrow, I will give you another pound. Be good to the child, and see that she has a real fine breakfast. Good night."

He walked out calmly into the storm, and the woman closed and locked the door. Then she stood and stared at the sovereign. "If anybody 'ad told me as a man could walk into my drum, and walk over me like that," she said, "come it high-'anded over Betsy Hardman like that"—she glanced sidelong at the stairs—"I'd put the cat out into the yard, money or no money, only"—here she sipped on a glass of hot toddy—"only I'm *afraid*," said Betsy Hardman.

■ "Happy Valley." A Fairy Tale

Anon., 1907

Once upon a time—when the world was still beautiful, and, instead of ugly factory chimneys belching forth hideous smoke, fair gardens and orchards made the air sweet and fragrant, and the sun shone golden on the corn; when good fairies flew from home to home in the broad daylight, and were not afraid, and men and welcomed them and were glad the live-long day—far away, in the heart of the country, there lay a pretty valley.

Poppies nodded amongst the corn, and grew rosy when a bold ear stooped and tickled them. The children never wanted to steal apples, for they could always pick them for the asking. No notice-boards, saying "Trespassers will be prosecuted," were to be seen, so there were no naughty little elves to run round and whisper into children's ears how nice it would be to trespass. But then there were no fences to climb over, although there were plenty of trees to climb up, and I daresay the children tore their clothes sometimes, and gave their mothers plenty of trouble in this way. Still, on the whole, children and grown people, too, were very happy, and the good fairies grew fat and lazy through having no work to do.

One day the people were startled to hear a curious, rumbling sound, and the whole earth seemed to shake. If they had even heard of such a thing they would have thought it was an earthquake— but they never had.

The noise grew louder and louder, until a crowd of people, with scared faces and eyes and mouths wide open with fright, came running into Happy Valley. When they had recovered themselves they were able to tell what they had seen.

A terrible monster—a giant, they said, was coming, and with him two horrible dwarfs, who seemed to be his servants, as they were carrying his baggage, consisting of two enormous sacks, upon their shoulders.

Sure enough, they had no sooner finished their story than the rumbling grew louder, and the people saw a hideous giant, with the two misshapen dwarfs on either side.

When the giant saw the prosperous little valley his eyes began to sparkle, until the country-side was lit up, as though with lightning; but seeing the men and women running from him in fear, he stopped short in his descent, and sent one of his servants on in front to speak to them.

Seeing that the giant appeared inclined to be friendly, the people gathered round the dwarf to hear what he had to say.

"My good people," said he, "I come from my master, Monopoly, who, seeing that you are unnecessarily frightened of him, bids me tell you to be of good cheer. For, though he could easily crush you with one stamp of his foot, he has no such unkind intention; but, indeed only wishes to be your very good friend and to render you all the service in his power."

At this the people began to pluck up courage, and although a few still had some misgivings (for the dwarf was so terribly ugly) yet most of them began to feel ashamed of their fears.

"My name," continued the dwarf, "is Capital, and I and my fellow-servant, Competition, have worked many years for our master, who is the best of all possible masters, and treats us exceedingly well. Seeing your poor little valley, with its miserable orchards, and knowing how hard you have to work to make your corn grow and how few nice things you get in return for your work—my master (with his usual kindness of heart) has taken pity on you,

Fig. 8. Walter Crane's illustration for Oscar Wilde's *The Happy Prince* (1880), in which the prince discards money and ornamentation to help the poor.

and will show you how, by working for him, you can have a great deal more comfort. Indeed, if you are industrious you may become rich as he—look!"

With that the dwarf opened the sack he was carrying, and poured out its contents—a number of glittering gold pieces, which came tumbling out before the astonished gaze of the people.

Now a curious thing happened—at the sound of the tinkling gold all the good fairies spread their wings and flew right away.

It was not long before the dazzled people were persuaded to accompany the dwarf to his master; and, following the servant's instructions, knelt at the feet of the giant to receive his blessing and words of advice. First he flattered them by telling them how sensible they were to come to him as they had done; and the people were just beginning to think that they were very wise indeed, when he began to call them fools.

"See here!" he said, "have you not been spending all the best years of your life in growing a little corn and fruit for yourselves, when under your cornfields there lies a gold-mine, which would make you and your children rich for ever?"

At this the people looked at each other in astonishment, and some were for running to dig at once to see if it were true. But the giant roared with laughing. "Do you think with your foolish, little spades that you can unearth the gold which lies deep hidden in the earth?" he said. "No, no! my friends." Then, seeing their disappointment, he added, "But I will tell you what I will do. I will give you spades with which to dig all the gold you want, but I shall expect you to give me a share in return."

At this the people were delighted and cried out how good and generous kind Giant Monopoly was, and they set to work to build him a great palace to live in; for none of their homes were large enough for him.

■ ■ ■

If you could have seen Happy Valley a year after the giant came you would have been surprised at the change which had come over it—surprised, and sorry, too, I think. For instead of the laughing cornfields and orchards, great ugly pits yawned everywhere; even the sparkling rivulets were turned to dirty, muddy streams, as the people threw the earth into them and washed their gold in them. Oh, yes! There was gold, plenty of it. The giant's spades (each of which took 100 men to dig with) tore up the whole cornfield with one spadeful, and there it lay—a great glittering mass.

But now, see how cunning old Monopoly was! He took a great sack and held it out before the people. "When this sack is full," he said, "the rest of the gold shall be yours, and I will only take this for my share."

"Very reasonable," said everyone; "of course there will be plenty left for us." So they shoveled up the gold with a will, and poured it into the sack.

But (poor, silly things!) they could not see the hole in the other end of the sack, and that as fast as they filled it the gold ran out, and was gathered up by Monopoly and carried off to his palace.

Soon, however, the people grew very weary of trying to fill a sack that was never full. They began to want food, but no one had any time to get it, and their orchards and cornfields had all been dug up. The giant, seeing that they were likely to die from hunger, and that he might have to turn to and dig up his own gold, called his servant Competition, and bade him throw a handful of gold amongst them. This the people scrambled for, and some were knocked over and killed in the tussle, and some who got a few lumps gave it away to their fellows in exchange for the food they were so sorely needing.

So this went on for years, and the people grew more and more afraid of the giant, and many hated him because they had seen the hole in the sack, but they dared say nothing about it.

One day, a young man called Fairplay, instead of going to work in the gold-mines, sat down to think. Now everyone knows that if you want to do more work than you can manage in a day, it is no use to sit down and think about it, or you will not do any at all. And this is what happened to Fairplay. The more he thought, the more disinclined he was to work, and the end of it was that, instead of going to work at the gold-mines he went wandering away and away, until at last he lost sight of Happy Valley altogether, and found himself in the heart of the country.

What beautiful fields and woods," thought he; "why should I not stay here, and live on berries and mushrooms!" So he set to work, and built himself a little home of wood, and here for a short time he lived very happily.

But he had not been long in his little wooden hut when he began to feel very, very sorry for his fellowmen toiling so miserably without enough to eat.

"How can I free them," thought he, "from that terrible tyrant, Monopoly? We must kill him; but I, alone, cannot do it. I must get others to join me."

So back he went to the Valley, but when his fellows saw him they all began to jeer. "Here is a lazy fellow, who won't work," said they; and they threw stones at him. "Better stone Monopoly," cried Fairplay, "for not only will he not work, but he grabs all the gold for which you work so hard for himself."

But they hooted and stoned him all the more for that; only some went home and thought over what he had said.

These few sought out Fairplay afterwards, and asked him what he meant.

"Have you seen the hole in the sack?" said he. And they nodded silently.

Then he told them his plan, of how they must free themselves from the giant and his servants, and they agreed to help him.

Lo! one night, when the giant was asleep, a long procession wound round the valley. First came Fairplay, with his followers; after them the women and children; and after them quite an army of fairies, each with a glittering sword in his hand. They knocked at the door of the palace, and killed the terrible giant, and his servant, Competition, ran away and was seen no more in Happy Valley.

"But what about Capital?" you ask.

Well, I'm coming to that. When they tried to find him they could not see the ugly old dwarf anywhere, but, instead, found a beautiful princess, whose long, golden hair reached to the floor.

"The giant wanted to marry me," she told them; "and when I would have nothing to do with him he turned me into an ugly dwarf, and made me work for him. Dear people, you have made me free! To show you my gratitude I will work for you all my life."

So Princess Capital married Fairplay, and they worked for the people, and were happy ever after.

■ The Peasants and the Parasites. A Fable

R. B. Suthers, 1908

Once upon a time there was a Peasant, who by diligence and industry wrung from the earth a decent living. And one day, while he was at work in the fields, he suddenly felt a weight descend on his shoulders. Without looking up he asked "What may this be?"

And a voice answered, "I am thy King."

"My King?" quoth the Peasant. "Whence and what are thou?"

And the King answered, "I come from the gods, and I have been sent to rule thy goings and comings, and to defend thee from enemies."

And the Peasant knelt and gave thanks to the gods.

Thereafter the Peasant was the slave of the King, and did his bidding in all things. And many times the burden was grievous to bear, but the Peasant complained not, for so he would have flouted the gods.

And it came to pass that one day, as the Peasant toiled, there came another stranger, and when he saw the King, he stopped and looked and a light came into his eyes. And he said to the King, "Who art thou?"

And the King answered, "I am the King of this Peasant."

"Thou a King," cried the stranger. "Who made thee a King over this man?"

"The gods sent me," replied the King. "And who art thou to question me? Go thy ways, or it may be worse for thee."

But the stranger stirred not. "If thou art indeed a King," said he, "show me the sign."

"What sign?" asked the King.

"Ah!" cried the stranger. "So thou knowest not the Sign. Thou art no King. Thou art an impostor. Thou has deceived this poor Peasant.—Thou—"

"H'sh!" whispered the King in terror.

"How if I denounce thy villainy to the Peasant," said the stranger. "Then would he cast thee down and throw thy body to the wild beasts."

And the King trembled with fear, and looked piteously at the stranger. And the stranger smiled a cunning smile and said, "Make room."

And the stranger climbed on the back of the Peasant, and the King made room, and the colour came back into his cheeks.

And the Peasant felt the new burden, and he said, "What may this be?"

And the stranger answered, "I am thy Priest."

"My Priest," said the Peasant. "What and whence art thou?"

"I come from the gods," replied the Priest, "and I have been sent to teach thee to love and obey thy King, and to guide thy King aright, peradventure he stray from the path the gods would have him follow."

And the Priest winked at the King, and the King was comforted.

And the Peasant knelt and thanked the gods for their great kindness to one so lowly.

So he had now to bear a double burden, and often his poor back ached. And the King and the Priest were as brothers, howbeit sometimes they quarreled as to who should be first. And one day, when they had nigh appeared to come to blows, a stranger appeared.

"Why revilest thou one the other?" he asked.

And the Priest was wroth and answered, "This impostor would fain rob me of my Priestly dues. Let him beware, lest I inform the Peasant that his King is no King, and carries not the sign of the god-sent."

And the stranger pondered for a time, and then turned to the Priest and said, "Hast *thou* a sign?"

And the Priest was covered with confusion, and spake not.

"Oho!" cried the stranger.

"Villain," raged the King. "Hi! Peasant—I will denounce thee—"

"H'sh!" said the stranger. "Make room for me."

So they made room and the stranger climbed up beside them on to the back of the Peasant.

And the Peasant felt the new burden and said, "What may this be?"

And the stranger answered, "I am thy Lawyer."

"My Lawyer! What and whence art thou?"

"I come from the gods," said the Lawyer, "and I have been sent to be a Judge between thee and thy King and Priest, to the end that they may not thoughtlessly deprive thee of thy just rights."

And the Lawyer winked at the King and the Priest, and once more they breathed freely.

And the Peasant knelt and thanked the gods for their gift.

So now the burden of the Peasant was still more heavy, and his eyes were always turned to the earth. And the years rolled on, and the King and the Priest and the Lawyer began to be afraid that the Peasant might sink under their weight.

And one day there came by a stranger, and when he saw the Peasant with his load he exclaimed, "Friend, thou art sick."

"Aye," said the Peasant, "I grow old, and my limbs are stiff—"

"Old! Thou old?" cried the stranger. "I will soon cure *thee* of old age. Wilt thou take my advice?"

"Nay, I follow no advice but that of my Lawyer, my Priest, and my King," replied the Peasant.

And the Lawyer said to the stranger, "Come up higher, friend."

So the stranger climbed on to the back of the Peasant beside the King, the Priest, and the Lawyer.

And the Peasant felt the new burden and said, "What may this be?"

And the stranger answered, "I am thy Doctor."

"My Doctor!" said the Peasant. "What and whence art thou?"

And the Doctor answered, "I come from the gods, and I have been sent to teach thee the laws of health, and to cure thy body of pain and disease." And the Doctor winked at the King, the Priest, and the Lawyer. And they smiled, and the anxious looks left their eyes.

And the Peasant knelt and thanked the gods for their goodness and loving kindness.

So now his burden was heavier than ever, but still he toiled on and never murmured. And the years rolled by. And in turn there came a Poet, to sing to the Peasant, and a Politician, to orate to him, and an Actor, to amuse him, and a Scientist, to bemuse him. And they all clomb[1] on the back of the Peasant beside the King, the Priest, the Lawyer, and the Doctor.

And one day a MAN appeared, and when he saw the Peasant and his terrible load, he was moved to anger. And he heaped scorn on the King and the Priest and the Lawyer, and the other riders, thinking to shame them out of their cruelty. But they heeded him not, and reviled him, and called him "Infidel."

So he turned to the Peasant and prayed him to stand up and be a man and cast off the cunning scoundrels who oppressed him.

And the King and the Priest and the Lawyer and the rest trembled and were afraid.

"If he should look up," they said.

But the Peasant heeded not the voice of the MAN.

And the Lawyer said to the MAN, "climb up."

And the MAN looked at him, and the Lawyer quailed before the MAN's eyes.

And when the others knew that the MAN would not climb up, their hearts sank within them.

And the Politician said, "Let *us* climb down."

And again and again the MAN urged the Peasant to stretch himself and to stand up, and assert his manhood. But for a long time the Peasant heeded him not at all. And at length, the MAN angered the Peasant, and he, too, reviled the MAN, and called him "infidel." And the King and the Priest and the Lawyer and the others jeered at him, and said, "We are safe again."

But the MAN clung to his task, and at last the Peasant began to listen.

And the Priest said, "I also think it is time to climb down."

And they quarrelled amongst themselves, and could not agree what to do.

And the Peasant has not yet stood up, nor have the Parasites climbed down.

But the Peasant is listening to the MAN with both ears.

■ The Eternal Feminine

C. L. Everard, 1908

"The country's going to the dogs!" said the Colonel, throwing down the "Times" in disgust.

"I wish I could say you surprised me," said the Doctor.

"Those wretched women, sir, have captured the House of Commons," said the Colonel.

"I wish them joy of their conquest," said the Doctor cynically. "But 'dogs' was hardly the word."

"What's the trouble?" asked the Barrister, who had just come away from a dreary debate at St. Stephen's.[1]

"Two hundred and seventy-one members in favour of Woman's Suffrage," said the irate Colonel, "and only ninety-two against."

"Majority, one-seven-nine," said the Barrister.

"Correct," said the Doctor, admiringly. "The whole ninety-two, to Prejudice were true."

"If you'll abstain from your flippant doggerel," said the Colonel, "I will proceed."

The Doctor's apologies were numerous.

"As I was about to remark," continued the Colonel, "this resolution will ruin the country."

"The road to Hell is paved with Parliamentary resolutions," commented the Doctor.

"There must be a permanent Paving Scandal in the infernal regions," said the Barrister.

"If the resolution means nothing else," said the Colonel, "it means that the government of the country will soon be handed over to the women—the shrieking sisterhood."[2]

"Rome was saved by the cackling of her geese,"[3] said the Doctor.

"The point we are dealing with," said the Barrister reprovingly, "is the question of the new political faith, I take it, of those members who voted for the resolution."

"Political faith be hanged!" said the Colonel.

"Can you hang what doesn't exist?" asked the Doctor. "The resolution was supported, not by faith, but funk. It only confirms my estimate of the House of Commons—a collection of fourth-rate politicians, with fifth-rate ideas."

"I'm inclined to agree with you," said the Colonel.

"I can't help that," replied the Doctor. "You condemn the Commons for being too advanced; I condemn them because they are not advanced enough—that's all."

"They represent the intelligence of the nation," protested the Barrister.

"I can quite believe it," said the Doctor, "since the British nation is principally composed of individuals who have lost all individuality."

"Yet you believe in the democracy," said the Colonel.

"The definition of terms is the Achilles' heel of philosophy," replied the Doctor. "I believe in Democracy as a principle of government. For 'the democracy' of which you speak—meaning the mob; for 'the democracy' which exults over a Boer War and whines when called upon to foot the bill;[4] which sheds crocodile tears over Chinese Slavery,[5] and is content to remain in a state of slavery itself—for this democracy I have little admiration."

"There is not much political difference between us," said the Colonel.

"As befits an old politician," replied the Doctor, "you do not study politics. Party politics is your forte. You believe—I do not impugn your sincerity—in Toryism, and beneficent feudalism, governed by a hereditary aristocracy; you stand for the party of yesterday."

"Quite true," said the Barrister, cheerfully.

"Our legal friend here," continued the Doctor, "as becomes a prospective Liberal member for Slumton-cum-Jerriville, was miseducated in the Manchester school.[6] He believes in the Divine Right of the Captains of Industry—the plutocracy of to-day—to govern us. He ably represents the party of to-day."

"And what of your noble self?" asked the Colonel, with a smile.

"As a Socialist," said the Doctor, "I believe in government by an *educated* democracy—not a mobocracy, mark you. I am content to support the party of to-morrow."

"'To-morrow never comes," said the Colonel triumphantly.

"Your originality is almost startling," said the Doctor; "but your party has not yet arrived at to-day. I stand by my definition, nevertheless."

"What of the party of the day after to-morrow?" queried the Barrister.

"On the day after to-morrow," replied the Doctor, "there will be no parties."

"We are apt to wander from the point in these discussions," said the Colonel. "We were discussing Woman's Suffrage originally."

"The Eternal Feminine is the Eternal Question," sighed the Doctor.

"Are you in favour of Woman's Suffrage?" asked the Barrister.

"I support the enfranchisement of women, certainly," replied the Doctor; "but I do not believe that the franchise should apply only to certain amiable females, who labour under the delusion— a woman without a delusion is like a fish without sauce—that a woman who pays rates is a lady. I think the vote must be given to all women."

"I hardly expected you to take up that position," said the Colonel, "after the opinions I have heard you express on the subject of Sex Equality."

"It is not a question of one's personal predilections," replied the Doctor.

"It is a question of sentiment," said the Barrister gallantly.

"It is a question of economics—a subject of which you, fortunately, know nothing," said the Doctor. "As a matter of fact, my position is logically consistent. I admit this with trepidation. The mind of the man who is constantly striving to be consistent is apt to attain to the consistency of mud."

"Joking apart," said the Barrister, who hails from Stirling Burghs,[7] "do you think it is desirable that women should have votes?"

"Plautus[8] says, 'there are some things which are admirable and desirable; there are more things which are necessary and inevitable,'" replied the Doctor. "The enfranchisement of the woman is, at any rate, economically necessary and inevitable."

"I doubt if Plautus said that," said the Colonel suspiciously.

"It may have been Herbert Spencer," replied the Doctor, "Or Machiavelli.[9] It doesn't matter much."

■ The Myopians' Muddle

Victor Grayson, 1909

In the land of Coma[1] dwelt the Myopians[2]—a strange people. Able and industrious were they, and the earth did yield abundance to their labours.

The sun sent forth his genial rays to arm and gladden the earth, and grateful showers did gratify its thirst. Thews and sinewa[3] of iron had the Myopians, and no task was too onerous for their enterprise. Yet were they not happy, for their vision was clouded. A few there were—yclpet[4] Panopians—whose sights were whole. And by reason of this they directed the labour of the others.

When the harvest was reaped, they of clear vision did appropriate the major portion. For the Myopians held their seeing brethren in humble fear and reverence. There was one among them, strangely garbed, deprived of physical vision; yet could he see with his soul. Him they called the Fakir. But, being a defective offshoot of the Panopians, he lived after their fashion and slept in their halls. When discontentment moved the Myopians to sighings and complainings, when they did whine of hard labour and small fare, he did endeavour to assuage their grief with hopeful prophecies. He told them of a happy land far, far away, where everyone would see; and those who saw least in Coma would see most in Utopia. He urged that the sight of the soul was better than the sight of the eyes, and taught them by precept, if not by example that frugal fare was best for the soul's vision.

The people heard his message with gladness, and the Panopians did pamper him in that he soothed the people. But it so happened in the inscrutable ways of Providence, and because of the

200   Victor Grayson

considerable appetites of its favoured ones, that there came a great drought.

■ ■ ■

And the Myopians began to murmur moodily. They said there was plenty to eat, as they had produced abundance. But the Panopians and the Fakir said that was an illusion due to myopia. They were short of bread because they were short of sight, and they could not see how that could be remedied until they reached Utopia. However, the matter had been receiving their consideration, and they had decided to construct, or at least to direct the construction of, a railway that would lead them to the happy land. And the poor people worked hard with little food, heartened by the hope of better things. At last the railway was completed. The Panopians charged them a goodly price for the journey; and one of them in a blue uniform drove the train, while another in a red uniform collected the cash as conductor. With hearts full of joy and hope the Myopians embarked. They could not see where they were going, but they could feel the motion of the train, and that did them good. For many, many days they rode in the train. The air became foul and noisome. The food was stale and inadequate. But they were buoyed up with faith in the knowledge and skill of the blue Panopian who drove and the red Panopian who conducted.

At last the train pulled up, and the Myopians sent up a cheer, thinking they had arrived at their destination. But the red conductor merely shouted, "All change here!" Then they dismounted, but owing to defective vision could not recognize that they were in Coma again. They had built their railroad in a circle. Then the conductor led them round into the same train, but from another platform. Yet they recked[5] not. The blue man went to the back of the train, and the red man to the front. And off they started again for the land of Utopia. They again rode for many dreary days. And they were cold and hungry, for they had paid their money to the Panopians for the journey. In due course, however, they stopped again. And this time the blue man shouted, "All change!" They were then led round the platform and entered the other side of the train. The blue man drove this time and the red man conducted the train. But some of the Myopians grew impatient and suspicious and some grew very angry. One said he did not think that either the driver or the conductor knew where Utopia was. And another said he thought they knew where it was, but for some reason or other did not want to go there.

■ ■ ■

In the end they sent a deputation of the Myopians to the driver to make inquiries. The driver, as was his wont, received them kindly and heard their complaints. They must not, he said, be led away by ill-disposed men of their class. They must learn to be patient. Utopia was a long way off, and the roads were very steep, and the train must of necessity move very slowly. Meanwhile, however, he was very, very sorry for them, and would be most pleased to pull up at Palliativo, where there was some fairly clean water to drink and a bit of grass to eat. He would give them some of his own stores gladly, but he needed all he had to feed the nerve necessary to his responsible position. So they returned encouraged to their unwholesome carriages.

So it fell out, however, that one of the younger Myopians suddenly recovered his full vision; and he bored a hole through the side of the carriage and watched the track. To his surprise and disgust he soon discovered that the train was travelling in a circle. Twice they passed through the land of Coma before he opened his mouth to inform his brethren. But, behold! When he told them, they called him "liar" and "malcontent" and "dreamer." And it came to the ears of the driver and guard that the young Myopian had recovered his sight and was spreading malicious rumours. So the Fakir was sent again to soothe the pilgrims, who were beginning to believe that there was something in what the young man said. The Fakir was replete with righteous indignation. He assured them that progress was being made, though very slowly. They had set out for Utopia. What was it and where was it? Utopia, he said, with touching solemnity, is not a place: it is a state of mind. If only they would see that truth, they would not care if they never reached Utopia at all. Life consisted in striving. Man never is, but always to be, blessed.

And the young man, being refined and courteous, was overheard to murmur, "Rodents!" And the Fakir, having taken a little collection for his stomach's sake, blessed them and departed.

■ ■ ■

The young man, however, persisted in his statement that the train was travelling in a circle. And he converted some. These went to the driver again, and he promised them that he would inquire into the matter. Day followed day, and they still went round and round. The young man grew impatient and angry. He even went the length of applying the brake and refusing to release his hold. And the Myopians had a meeting and dissociated themselves from his action. The proper way to solve the difficulty was to use moral suasion on the driver and conductor. They admitted they were going in a circle, but they contended it was better to travel in a circle than not to travel at all.

The young man was seized by the driver and dropped off the train amidst the applause of the Myopians. They were last seen in a compromising position approaching the brake.

■ A Martian's Visit to Earth. Being a Literal Translation into English of the Preface to an Account by a Martian of his Visit to England

A. L. Grey, 1909

To those of my fellow Martians who hoped to learn something fresh in the domain of sociology, to add something to their science of politics, this account will certainly come as a disappointment. Instead of revealing an advanced, highly organised, highly differentiated civilisation from which we might construct new ideals I have to tell of a quite primitive state, to find a counterpart to which we must go back in our own history some thousands of years. To bring this fact home to my readers I need only refer to one fact, that upon Earth the "strife" age is still in progress. There have, it is true, been a few moments in history when a vision of a better state, in which help shall replace strife, moral strength replace cunning, and in which men shall recognise that the welfare of all is the highest good and rigidly entails, in the surest and best sense, the welfare of the individual—when such a vision has appeared to a select band whose philosophy surrounding influences too unfavourable, died an early death.

The etheroplane, which had cost us so many years' thought and labour, fully justified our efforts by a smooth and uneventful journey across the intervening ether. We chose for our destination the largest collection of habitations—a place called London, the metropolis of the British nations, as we considered that we should here be able to study society in its most advanced form. As we slowly descended upon this great collection of houses I noted a few particulars which I may as well describe here.

The first impression I got from the hurrying crowds of black-coated men in the streets, the knots of manual workers near the docks, upon the buildings, and passing to and fro in the factories and workshops, was that the whole was a great penal settlement where men were condemned to labour of varying degrees of irksomeness. Insufficient nourishment was betrayed by the pinched, pale faces of the sweating manual workers; worry, care, and anxiety furrowed the faces of the men in the streets, and even of the gaily-dressed crowds who were strolling about in the parks. The heaviest punishments seemed to be those of the manual workers, for they are at work long before other people are awake; they are exposed to many dangers to their lives, and frequently work without any protection against the rain or piercing cold. I concluded that they were the greatest criminals, probably murderers, for I could not conceive that for any less crime the State could condemn a man to pass the whole of his life in such discomfort and misery as these have to do. Those guilty of less, but still grave, crimes, I imagined, were the lowest grade of the black-coats who work nearly as long as the manual workers, sometimes even longer. They are cooped up in incredible numbers in badly lighted, comfortless rooms, where they spend nearly the whole of the day bent over books in which they write with a pen. I am informed that it is a very rare occurrence for one of these "clerks," as they are called, to be promoted to more responsible and better paid work. Compared with the first class, indeed, they were as regards physical well-being in even worse plight. The dull, unhealthy monotony of their lives of endless routine was expressed in the apathy and inertia of their minds and bodies. In prominent contrast to these was a small coterie of individuals who seemed to have been selected from the nation at large, set apart, and supported at what was in effect the State expense, either as a reward for great and meritorious services to the State, or because their transcendental mental and moral qualities marked them out as teachers and advisers of the fellows, or because they were in some way indispensable to the general welfare. Their dwellings were the most magnificent of all; their evenings were spent in feasting and gaiety; they dressed sumptuously and were attended by numerous personal servants who observed towards them the greatest deference. My first conclusion was that they were sacred personages or comprised some high religious caste, but when I observed that there was a separate priestly caste with which, indeed, they seemed to have rather less connection than the rest of the community, I was obliged to revise this opinion and formed the one I have already referred to. I was early brought, however, into contact with a considerable number of this leisured class; and to my surprise I was unable to detect any of the superiority I have imagined to be theirs. On the contrary, their moral and intellectual standard was undoubtedly below that of their fellows. One of my first inquiries was with regard to this anomaly. It appears that it is the custom on Earth for property and land to be parcelled out among individuals, and that a father leaves at his death almost the whole of his possessions to his children, only a small fraction passing to the State, the result being that a wealthy caste having no regular occupation other than that of disposing of possessions left to them has gradually come into existence. Now mark the consequences. In the course of generations the qualities which originally distinguished the members of this caste gradually atrophied through disuse, for it is one of the strange laws on Earth that, although a man can only amass wealth by his own efforts or by the efforts of other individuals, when he has got it, the continued possession of it is assured him by the State, an attempt on the part of another to deprive him of his possessions being an offence punished by the State; there is, therefore, no need for the possession by the son of the qualities of the ancestor who collected the wealth. In fact, at the time of my visit to London there were persons of notoriously weak intellect in the possession of vast wealth which had passed to them from a relative.

Not only is wealth transmissible in this way, but also, in this extraordinary country, the power of government! A certain section of the idle rich caste, known as the "titled nobility," inherit the right of taking part in the making of the law. There is, however, in the Legislature a House of elected representatives, and, as might be expected, the relations between the "Lower" House, as it is called, and the "Upper" House,[1] in which these persons of atrophied mentality and morality may sit, are often far from cordial. It is a significant fact that the progress of the nation has proceeded *pari passu*[2] with the decay of the power of the Upper House. Originally, the Upper House, or House of Lords, was a meeting of martial chieftains and men noted for their cunning or wisdom and prowess in debate, and was called as a rule for a council of war. As such it was indispensable, and even after its function as adviser to the head chieftain or king in matters relating to hostilities with neighbouring tribes or nations had undergone transformations and attenuations, the Council served a useful purpose in troublous times when each member or chief was the actual head of a band of warriors or retainers. A change, however, has taken place since the origin of this part of the Legislature in the social conditions of the race. In the case of the nation I studied the more especially, known as the English nation, this change, the change from the military state to the industrial state, was, perhaps, more complete than in any other terrestrial race, but such is their reverence for ancient institutions that they will retain them, not only after they have ceased to exercise their legitimate powers, but even after their influence is admittedly harmful. In no case is this more apparent than in the case of the British House of Lords. The Lords have ceased to be heads of bands of warriors; they are not necessarily warriors themselves; they have crests, but no helmets; armorial insignia, but no arms; territorial titles, but no consequent jurisdiction; in short, there is no vestige remaining of the right they once had, in the ages of physical strength, to govern their fellows—in the age of Intellect their only interest is for the historian, as Vestigial Rudiments.[3]

It will seem incredible, but it is nevertheless a fact, that all terrestrial nations who make any claim to civilisation are divided socially into two great classes, viz., workers, and capitalists or shareholders who own what the workers work with! And not only this, but under the present conditions the two classes are engaged in endless strife, each wishing to increase its share in the wealth produced at the expense of the other! Hence the social and political quagmire in which all parties are floundering. Most of the members of both classes may take a part in the election of representatives to the "Lower" Legislative House, called the House of Commons. At the time of which I write the electorate numbered 7,500,000, of whom 6,500,000[4] belonged to the classes of workers, so that they are an overwhelming majority at the polls. In spite of this, however, the special representatives who look after the interests of the "lower" classes form less than one-twelfth of the whole House![5]

There are very few constituencies in the country in which the shareholding class is sufficiently numerous relatively to be the dominant power on polling day. That this is recognised by the "upper" classes themselves is shown by the tone of the press, the addresses and speeches on such occasions of the political leaders, national and local, which are usually adroitly framed to inveigle the working man. Polling day is the one day in the year on which the working man feels that he is indeed a separate entity, and not an insignificant detail in the organism, which, like Sisyphus,[6] rolls the boulder of capital up the industrial mountain only for it to return for a fresh ascent. As will be already apparent, there were many features of the present civil and political life of a typical terrestrial nation which seemed out of date, anomalous, or ludicrous, but none more amazing than this, that though industrially the workpeople recognised clearly the consequences of the antagonistic nature of their relation to the shareholding or capitalistic class and had formed themselves into unions to strengthen their positions, politically this recognition had no existence. The workers have a majority at the Parliamentary polls; they have men of intellect and learning ready to come forward as their representatives; they have, collectively, the necessary funds; they have, in short, all that is necessary for them to reconstruct the industrial system on an equitable and rational basis, a basis upon which they will be able to enjoy the whole fruits of their labour. But they do not move; the handful of

Labour Members in Parliament is impotent in the face of the number of the capitalist class arrayed against them. I looked around and saw the squalor and thraldom of the many, the luxury and license of the few, and marvelled greatly. But at last I saw the reason. Why is the elephant obedient to the prod of the mahout upon his head, whom he could crush to a lifeless pulp in a second's grip of his trunk or beneath the bulk of his mighty body? The man knows, the animal does not; that is the reason. So does the capitalist know, but the worker does not. But, unlike the elephant, the human worker has the capacity for knowledge, and once let him wake to it the time of the shareholder will be over, his place will know him no more.

I cannot better conclude this preface than by making a few reflections on more general aspects of this antiquated system and on the political state of Earth in general. The planet at present is divided among a large number of "nations," as they are called. Each nation has its little plot of land, which it considers to be its own inviolable property, and it is considered one of the highest virtues of man for him to do all in his power to render secure for the nation in which he was born the exclusive right to its particular plot of land, even to the extent of losing his life in its defence. Each nation guards its land with the utmost vigilance and jealousy, although its right to the particular area it occupied at the time of my visit seemed problematical in most cases, as it had often been previously taken by force from another race; this species of robbery had, indeed, on Earth at all times and by all races been considered to be creditable rather than otherwise, and those warriors who have plundered other nations most and driven them from their own formerly peaceful and often prosperous land into sterile and mountainous countries have been hailed as heroes on their return, and have received great rewards and honours. It is curious that while in the individual rapacity of this kind and the taking over of other persons' property by force is regarded as immoral, … a State, [is] quite at liberty to seize the property of other States. Speaking generally, the morality of the State lags behind that of the individual. It so happened that the English nation, of whom I am speaking more particularly, governed directly from London, or indirectly at local centres, a greater portion of the land of the globe than any other nation, for the defence of which, as the territories in question were most easily or of necessity approached by sea, a tremendous navy was kept, at great expense both in men and money. With regard to this colonial question, affairs are rapidly approaching a critical stage. The population of the older and more congested portions of the globe such as Europe is increasing by leaps and bounds. England has millions of square miles of sparsely inhabited territory to which her surplus population may emigrate, and this is naturally regarded with covetous eyes by the other nations who have no outlet of their own. It will not be long, in my opinion, before there will be a world-wide upheaval, either peaceful or bloody, which will result in a more equitable distribution of the land as a preliminary to the final obliteration of the artificial division of the human races into hostile nations.

In many cases the annexation of territory has been peaceful, and has finally been acquiesced in by the minor nation upon which it has conferred many benefits. In such cases, of course, very little criticism can be made, but in other cases, when the conquest has been by the edge of the sword the wound has ranked[7] and produced an embittered, crushed people in whose midst the agitator, traitor, and anarchist have always found a home. The cases of Poland and Ireland come in this category, and in no case is the injustice of superior might more evident than in the case of Ireland, which has chafed against English rule for seven hundred years. To-day the wound is as sore as ever. The Irish race are the descendants of the primitive tribes who were expelled from England, Wales, and Scotland by the Romans and Saxons. They belong to an entirely different stock from the Anglo-Saxons and have quite alien racial characteristics. It is probably this fact which has prevented anything like a reconciliation between the two peoples. Ireland was first brought under English dominion some seven hundred years ago, but it was not until several centuries later that the country was finally conquered—if it can be said ever to have been so in view of the numerous armed insurrections which have taken place at various times since. It is true that Ireland was in a turbulent state originally and was racked by internal dissensions between various independent chieftains. It is also possible that it would have remained in this state to this day if Irish soil had never received an English foot. But this is a question for the Irish and the Irish alone, and not for the English or any other nation. To say that Ireland is better off under English rule is no extenuation—the Irish are the best judges of their own happiness, and they want the English out. Possibly France might be better off under English rule, but (such is her blindness) she thinks otherwise, and the last vestige of English property on French soil disappeared four hundred years ago. I can find no justification at all for the continued occupation of Ireland by the English. It is an act of unprincipled aggrandisement. Surely the keeping of four and a half millions of people in a political yoke which is intolerable to them, by a nation alien in origin, in religion, in almost every racial characteristic, is an act of political immorality which a nation whose policy is supposed to be dictated by principles of justice and humanity should repudiate!

There are many aspects and problems of human life on Earth which I am unable to deal with in this short sketch, but those which I have touched upon will, I think, afford sufficient grounds for my general condemnation of the present system as cruel, wasteful, and, above all, aimless and vague. What is the object of the activity of the nations, *as nations?* Evolutionally speaking, they are in the "amoeba" stage; their sole aim in life is existence; they seek to survive—that is all. They have yet to realise that they are only component parts of a higher organism, the world, and that strife between those parts reacts upon even the victors through the injury to that higher organism.

The same pathetic aimlessness marks the growth to maturity of the individual. His natural aptitudes and the needs of the State are often the last things considered in determining his life's occupation. The State maintains an attitude of indifference on the point of a boy's suitability for his occupation. He may wish, for example, to be an engineer (as many boys do), and may, or may not, have a genius for engineering, but his father, who is a doctor, wishes his son to join him in his practice. The State supplies no information as to the total number of medical men it requires for the efficient care of its sick or whether the supply already exceeds the demand; nor could it do so if it wished; it has no information, for it takes no interest in these things, being, as a rule, more intent on acquiring some desolate tract of land ten thousand miles away. The same vagueness applies to all human activities. A man's occupation, his make, his philosophy (if any), his outlook upon life, are all allotted to him by a process of which chance is the greatest ingredient and his own needs and the nation's needs the smallest. So long as those in power and affluence on Earth continue to lack the insight and moral stamina to prefer a happy community to a surfeited oligarchy, though the latter be themselves, so long will Earth be unable to progress toward the Martian polity in which, given an individual's mental ability, special talents (such as for art, music, engineering, scientific research, etc.), character, desires, and disposition, the State, acting on these data on the one hand and its own requirements for its most efficient equipment on the other, allots a definite career and prospect for that individual. On no other principle will it be possible to secure justice and contentment to the man and prevent the great loss to the State of intellect and talent which takes place to-day on Earth.

◼ Nightmare Bridge

Glanville Maidstone, 1910

I knew in my dream that I was lost. Weary and cold, with aching feet and heavy eyes, I plodded along that silent and solitary thoroughfare of a great city. The vista seemed endless; the winking lamps stretched on as far as one could see. Far as I walked I had met no one, not even a policeman. Stay! There is a constable standing in the shadow of a gateway. I stop before him; I ask him whither does this road lead. He looks at me with strange eyes; he does not speak, he whispers: "To the bridge." He is very pale, the constable, and very lean. His face—his face is like a skull: it *is* a skull. No; but how hollow are his eyes! How sharp and prominent are his cheekbones! And as I turn away he laughs. His laugh puts fear into my heart. I turn cold with fear. I try to walk rapidly away from him, but my feet are like lead. And he follows me. I hear the sound of his feet, and the echo of his measured step comes back from the dark and silent houses. Will this road never end? Do those glimmering lamp-lights stretch on, an avenue of stars, to the edge of the world? Where is this bridge? Why did he call it *the* Bridge? I tramp on, the constable following without a word. Then—then I see the Bridge. I am on the Bridge. It is a wide bridge, brilliantly lighted, exquisitely paved. There is a broad footpath on either side, and lines of gilded railings. Overhead stretch festoons of beautiful flowers. The road is used by motor cars and handsome equipages drawn by noble horses. In the carriages and cars are men and women dressed luxuriantly. I can see the sparkle of gems and hear the sound of conversation—conversation gay and witty, carried on in high-pitched aristocratic voices. The traffic in the roadway is not dense: there is ample room. On the footpaths there are but few people; they are the counterparts of those in the carriages: men and women, handsomely dressed lounging easily, laughing and talking: a picture of wealth and happiness. Outside the railings?—outside the railings it is dark. There seems to be partly visible through the shadowy obscurity a moving crowd, a dense traffic. There is a great deal of noise: the noise of tramping horses, heavy wheels, cracking whips; the noise of angry voices, or curses, sobs, and groans. What goes on there in the semi-darkness? Is it a riot? Is it a battle? Hark! a scream!

What bridge is this, then? What does it span: a river? I look for the terrible constable. He is at my side. He shrugs his shoulders and says, in his horrid whisper: "You do well to choose the middle of the Bridge. You would not enjoy the outer roads. I know: I used to be among it."

"What does it mean?" I asked. "What is it? Let us go there, where the noise is. Let us go and see. Come, come, come; let us go to the side of the road, where the crowd is."

"Come," said the constable, "I don't care. I'm safe enough—unless I lose my feet or my head."

"Lose your feet? What do you mean?" I asked.

"Come and see," says the constable, with a grim smile. "If a man goes down in that crush he gets no quarter: not from *them*."

"From whom?"

"From his fellow creatures." The constable leads me back towards the entrance to the bridge. "If you fall," he says, "do you know what they will do to you?"

"Tell me," I ask him.

"Well," he says, "you be careful. If you fall they will kick you; they will trample on you; they will hustle you over the edge, into the river."

We are on the Bridge—on the outer road. What dense traffic! what a terrible crowd! There is not room. There are no footways, and the heavy traffic is mixed with the struggling pedestrians. On the outer side, next the river, there is no parapet. The people fight frantically to keep away from that edge. But they cannot. Hark! another scream! "What is that?"

"Another one gone over," says the constable, "a woman. She's too old and weak to fight. Many of the weak ones go: men and women, and children, too—very many children."

In appearance this crowd resembles an ordinary London crowd—of poor people. The crush is so severe that at every few yards distance we see groups fighting—fighting like animals—fighting as I have seen women and men fighting round the tram cars and the motor omnibuses. And the constable spoke the truth. When a pedestrian—man or woman, yes, or child—goes down, the case is desperate. A girl falls close by us. Another woman kicks her, a man treads upon her; when she screams a second woman strikes her in the face. Then—oh, a huge wagon laden with iron crashes through the crowd. A man is down—down under the wheels!

"In the name of Heaven," I cry, turning to my sardonic guide, "what does this mean? Why do they not widen the Bridge? Why do they not put a parapet on the outer side?"

"No money," says the constable. "Who's to do it?"

"Do it!" I exclaim. "What kind of city is this? Is there no government—no authority?"

"Of course," the constable answers. "This is a civilized country: a Christian country. Government? What are you thinking about?"

"Then," I say, "tell me, who governs this city? Who is responsible for this bridge?"

The constable nods his head towards the wide and beautiful central roadway. "Those," he answers; "those ladies and gentlemen, there."

"But," I cry, "those people take no heed. They are lounging, talking, trifling, laughing. Do they know that men and women are being crushed to death? Do they know that little children are being hurled into the river or crushed under foot? Why do they not stop these horrors? Why do they not widen the bridge?"

The constable shook his head. "I told you," he said, "you would be better in the middle—seeing you'd had the luck to get there. They cannot widen the bridge, do you understand, outwards; they could only relieve the crush by throwing down the railings and throwing open the wide middle road. That's the difficulty."

"But," I said, "in the presence of this awful crush and struggle, this terrible suffering and loss of life, surely they could do as you say! There is room on the bridge for all and to spare."

"True," the constable nodded. "But," he said, "the middle way is *theirs*, do you see? Naturally they will not give up any of their room; that is why they have put up those gilded railings. There are very few can climb those railings."

"But the crowd," I said, "will the crowd endure this? They are so many. They could pull the railings down."

"They are very strong," said the constable.

"If they are made of steel—" I began.

"Steel?" The constable laughed his horrible laugh. "They are made of something stronger than steel," he said.

"Of what are they made?" I asked.

"Of lies," said the constable, and kicked a fallen man out of his way.

"But," I cried, "Lies can be broken with truth. I will speak to the people. I will appeal to them for the sake of their women and children. I will give them the truth to break these lies."

The constable shook his head. "Do nothing of the kind," said he. "Go back to the middle way. You will hardly be heard in all this noise; and how can men listen or understand when they are fighting for dear life? They will pay no attention to you; or they may throw you down, and then they will trample on you. Go back to the middle way."

"Then," I said, "I will appeal to the ladies and gentlemen of the middle way. I will tell them what I have seen."

"No use," said the constable, "those people on the middle way like a lot of air and space; they like to be grand, and they like to be happy. They keep their eyes away from the side road, and talk beautifully about all kinds of noble ideas and pleasant things. But they'll see you damned before they will give up an inch of their room. Try them. Nice, polite, refined, well-spoken ladies and gentlemen they are; but try to take a foot of their road, and you'll think you have been thrown to the lions."

"But," I said, "it is horrible. It is infamous. These people are worse than savages. This city is a disgrace to humanity."

"Steady, steady," said the constable. "What city do *you* come from?"

"I? I come from London."

The constable laid a bony hand on my shoulder. His pale face grew redder, his smile became more human, his baleful eyes twinkled humorously, and his whisper rose to a firm, deep voice. "Why," he said, "London? Bless our two souls! London! Don't I know London? Don't I know that London is just exactly like this? Why, governor, this *is* London. What part is it you want to go to? Now then, wake up, mister; you must not sleep here."

"Good heavens! Why—fancy my falling asleep in a railway station! In the refreshment bar—"

"Well," said the constable, "the bars are closed, sure enough. Not," he added, "but what there might be ways of getting something if you really feel the want of it, sir."

And there were.

■ The Fool and the Wise Man

W. Anderson, 1910

Once upon a time two men met. One asked the other, "Who are you?"

He answered, "I am a fool, I am called a worker. Now tell me, who are you?"

"I," replied the former, "am a wise man; men call me a gentleman."

"What do you do?"

"I teach fools like you."

"Will you teach me?"

"With pleasure, come with me."

The fool went with the wise man, who took him to a pile of bricks and a quantity of wood.

"Build me a grand mansion and a small hut," said the wise man.

The fool did so, and when he had finished the wise man gave him some money, saying: "I will live in the mansion because I have earned it by my intellect; you will live in the hut, which will be better for you as you are a fool; you would not appreciate the artistic merit of the mansion, and the nails of your boots would destroy the rich carpets; and as the hut belongs to me (you know you made it for me), it is quite correct you should pay me rent for the right to live there."

The fool lived in the small hut, and paid the rent, saying: "What a clever man; I should never have thought of building a hut for myself if he had not mentioned it, and I could not pay the rent if he did not pay me a daily wage."

The wise man took the fool to the entrance of a mine, saying: "Draw out the coal from the bowels of the earth, and when I have finished with it you may have the cinders to warm yourself."

The fool drew out the coal and said: "This man is not only wise but good, because he gives me the cinders to warm myself when he could easily have thrown them away."

The wise man said to the fool: "I require someone to dress me, to prepare my food, etc.; give me some of your children to wait upon me."

The fool sent his children, saying to himself: "This is good, he will teach them to know as much as he has me, and some day they will become gentlemen like him."

A few days afterwards the wide-awake one said to the other: "When I took your children into my service I was compelled to increase my expenses; such being the case you will have to be content with a lower wage so as to enable me to remunerate them fairly."

The simpleton scratched his head for a while, but said at last: "Oh, yes, my children must be paid for by all means. Very well, we must all live."

The man of brains said to the ignoramus: "Build two schools for my use, a spacious one and the other of smaller dimensions, where our children may be educated."

"Why," said the latter, "should one be larger than the other?"

"The reason is, that my children being gifted gentlefolk, like myself, require a high education in order to develop their intellectual faculties, hence the need of a large school. On the other hand, your children being the issue of a fool will have to do manual labour, the same as you, and therefore the smaller will suffice them.

As a matter of course you cannot expect your children to be educated for nothing, so you must pay for the service."

One day the clever one betook himself in a very bad mood into the fool's presence, saying: "You have been thinking?"

"Yes," answered the other.

"I will not allow it; if you do it again I shall punish you."

"Oh!" cried the simpleton, dropping his tools, "you have given yourself away. Were you as intelligent as you imagine you would be aware that it is an impossibility for even fools such as I to forego thinking at some time or other. I know you now, you are a knave!"

The following day the slave hoisted a red flag. Armed himself, and rebelled against his master. Thinking was the beginning of the revolution, the consummation of which has not yet arrived.

■ The May-Day Festival in the Year 1970

'*Optimus*', *1911*

On April 29, 1970, the "Volkstribüne," official organ of the Socialist administration for the district of Lower Austria, published the customary order of the President that all work should cease on the First of May. Only such work as was necessary for the festal celebration of that day was to be allowed, but even with regard to the latter the President's message desired that the decoration of the streets and the preparations for the festival should, as far as possible, be carried out on the preceding day.

On the morning of the First of May the great garden city of Vienna, which now extends from Stockerau to Mödling,[1] lay in deep repose. The many bright-coloured little houses, in Cotta style,[2] each surrounded by a small green garden, had been already decked out the night before with red flags, and so it was half past six o'clock—the sun had long ago risen brilliantly—before the first of the green blinds in the workers' little one-family houses were drawn up.

Already the evening before the young people had planted flag-staffs between the blooming chestnut trees, and many hundreds of red flags were already waving merrily in the breeze. The regular roads were strewn with freshly mown grass, and in every district—from Stockerau to Mödling—a large platform was erected in the principal square, with a small platform and speakers' desk opposite to it, which was also to be used by the conductor of the district orchestra.

At 7.20 a.m. the motors from the milk co-operative and other food supply stores, which from old association still kept the name of "hammer-works," ran through the workers' cottages, and deposited in the breakfast receptacle which is built into the front of each house the necessary provisions for the festal day, milk, eggs, bacon, or fish, fruit, vegetables, coffee, cigars, etc., according to the orders given the preceding day at the food centre. At 8 o'clock smoke was already rising from the chimneys of all the pretty houses, and whoever entered any of the clean, white-washed halls was met by an aroma of fresh coffee and newly-baked bread. And at this time many a housewife might be seen going up and down the garden with large scissors choosing the peonies and tulips which were destined for the festal board.

At 8.30 500 bands of music marched through every division of the garden city, except, of course, the inner quarters, on feast days resembling cities of the dead, which are exclusively given up to

Fig. 9. Walter Crane's poster for the International Socialist Trade Union Congress (1896). Private collection, photo © Ken Welsh / Bridgeman Images.

workshops, factories and offices. The underground railway, which takes one in 4 to 6 minutes from, for instance, the St. Viet garden city to the factory quarter of Brigittenau,[3] rests to-day. But at certain headquarters of each district one can—after previously giving notice at the traffic centre—have one of the motors which stand there, which indeed one must drive oneself, in order to do which it is necessary to have passed the chauffeur's examination, a thing which is, in general, done by one member of each family. There is, however, no very great demand for them, most of the comrades preferring to pass the day with companions in the same district, to which they have been drawn in order to be near the friends of their choice.

The silver trumpets of the bands bring jubilation, noise, movement, confusion into the quiet garden city streets. In a twinkling the battalions of the "Youth" were drawn up, and, headed by the bands, marched rank after rank to the platforms on the public place. The orchestra played historical battle songs from the old departed times of oppression, and the choirs of youths chimed in with clear voices. By 9 o'clock everybody was on their feet; 800 platforms in all the great squares were crowded, and from millions of throats now rose a real true hymn of the people into the stir, a song of joy and of labour, a paean of youth and strength, a song sung by awakened mankind in its own honour.

Then all became still.

An old man mounted the tribune (the procedure was the same at all the centres of festivity) and spoke: "Comrades, brothers, fellow citizens! Let no man to-day forget the times of struggle! You rosy-cheeked youths, from out whose eyes life sparkles, you know not how black and threatening it was, here on earth, even as late as 60 years ago. You never knew the horrors of exploitation, the misery of those who had deadened themselves with drugs, the hopelessness of those who were utterly weary. We elders, who were witnesses of that dread epoch, we are dying out. But yet to-day I remember with a shudder the days of the horrible tenements in the narrow alleys of the large towns, of the neglected children roaming naked about the streets, of the torture of unemployment and of dependence on an employer—that life led by millions of proletarians, which was no life, or would not have been if it had not been spiritualized by the burning desire to destroy that world of oppression! You, who are growing up in light and sunshine, in the strength and fullness of a free life, think of the hell of capitalist society whose portals we have successfully broken down."

The words, spoken with trembling lips by the old man, were listened to in breathless silence.

Then a young woman, slender as a girl, in a long flowing robe which showed the chaste beauty of her noble form, mounted the platform and spoke with impressive nobility of manner, without undue heat and yet full of life: "Comrades, sisters, brothers! The words of the fatherly veteran have sunk into our hearts. We know, indeed, that there was once a time of the madness of possession. We know that the soul was once fettered by the demons of selfishness. We know it, but we can no longer fully realize what it was. For how is it possible that human beings themselves should have maimed their own souls and bodies? How was it possible that thousands should slavishly serve one? How was it possible that, instead of becoming strong and free in light and air, well cared for and well educated, men should pine in pestilential air, in ugly homes, untaught and half-starved? At that time man only knew *himself*, and that made him small! We know that man and woman, flower and animal, the blade of grass in our garden and the stones on which we tread, are all parts of the same world, and only he who feels himself at one with all creation, he alone is worthy to be our brother. Whoso finds himself anew in others, whoso has conceived the great law of fellowship, he who will not tread down a blade of grass unnecessarily, whose glance caresses every child, he who feels and knows what is taking place in the soul of his neighbor, he is rich. To the slave of the vanished state of society his possessions formed a world, to us the whole world had become a possession!

No applause was heard. No evil look fell on that proud figure. But a thousand youthful, sparkling eyes looked at each other, filled with the noblest emulation to become prominent in the service of the whole.

Music struck up. The youths sang. The crowds then went leisurely home. In the group in which the old man walked someone pointed over to the factory district. "Yes, indeed," the old fellow related, "the factories then were not worked by electro-dynamos as now; there was infernal black smoke in almost every workshop, and our hands were covered with soot; and where was there ever a chance that a gifted workman might study or ever leave the factory to be admitted to other social work? When his strength failed him—well then …"

But the old man had now reached his goal. They led him to the gate of the palace which bore the inscription "The Castle of Peace." Such places 60 years ago, miserably arranged, were known as "poorhouses" or "alms houses."[4]

The middle of the day was passed by each one in his own family circle. On each table was a beautiful bouquet. After dinner the old people lay themselves down in hammocks, the young ones went into summer-houses, taking with them this or that book from the central library which supplies every citizen daily, as gifts or loans, with the books he desires. The little ones ran to the great public playgrounds.

At 3 o'clock trumpet blasts called once more to the feast. Now the masses made a pilgrimage to the 50 great arena buildings, the people's theatre, in which to-day festive performances, free to all, were held. The great orchestras played, glorious voices sang hymns of freedom, and at last the rising of the curtain disclosed the stage. Goethe's "Faust,"[5] still as ever the symbol of struggling humanity, was performed. Breathless stillness in the whole arena, a hundred thousand human beings feeling the words: "Wer immer strebend sich bemüht, den können wir erreten."*

It is evening; the inner districts lie in darkness, but in the garden city quarters there are lights shining from many thousand houses. From the Kahlenberg[6] thousands of rockets ascend flaming through the sky; on the Danube boats with bright red lamps are sailing. From the gardens before the houses sound violins and flutes; the children sing till they are tired. No drunkard reels through the peaceful streets. From the "Castle of Rest" may be heard the voice of a happy old man. He is weeping for joy.

---

* "Whoever struggles with difficulty himself to redeem, him we can save."

■ Mary Davis; or the Fate of a Proletarian Family. A Lesson Given to the Glasgow S.L.P. Socialist Sunday School

Tom Anderson, 1912

Comrades, Girls and Boys, and Grown-ups,—

The lesson[1] I am going to give you to-day is in the form of a story, and the story is about a young woman—her name was Mary Davis. She was the daughter of a coal miner.

This is a true story, and it happened fully twenty-five years ago.

Two miles east from here is the mining district of Lanarkshire, and it was there that Mary was born and brought up.

Mary had two brothers, Tom and James, and they were both miners.

We had been companions from our school days, and I was a regular visitor at their house from my boyhood up till I became a man of many talents, and I want the girls and boys here to remember, and to be on their guard, when they hear their teachers in the day schools tell them of the great men and women in history.

We have a text, which you all can repeat, but which possibly you cannot understand quite clear as yet. It is: "The Great are only Great because the Workers are Wage-Slaves. Let us organise." This little incident of Tom Davis will help you to understand what I mean.

Old Tom Davis was a coal miner,—a wage slave. If you had met him coming home from the pit, just as you were coming home from school, you would have seen a big burly man, with a very black face; his clothes were coarse, his jacket, trousers, and vest were all begrimed, just as his body was, by his occupation. His master, I am sure, would never have allowed him to come into his house with such clothes on. He, to his master or his master's friends, would not be a great man; he, to them, would only be a common miner. Yet he was a truly a great man. The great men you are told about by the lackeys of the master class live in big houses and have servants to attend to them, they own a great deal of wealth, and you are told stories about them and of their greatness, to cloud your brain and make you servile. Do you know, that if you are told a lie often enough you will believe it,[2] and these stories of the great men you are told about are not true, but your fathers and mothers were told the same stories that are being told to you, and they believed them all their days to be true. Nearly all the workers believe them to be true. It is only the revolutionary worker who knows them to be false, and the master class is afraid of these men, lest they should be able to explain to the workers the true position.

Now, let me tell you something about old Tom's talents, or his greatness. We called him "old Tom," not that he was very old—he was only forty-five—a younger man at that time than I am now. Well, he was a splendid violinist, one of the best reel and strathspey[3] players in the district. Many and many a time has he played at the marriages of the miners and others, just for the love of playing. He was a good quoit player,[4] and at the local flower shows he took prizes many a time for his flowers. He was an authority on dogs, birds, and poultry, and as a debater on politics and history he was looked upon as a master. And he was only a coal miner. His name does not appear in any of your history books. That would never do. Your father's masters would not suffer such a thing to be.

Now, let me give you a description of the Davis's home. The Davis's lived in a room and kitchen house—it was called a "butt and ben," that is, the room went off the kitchen. That was the usual kind of house occupied by the miners, and it is the same to-day. This "butt and ben" of the Davis's will always live in my memory. It appeared to me a palace in the true sense. The floor was so well scrubbed that it always looked nearly pure white, the polished parts of the grate were always very bright, and the old-fashioned sweay,[5] with its large chain links, I think I can still see hanging down into the center of the fire. The set of "cans," a marriage present of years ago, adorned the shelf, and on them were inscribed the names of Tom and Mary his wife. On the right hand side of the fire hung the old "waggity we-clock,"[6] with its brass chains and brass weights. The old style kitchen dresser, with its display of plates, was always to my mind a work of art. There were two beds in the kitchen: we call them built-in beds. The coverings on them were pure white, with an embroidered border, the work of Mary the mother. This "butt and ben" was a marvel of order and brightness. The walls were colour-washed, the bottom part pale green, the top and ceiling pure white. A few pictures adorned the walls, but none of the pictures were of saints, or of kings and queens. The pictures were a few photographs of the family, of a prize canary, and of some prize flowers. And in the room was a good-sized bookcase packed with books.

The Davis family did not go to any church; this at that time was a great sin. Many a time have I heard old Tom laugh when a busy-body from the church would call to see if he would send his family to the church. He would ask his visitor *why* he should send his children to the church, and the visitor would say, that they might be saved. "Man," Tom would say, "I am astonished at your simplicity." He would then rise and go to the room and bring a few books from the bookcase. Then he would ask his visitor if he had read *that* (Gibbon's "Decline and Fall of the Roman Empire"[7]), handing him the work. This always closed the conversation, the visitor always preferring to go away without saying any more on the question.

Sunday was a great day in Davis's house. Breakfast was at nine o'clock, then all the topics of the week were discussed at the table; dinner at two o'clock was the same, the only difference being, one or two men folk (friends) would be there, and the discussion took a wider range. Supper at six was on the same lines.

Mary Davis at this time was a young woman of eighteen years of age. She worked in a weaving factory. She was a fine, bright young woman, tall, and of good appearance. She was a born rebel and a strong supporter of all her father's views. She had tried on several occasions to improve the conditions of labour in the factory, but the results were so small that it daunted her spirit; still she headed every revolt that was made to secure improvement. One day, as she was engaged at her looms, the manager's son came along to where Mary was working. He had heard a great deal about this rebel woman and he wanted to inspect her. He stood behind her, and, being the son of a rich man and a boss, he put a hand on each of her shoulders. Like lightning the daughter of the miner wheeled round, and with a shuttle which she had in her hand struck him across the face. The young snob was upset. He was smarting from the blow, and he turned round as if to strike back, but when his eyes rested on the brave woman standing ready for him, he shewed the white feather.[8] There was great excitement in the mill all the afternoon, for the news spread like "wild fire." All the women (and there were nearly 1,000 employed in the mill) were inwardly delighted.

When Mary reached home that night—the news had arrived before her—there was a big crowd standing at her home to see her. To Mary the incident was nothing; she considered it her duty to do as she had done, and she said had she not done it she would have been a coward. In the Davis's house that night a concert and dance took place in honour of Mary. Next morning Mary turned out to her work as usual, but the gatekeeper had strict orders not to admit her, and as she entered the gate, this white servile wage-slave, according to orders, stopped her, and said, "You are not to start work here again."

"Brave man," said Mary, "noble slave, go now and lick your master's feet; and for so doing you will be allowed to work all your days in the mill," and with that she turned and walked home.

Some time after this incident the miners were on strike, and a meeting of the men was being held on a piece of common land near the town. Mary went to the meeting; her father was chairman, and the principal speaker was a young man—John Sneddon, a rebel of his time—and he was Mary's lover. There was a big crowd at the meeting. After the chairman had spoken, he called on John Sneddon. This young man's speech had a great effect on the miners; he was one of themselves. He put the case clearly before them, and asked, "Are you going to give in?" "**Never,**" was the unanimous reply. There were several policemen, along with several of the highly paid lackeys of the coal masters, moving around the meeting, and it so happened they halted just where Mary was standing, and one of the lackeys said, "Listen to that fool Sneddon." Mary was so enraged that she turned on the man and struck him. The police seized her, then a free fight ensued, in which the police and the lackeys came off "second best."

During the night the arm of the law visited Mary's house, and she was dragged from her bed and taken to the office. After a delay of several weeks, she was tried and found guilty, and sentenced to three months' imprisonment with hard labour.

A great fete was arranged for the day on which Mary was liberated. The largest hall in the district was taken, and Mary and John Sneddon were married. The event was one of the greatest ever known to have taken place in the district. For years after it served as a date; "It was on the night on which John Sneddon and Mary Davis were married," was quite a common saying.

For the next few years the Davis's and the Sneddon's had to move all round the district to get work, for Capitalism makes you pay for it, if you attempt to assert your manhood, and this is one of the great levers that makes many of the workers cowards. It is not that they have not the desire to fight, and they know that they should fight, but they are afraid of the starvation of their women and children. They go back to their work defeated men, they hope that their fellows will soon give in, and that the strike will be settled, and that it will soon be forgotten, and they endeavor to make themselves believe that there was some excuse for their going back. That their fellows will excuse them for "blacklegging" is their one anxious desire. They know they have been "Rats," but they feel that the loss of their manhood is a great price to pay to get bread, and in silence they curse their fate, and their one desire is, that some day may come, in which they will join with their fellows and fight like men, and so the hope of this keeps them from sinking.

Time, however, brings changes. Old Tom suggested to his sons and John Sneddon that they ought to try their old district again, for it was in that district the greatest part of his life had been spent: his boyhood days, his days of love, courtship, and marriage; there his children were born; there his old "butt and ben" awakening memories of the happy days spent in it—the old man yearned to go back, yes, even to go back and work in "Number 3 Pit." And back they went. They all started in "Number 3 Pit." The men in the pit were well pleased to see their old friends back. These are good men, the manager said to himself, and they have had a good lesson. So there they worked. Nothing of any importance cropped up during the next year or two, and the family were all back again into their old way of living, spending their spare time as they did in the good old days.

One beautiful afternoon in June there was a great stir in the street the Davis's lived in. No one could tell what was wrong, till, late in the afternoon, the news came—there had been an accident in No. 3 pit. Then the frightful truth was known. A "fall from the roof." Everyone was afraid to say who was hurt. But the news leaked out—"the Davis's." At the mention of these names many an eye became moist. Still, no one was sure. It was an anxious time. The crowd in the street began to open out, some men were coming. They were middle-aged miners, and they were walking with their eyes cast downward. They were coming to the Davis's house, to break the news and condole with the bereaved ones. These men walked as if they were blind; their comrades were killed, how would they break the news to the women? Their hearts were full, they knew their duty, and so they walked, knowing not how. Not one in the crowd attempted to speak to these men, theirs was a holy mission; rather did they stand aside reverently, with a slight bend on the body, as a mark of great respect and sympathy. The miners entered the house, while the crowd stood in silence. They knew, from experience, that it was death; no one spoke. They waited, and in a short time the miners came out, with their heads bare, and a glance at them told that these strong hewers of coal had been shedding tears. The three men halted on the step of the door, and one of them said: "Tom Davis and his two sons, and also John Sneddon, have been killed by a fall from the roof." The miner said no more. The crowd was speechless. "It is terrible," was the expression on all lips. Terrible, children, yes, terrible, the price the workers pay for their bread.

Three days afterwards, the remains of the four men were buried in the old chapel graveyard. All the pits in the district were idle, and hundreds of the miners attended the funeral. They came just in their ordinary clothes. The four coffins were carried by the miners shoulder high, and Mary Davis, her mother, and old John Sneddon and his wife, were the chief mourners. The cortege was four deep, and it extended to a great length. They walked from the house to the graveyard, which was fully a mile. There was no priest at the funeral; Mary and her mother desired it so. Old John Sneddon was asked to officiate, and for the memory of the dead, he was only too pleased to do so. His words were few. Just before the coffins were lowered, he said, "Friends, four brave men have been killed, whom we all knew. Let it be the duty of us all to cheer those who have been left, and if we do that, we will have done our duty, and we shall have nothing to fear. Those who are gone had no fear, they were good fighters; their battle is ended, let us continue it in their spirit is my earnest appeal to you all."

Mary and her mother bore up well under their great misfortune but the blow was too great for the old woman. By the close of the year she had also passed away, and was laid beside her husband and her sons in the old chapel graveyard.

Mary was back again working in the factory. She was a different woman. She seemed as one who was waiting and waiting. She had one girl, who was now twelve years of age, and the child kept her in life.

The women in the "pass" in which Mary worked had a grievance against their tenter or "overseer,"[9] and they approached Mary to be one of a deputation to go to the manager to state their case. Mary was silent, till one of the women said, "Are you afraid, Mary?" She looked up and said, "Of whom? I will go." The deputation was successful in getting what they wanted. It was a paltry matter.

The following week after this, the "tenter" came to her and said, "You will have to leave on Saturday, Mary." She looked him straight in the face, and said, "If I leave on Saturday, *I will kill you before next Saturday.*" The man turned white, he was afraid of this woman. He went, however, and got another "tenter," and brought him down to where Mary was working, and said to her, "You might just repeat what you said to me a few minutes ago." Mary laughed and said, "What are you joking about?" The "tenter" was foiled, and Mary was allowed to work away, he being afraid to pay her off.

Some months afterwards Mary left and went to work in a mill in the North of England, where a friend of hers had gone. Just at this time the Labour Movement had taken birth in this country. Mary became one of the pioneers. She began to live again as in the days of old, but the master class or their lackeys always watch these brave, outspoken people, and the master class is the same the world over. Starvation and death they mete out to any one who may rebel against their rule. This woman became known to them; she must go. She was hounded from one factory to another. One poor, brave, penniless woman capitalism meant to kill, in quite a legal way.

The pity of it all was, the workers for whom she worked so hard were blind and servile slaves. The promise of a little bit of extra bread kept them quiet. They did not see that their bosses were giving them a trifle, so as to keep them sleeping, as it were, and they were using many of the weaker ones among them, through their lackeys, to speak ill of Mary. Mary was forced to look for work elsewhere, so she decided to move on to the great City of

Death—London. She had decided to walk all the way,—nearly 200 miles,—so the two started. It was Mary's expectation that she would find some work for her daughter and herself in some of the smaller towns they passed through.

It is very strange, girls and boys, and yet it is true, when men or women get crushed down, when they feel they are sinking, all the hope and love of life leaves them. The great capitalist society disowns them and calls them wastrels, their once fellow wage-slaves give them the cold shoulder, just as the masters do. The world is against them; wage-slaves are of little value, and so they sink and sink, and then they have no labour-power that any one will buy, they are of less value than rags thrown into the ash pit, and yet at one time they were as you now are, cheerful girls and boys, full of life and joy and love. So I would counsel you to have mercy—you who are just entering into womanhood and manhood, you so full of life and vigour, hope and love; you who think that the world is beautiful and the road is smooth and plain, and nothing but happiness in front. You have not met as yet the vulture Capitalism, your young minds have not yet grasped its power, you are chained to it, but you do not know it yet, and you laugh, and are merry, as you should be at your age, but what awaits you when you reach thirty years of age? The same lot as your comrades in chains— hardships, trials, suffering, pinched and wan faces, love gone, poverty eternally hunting you, hope gone. And the young slaves come along, and they are laughing and singing, and they are dreaming the dreams you used to dream. Little comrades, this is a true picture, and there is only one hope left to the wage slave to keep him alive and above water, and that is to become a rebel, to sound the slogan of the Class War, to consecrate his life to the organization of his fellows, so that they may be organized into one vast industrial army, to take the means of life into their own hands, and so kill this vulture Capitalism.

It was harvest time, and Mary and her daughter got work with a farmer. The work to them was hard, but they kept at it. The folks whom they worked along with were plain, simple, country people, full of sympathy and kindness, cheerful in nature, and ever telling simple stories of the district and its people. Capitalism had not as yet got those people into its tentacles and debased them; they lived in a different world from the industrial wage-slave, and so with the work and the people Mary's spirits began to revive, and by the end of the season she was feeling quite at home. Being only an odd hand taken on to assist at the harvest, with its finish she had to go. So once more the two of them faced the Great North Road. And on the same road many hundreds of industrial slaves have trod. Many a brave man and woman have walked as Mary and her daughter walked—knowing not the end. They had walked well on to the outskirts of London without being able to secure any work—they were not alone. They met very many people on the road, many of whom were on their last walk, for soon, very soon, that little power they had to labour would be gone for ever. This they knew, and could not help. They marched on, and when the darkness of the night set in a few of them passed over to walk no more. No one knew, no one cared; useless wage-slaves—dead— the best thing that could happen to them; and they were buried, not for love, but for fear of pestilence. And capitalists sit securely in their mansions, surrounded by all the luxuries of the world, self-satisfied.

Mary was successful on the outskirts of the great city of death; she got a job in a laundry to work a steam mangle. Her experience as a weaver induced the boss to give her a job; she also looked a fine, healthy slave, and likely to be steady, judging from her appearance. Here she and her girl worked till near the end of the busy season, but just before its close, they had been working all night to finish a large order. They were on their last hour, when one of the sub-foremen (a man who had a grudge against Mary) who was carrying a large basketful of clothes in front of him, knocked against Mary as he was passing her. She was feeding the roller at the time, and her hand slipped and caught in the rollers, and was fearfully mutilated. The brave woman uttered not a sound, the machine was stopped at once, but too late, the arm could not be saved. An ambulance was sent for and she was taken to the hospital. A worker's arm is nothing, another worker can be had with two arms, and another was willing to take the place of Mary, who had left to get the right arm taken off above the elbow. The nurse who had care of her was struck by her remarkable appearance and fortitude, and as she grew better she began asking Mary questions. Mary for a long time said nothing, she could not be induced to speak; she had made up her mind to die—to end it all. But the nurse won her sympathy, and Mary told her the story of her life. "I have a little book." She said, "it is in our lodging; my girl shall bring it to-morrow. In it I have entered the principal events of my life since I was fourteen years of age, up till I came here; and I want you to keep it for me, and should anything happen to me, send it on to the address given on the first page." The nurse promised to do so, and she also got Mary's girl a place in the hospital. A few weeks after she was better, she was visiting her daughter at the hospital, and a deputation from a town in the North of England was being shewn through it. Mary was standing in the corridor as they passed, when one of the deputation stopped, stared, and said to her "Are you Mary Davis or Sneddon?" She answered, "Yes." He said, "I thought so," and passed on. This angel of capitalism, at the luncheon given in their honour that afternoon in the Board Room, told the story of the dangerous woman Mary Davis, to suit his class interests. All the other angels at the feast were agreed on the suggestion by the angel from the North, that this woman and her stock should be removed from all respectable society.

Some one may say, such is not the case; they, I am afraid, know little of these men. They will call themselves Christians and make a pretence of worshipping the meek and lowly Nazarene, but on the Monday some of them will go to their factories and make little brass gods to send to the heathen, at a profit,—for profit is greater than all the gods ever created, and they would shed the blood of the nation to retain these profits.

Why, then, do you think, they would scruple at killing one woman and her child. Look at the death roll of Labour's Army, a 1,000 workers are nothing, 10,000 are nothing. It is, how do they stand? They, with mock solemnity, send condolences to the widows of the murdered miners, when it happens to be a batch of 200 or 300 killed at one time; when they are killed by the dozen they say nothing, it is not worth taking notice of.

If it were to serve their purpose they would turn the army on the works to-morrow and kill them by thousands, yes, by tens of thousands, if it were required. If the workers were to become class-conscious, (a sufficient minority of them), and put up a good fight, these men would then shew their hands, blood would flow in every street in the kingdom. These men know not any thing that is sacred, except their class interests. Religion, family, love, honour, friendship, courage, home, or country, none of these things count to them; their type is the lowest, despicable type the human race has evolved.

Their class is all they know, everything is justified by that standard, and if you tried, as an individual, or as an association, to stand up for your rights, WOE UNTO YOU. Look at the fearful position of the wage-slaves to-day in any modern factory. They are given on starting work a small brass token with a number on it, slave number 22. He takes it off the board in the mornings as he enters the factory gate and puts it in a box. He has no option, he is not John Smith or Tom Scott, he is number 22; when the boss enters he looks at the board to see if all the slaves have started; if any numbers remain on the board he gets the time-keeping slave to take a note of them, and the slave or slaves must appear before him and tell him WHY they were not at their work.

Some years ago I was working in a large joinery factory, where nobody but craftsmen slaves were employed at "test work" (work that must be done in a certain time or else the slave would be paid off). I was the shop delegate, and I called the other shop delegate a wage-slave; he was very angry and denied it, and wanted me to prove it. The other craftsmen slaves got interested in our discussion and they raised their heads from their jobs to listen. Just as they were all leaning forward so as to better catch what was being said, the door at the far end of the building opened with a bang, and the master of the slaves stepped in. Transformation of transformation, every craftsman wage-slave had bowed his head in double quick time. I shouted to the men near me, and especially to the wage-slave who was on the other side of the bench to me (with whom I had been discussing), "*Raise your heads, you wage-slaves, raise your heads: be men.*" But, no, the man at the far end of the shop was still standing there, they could not raise their heads; they had not the power. Such is the power capitalism has over the worker to-day.

But when a brave woman like Mary Davis defends herself against the master class, many, very many, of the workers marvel and say it is not true. They say to themselves, how could she do it? They feel they are too well bound. Take courage, take courage, it can be done, once you get started on the way. The chains that bound you in the past are useless, they can bind no longer.

I have given you a short description of the workshop to prove that Mary Davis's case is not an isolated one.

Mary's end was drawing very near. She and her daughter decided to try the centre of the big city. Mary was not living now, she was an automaton. She was also a woman now without an arm, and women in the big city are very cheap. No one can tell how very cheap they are. You can buy them for a few pence, yes, even for less than that; you can buy them for a shakedown of straw if you happen to own a small attic in any back street. They are not human beings now, these women; if they were, they would be revenged, and then die. But the paid hirelings of capitalism have drugged them from their birth, and even in the degradation they keep on drugging them, that they have no will power of their own.

Mary and her girl wandered about for a week or two without hope. Footsore and weary, they arrived late one night at Trafalgar Square, the hub of the great city. They were hungry and the girl wanted to beg from some passers-by, but the mother would not hear of it; her proud spirit arose within her; it was nothing to die, why beg? At last she turned to her girl and said, "Go and ask the workmen in the trench for a piece of bread." It was then near midnight, and the workmen were making a big trench across the street, just at the Strand, for a main sewer. They were labourers, big, burly men; they had come from the sort of men that ordinary craftsmen despise. They were men of open countenance, men you could ask for a match or a pipeful of tobacco and get it. They were merry at their work. It was to these men Mary sent her girl to beg. The girl approached the first navvy, and said, "Could you give my mother a bit bread?" The man lifted his head and looked at the bright girl and then casting his eyes to the Square, he saw the form of a woman there. "A bit bread, my lass; yes, my lass, with pleasure." His coat was lying by on a mound of turned clay; he got his coat and took from his pocket his supper—it was wrapped in a red cotton handkerchief, and as he was opening it, the other navvy next to him said, "I will give a bit, too, Bill, there is no need of your giving it all." And these men, at the very bottom of Labour's rank, shared their supper with an outcast woman and her child, simply because they asked for it. It is the poor, children, who help the poor.

That night the world knew Mary Davis no longer. Less than 200 yards from the square is the river Thames, and in its icy embrace Mary Davis, the woman of large heart and soul, gladly found rest.

■ The Lost Vision. A Spring Fantasy

Victor Grayson, 1912

On a sunny day at noon in the early spring, a young man loitered in the shade of a green-budding wood; all around him the stately trees were putting on their verdant robes, and the filtered sunshine wrought a carpet of curious and beautiful design for him to walk upon. The earth was wrenching itself from the cold clasp of winter; the air throbbed and trembled with the ecstasy of awakening life, and the pregnant earth seemed to heave with the bitter-sweet yearning of maternity.

A song was singing in the young man's soul. His eyes beamed with the light of joyous vision. He was sharing Nature's dream of coming glory; in his heart fresh shoots of hope were springing; he bathed his spirit in the gladness of the world's new birth. From sheer joy of existence he shouted aloud, and a thousand birds responded with an anthem of confident and forward-looking faith.

The young man had a priceless dowry that only Nature can bestow. He was strong, lithe and handsome; he was conscious of all the richness and beauty of the earth; the wonderful universe was his—and he knew it! His path was bright primroses, and his sleep would be canopied by myriads of lustrous, mystic stars. Flowers, too, were coming—thousands of beautiful flowers—to fill the air with their fragrance; and in return for his loving labour Nature would give forth its bounteous tribute of good things to feed and clothe his graceful body. Somewhere in the world's quiet places there was preparing for him a tender, lissome mate who would bear him robust children, and he would watch them grow up in the sunlight as he was growing now. He lay down and embraced the warm kindly soil with the grateful reverence of a child for its mother.

He was indeed blessed above his fellows. With lilting step the young man fared forth from the wood and returned to the "hum and shock"[1] of mankind. Boldly he trod the sinuous mazes of the social labyrinth, and beheld with truthful, fearless eyes all there was to behold. He saw the rows and rows and rows of putrid hovels where starved and hopeless slaves breathe out tired and paltry lives; he watched these dens at sunrise spawning forth their semi-human contents into the congested reek of mean streets and alleys; he saw the dirty children—sweet little flowers of humanity soiled and bruised in the bud—he saw these in their tens of thousands stewing in the foul cauldron of grime and crime and poverty; he saw their little skeleton arms and hands grasping at the disease-fouled air as they yielded back to nothingness the meaningless fragment of their lives.

He saw broken-hearted mothers bending over little graves, and heard cries of anguish as they gave to Moloch[2] other bairns to glut his maw; he saw their parched, milkless breasts and their backs bent and distorted with inhuman toil; he saw them cooped for long hours in sultry factories, and being done to death in accursed sweating dens; he saw the daughters of the poor with rouged cheeks and leering eyes, plying their debased bodies for hire in the public thoroughfares; he saw them in the death agonies of unspeakable disease, in hospitals provided by the kindly rich.

He saw men tramping the streets in rags and misery, begging in vain for employment for their hands; he saw the tears stream down their hollow cheeks when the little ones asked for bread; he saw them in the workhouse wards and the prison cells, being drilled and bullied and damned by the disciplined flunkeys of their own class. He saw the workers toiling patiently in the mines and the mills, and he saw them shot and bludgeoned at the masters' behest when they tried to increase their pittance. He saw all the horror and squalor of the veritable hell upon earth which is known as "the workers' lot."

■ ■ ■

Other sights also the young man saw. He saw the fat and insolent plutocrat lolling in idle and superfluous luxury; he saw him strutting truculently in mansions whose bricks were compounded of the wage-slaves' flesh, and whose mortar was their blood. He saw their fleet motor-cars and their floating castles, their priceless wines and dainty viands, their bejeweled wives and expensive concubines. He saw crafty lawyers—out for gold—and ambitious politicians —out for place—sitting together in the seats of the mighty— protecting the Constitution. He saw the whole tangled mass of lies, cunning, cant, chicane and fraud which buttresses and sustains the vast structure of privileged tyranny.

■ ■ ■

The young man returned to the wood and considered these things he had seen. Rain had fallen, and the tears of the sighing trees fell quietly into the sodden earth; the wet branches drooped as with dismal disappointment; the birds were singing, but their song was a wistful threnody; the air was pervaded with melancholy tenderness. The young man wept for that he was born into a world of strife and sadness. His sight of the ways of men had shown him Spring as Winter in disguise. Near by him a mighty tree was being slowly strangled in the merciless embrace of its creeping parasite; tiny insects were destroying the green leaves—thus preparing themselves to form a future meal for insects of stronger and subtler growth. A spider was patiently spinning its gossamer web to snare the feet of the trusting fly. Here in the wood, as in the world, were paupers and criminals and idle rich; the prevailing law was the pitiless "law of prey"; the teeth and claws of nature were red[3] with the blood of the mangled weak. The young man shrank back from this revelation of universal horror. He felt helpless and hopeless in the face of life's sinister mystery.

But as the sun shone suddenly through the trees, he ceased weeping, and a strange light kindled in his dark blue eyes. He seemed to be listening to far-distant voices, to be watching the world's chaos swinging into ordered harmony. The birds burst forth again into a song of hope. With head erect, clenched fists and shoulders squared, the young man walked resolutely back into the human battle-field.

For he had found the Vision.

■ ■ ■

It is winter in the wood, and an old man picks his way with feeble steps through the winding avenues of bare trees. His skinny yellow fingers are encircled with costly rings, and he is clothed in the manner of those who command great wealth. There is something hard and repulsive in the wrinkled face, the mouth has a sordid droop, and he stares at the ground with bleared, expressionless eyes. He would seem to be seeking something, this old man, for now and again he mumbles to himself in a husky, quavering voice, and peers inquiringly about him on every side. At an old dead tree he pauses, and with trembling hand plucks a spray of ivy from its decaying bark. As he holds it in his fingers the crafty lines of his face seem for a moment to disappear and his dull eyes moisten with reminiscence. He is trying to recall to memory a day in an early Spring of long ago, when the great road stretched in front of him right up to the celestial heights, and his soul had caught the sudden gleam of the ideal. He remembers the first few battles with greed; the glamour of power, the cunning deals, the attainment of riches—and now he realises that though he can *buy* anything, he can truly possess nothing!

So the old man goes doddering sadly through the wood, staring about him with pathetic appeal, as if he thought he might find again the Vision that he had—somehow, somewhere—lost.

■ The Aerial Armada. What Took Place in A.D. 2000

Frank Starr, 1913

"Grandfather, will you tell me the story of the Armada?"

"The Armada, sonny; why, certainly I will. You mean the Armada of the Air, of course. Well, it was on July 29, 1938, that the events I am about to recount took place. It was rather odd that the Morgulian Admiral of the Air should have chosen the three hundred and fiftieth anniversary of the Spanish Armada disaster for his aerial invasion of England. But in selecting the date he was guided by the fact that all the junior officers of the Army and Navy would be at Goodwood,[1] and all the senior members of the service, to a man, would be at an Alhambra matinée, at which a ballet of the Maud Allen species[2] was to be produced. By directing his airships first to Goodwood and dropping a few hundredweight of bombs on the grandstand and the paddock, and then flying off to London and removing Leicester-square,[3] he calculated upon paralyzing the whole of the services, including their flying wings.

"But the Admiral reckoned without Captain Stedison, the commander of No. 49 Aeroplane Squadron, whose size in field service caps told that he possessed more brains than the average army officer.

"On the morning of July 29, Captain Stedison had tethered his tiny visiting biplane to the hitching-post in the roof garden of the Caravanserai, a huge hotel which used to stand on the site of Charing Water-Gardens, and which commanded a view of the Thames from Vauxhall to the old Tower. Stedison was in the Caravanserai billiard-room playing a thousand up with one of the half-dozen professionals kept on the premises, when his squadron sergeant-major, who had just flown from the Nore observation station,[4] entered excitedly.

"Saluting his superior officer, the sergeant-major gasped, 'I have just received information that the Morgulian dirigible[5] fleet is preparing to start from Bluephalia. Air Scout 2579 brought the news, and her observation officer reports that the fleet is ten times as large as we have ever imagined; that its battle "dirries," with manoeuvring distance between each, extend for eight miles in two parallel lines; and that they are followed by clouds of smaller craft; I have wirelessed to every station along the coast and there is not a single air-pilot on duty. What shall we do? They will be here in six hours.'

"The commissioned officer bit off a fresh supply of chewing-gum[6] (smoking was forbidden to flying-men, and in those days, when six out of seven civilians were professional footballers, everybody chewing-gummed). Then with the nonchalance of Ouida's guardsman[7] he said:

"'Tut-tut, Marshman, have you got the jumps? What do the papers prophesy regarding the weather?'

"'The *Daily Wail* and the *Daily Distress* both predict continued east wind and fine weather, sir.'

"'And the *Morning Toast?*'

""That says the same.'

"'With such unanimity then we may undoubtedly expect a change within a few hours. I shall therefore finish my game at bowls— I mean billiards.[8] We have plenty of time for the Spaniards—I should say the Morgulians. Meanwhile wire to the headquarters of the United Longshoremen these three words: "Prepare to charge," and then return to duty.'

"Three hours later Stedison was opening the door of his own private hangar, whose secret till then had been his alone.

"There stood the darling of his heart, his own invention: a gigantic monoplane, four times as big as anything in the service, driven by a 2,000 h.p. motor, and bristling all along the edges of its planes with long razor-edged blades like a steel-quilled porcupine.

"'There is plenty of time, Marshman,' said the Captain, as he climbed into the pilot-seat. 'Send an orderly with another wire to the United Longshoremen telling them to charge for all they are worth.'

"Within five minutes this command had been executed, and the sergeant-major was in the observer's seat behind his captain. Stedison touched a button. In a second the machine was off the ground. In 60 seconds she was a mile in the air and speeding at the rate of eight miles a minute towards the drawling fleet of dirigibles, whose greatest pace was 70 miles an hour.

"Soon they were a speck in the air three miles above the great airships, whereon, as Stedison knew beforehand from his spies, were to be found not only the Great Morgul himself, but all the financiers and Bourse thieves[9] from Morgulia; for the expedition to England had been long planned and they intended to be on hand when the loot commenced.

"The British coastline was but two miles distant when, like a stone, Stedison's craft dropped to the level of the huge envelopes.

"It was all over in two minutes. Racing along the line of balloons at eight miles a minute the razor-edges of the monoplane cut through the silken fabric of the dirigibles with a noise so like the tearing of calico that Marshman, who abandoned a drapery counter for the Army, had murmured 'And the next article, please, Madam,' before he realised what was actually happening.

"As they turned at the end of their eight-mile run and commenced to slit the parallel line of gas bags, the sergeant-major saw the balloons—dirigible no longer—sinking, flapping and sagging, to the sea level.

"Then he understood his captain's message to the longshoremen. From the beach flew boats by the hundred—motor boats, sailing yachts, rowing skiffs—everything, in fact, that would float.

"The deflated envelopes had drifted to within three-quarters of a mile of the shore, so that the boats soon reached the slowly submerging cars.

"'For the shore, sir; for the shore. Anybody going ashore?' shouted the boatmen in chorus, as they lay on their oars and watched the water creep up from button to button of their victims' waistcoats.

"'Yes, oh, yes,' cried the Morgulian raiders. 'Save us, oh, noble seafarers.'

"'Charge for all they are worth,' rang the clarion tones of Stedison from his megaphone above their heads.

"'Right-ho, guvner!' answered the boatmen; and then, to the sinking Morgulians: 'Two hundred thousand pounds a piece for putting you ashore, gentlemen.'

"The sinking men raved, but when the water reached their collar studs they capitulated with curses in 15 modern languages.

"But they were not yet out of the wood. At the pierhead they were charged £200,000 per head as landing dues; the bandsmen in the pavilion made a gold collection; the skating rink attendants sold them skates at £50 a pair; so that by the time they were clear of the pier-gates the whole lot of them were not worth a promissory note[10] for the price of a drink.

"They reckoned, however, on being able to repudiate their liabilities once they regained their ancestral halls in Morgulia. But they had counted without Baron Isaacstein. That worthy scion of a fine old English house was cruising off the coast in his steam yacht when the Armada was shattered and his instinct prompted him to do a little bit of business on his own. He recognised the Great Morgul on one of the sinking dirigibles, and cutting the car adrift he towed it another two miles out to sea before he persuaded the G.M. to surrender his sovereignty as the price of a ride to shore and safety.

"Isaacstein was no fool. He had the transfer of the monarchy to himself drawn out in *propria forma*[11] before he parted with his royal prisoner. Once installed on his regal throne as the Great Morgul, Isaacstein discounted the whole of the longshoreman's bills at 50 per cent. and collected the debts himself."

"And what happened to the shoal of little air-craft that you mentioned, grandpa?"

"Oh, the newspaper weather forecasts were, as usual, incorrect. The wind swung round to the south-west, a storm sprang up, and the rest of the fleet was blown away North. It was thought that the crews perished; but the discovery of a new race of white Esquimaux recently has rather modified that theory."

"Grandfather, shall I tell you a story, now?"

"Why, certainly, my lad, I shall be delighted."

"Once upon a time there was a little boy named George Washing—"

"What do you mean, you young scamp? You get off to bed at once."

■ Mr. Prowser-Wowser

Edward Hartley, 1913

New Zealand trains are not very fast, and New Zealand railway journeys are a wee bit wearisome.

In going from Wellington to Auckland most of the passengers drop off and stay overnight at some hotel, finishing their journey on the second day.

A gentleman in one of these trains began to praise them, and pointed out the speed (?) at which we travelled. I told him that when at home I could receive a wire calling me to London 200 miles away, pack my bag, get some lunch, and be in the centre of London in less than five hours.

"Oh!" said he, "I wouldn't travel on a train like that! I'd be afraid!"

It is, however, possible to have a conversation, and there is certainly plenty of time. It was on one such journey when, after reading, and looking out of the window at some striking scenery, which, however, had a tinge of sameness, that there entered the carriage a gentleman who had asked questions at a meeting I had held, and who afterwards came and spoke to me, and said how pleased he had been with both the address and the answers.

He saw me at once, and, taking the adjoining seats for himself and companion, introduced me to one whom we will call Mr. Prowser-Wowser.

The Self-Made Man

Mr. Prowser-Wowser was a man to whom the word "smug" is most appropriate. A smug complacence literally oozed out of him. Life for him was obviously prosperous. His neat grey suit, his soft grey hat, his plump white hands—in fact, his whole appearance said, "Look at me! I've done well!"

He was the kind of man who would be an excellent husband; a good, kind father, if his children were submissive and obedient, but who would not brook much opposition; and in business matters be much like "Scrooge," a tight-fisted hand at the grindstone.

Still, life as a whole had been so good to him that this streak of hardness had not been over-developed. He would have been a real good fellow if he had not been so prosperous.

We talked for a while about general matters. Then the strike at Waihi[1] was mentioned. My first acquaintance said, "You know Mr. Hartley is a Socialist."

"A Socialist," said Mr. Prowser-Wowser, with something like astonishment. "A Socialist! Why, Mr. Hartley seems a very sensible man."

I laughed and said: "Yes, that is why I'm a Socialist. All sensible men who have considered the subject are Socialists. Some are either loth or afraid to admit it; but if they understand they know it is true, and they know it is inevitable."

"Well, now! I'm not a Socialist, yet I've been called a sensible man."

Socialist and Sensible!

"Do you know what Socialism is? Have you studied it?"

"No. I've never had time."

"Are you opposed to Socialism?"

"I certainly am!" And he was very emphatic.

"And you don't know what it is!"

This brought silence for a while, and his friend's eyes twinkled.

"May I ask why you are a Socialist, Mr. Hartley?"

"Because I'm tired of the present system."

"Oh, the present system is all right." And Mr. Prowser-Wowser looked himself over and regained his self-possession.

"It may be all right for you and me, but it is not all right for the great mass of the workers."

"Oh! they seem to be all right generally. But what's wrong with the system?"

"It's so unfair! The hardest, the most dangerous, and most disagreeable work gets the least pay; the easiest and most pleasant work the biggest and better pay; and when you get to the gentleman he does nothing at all, and gets the best income of the whole lot."

What Is Hard Work?

"Come, now! It depends on what you call hard work. Would you say that a judge's work was hard work?"

"Not very hard. Which would you rather be, a judge or a policeman?"

This rather startled him, but after a pause he said: "A judge, certainly!"

"Why?"

"Oh, I suppose for several reasons; but it would be much pleasanter."

"Exactly so! Now, I think one miner is worth all the lawyers and parsons in a country."

"What about the teacher? I suppose you would call him a worker?"

"I never mentioned the teacher; but I want no mistake made about my opinion of him. I count the teacher the most important man in the community."

"Then you will include the parson in the most useful men."

"I don't think so."

"Why not? What's the difference between the teacher and the preacher?"

"A vast difference! One teaches something he knows all about, and the other talks about something he knows nothing about. What can the parson know about Heaven?"

"He knows as much about it as you do." This somewhat stiffly.

"Probably; but that may not be very much. I don't know much about Heaven and the future life."

"No. But he may know as much, or even more."

"Not more! He cannot! Speculations we may have about future life and places; there can be no knowledge."

"But you admit he knows as much about these things as you do."

"Exactly! But I know nothing, neither does he."

"Well, he can tell you a good deal about these things."

"Likely! That is easy enough. I could tell a lot of what I think about a future life; but it is all speculation what I think and fancy. I can give you no proof; neither can any other man."

The Waihi Strike

This finished the conversation for a while. Then the talk drifted back to the Waihi strike. Both these gentlemen were opposed to the strikers. I find most people who ride in first-class carriages usually are opposed to all strikers.

I pointed out that even if the men were wrong there was not justification for the masters. Their profits were big enough to give the men both better wages and better conditions.

"But the men have both good wages and good conditions. A member of our church worked there for several years, and he told me about the place and its workings."

I had discovered that Mr. Prowser-Wowser was the main financial supporter, and practically the head of a Methodist church.

"Did he tell you the enormous profits that had been made? Did he tell you the men's wages averaged less than £3 a week?"

"No. He probably didn't know. But surely these people are entitled to the results of their brains and capital."

"Of course they are! Only the profits are not due to their brains and capital."

"Really, Mr. Hartley! You astonish me."

"Perhaps so. I don't want to astonish you. I want to convince you."

Our Foolish Talk!

"But you talk so foolishly."

This is the usual way when people have no answer to Socialist arguments. They generally suggest that we are fools. I paused, and he continued:

"To say that the profits are not made by brains and capital is mere rubbish." Here his smug self-complacency was almost irritating.

"Of course, something is due to the working men," he added, grudgingly. "But most of the wealth is made by the brains and capital of the managers and shareholders. Even you will admit that, Mr. Hartley."

"I shall not. I shall maintain that the real wealth production is done by the workmen. The previous wealth-production of the workers, which we call capital, is useful, and so are the brains of the managers, when they've got the right kind of managing brains; but the real wealth-making is done by the men who work."

"But this is ridiculous. What could you do without capital?"

"What could you do without labour?"

"Well, nothing, of course; neither can you do without capital."

"Yes, we could do without capital, though we don't want to do without wealth."

Here he got impatient, and said he'd "no time for hair-splitting." I don't like hair-splitting, and was tempted to follow him, but refrained, and said, "Labour has produced the capital."

"Nothing of the kind."

Capital and Labour

"Yes. Abraham Lincoln put it very well when he said, 'Labour is prior to and independent of capital. Capital is the fruit of labour, and could not exist if labour had not first existed.'[2] All the capital in the world is the stored-up labour of the working men, past and present."

"Hear, hear! Bravo!" said both Mr. Prowser-Wowser and his friend. "I'm glad you admit that capital is stored up labour."

"I must admit that. The trouble is that one man generally does the labour, and the other man stores it up."

"I'm not so sure about that. But do I understand you to say that it is not the brains and capital which are the main things in

Fig. 10. Walter Crane's "The Capitalist Vampire," from *The Comrade* (1903).
Private Collection © Look and Learn / Bridgeman Images.

the production of wealth? Of course, the workmen help, but the main things are the brains and capital of the rich men."

"I deny that altogether. The workman could manage without the capitalist, but the capitalist cannot do without the workman."

"Really, Mr. Hartley." This in a tired tone, as who should say, "There is nothing more to be said."

I took up the newspaper. "Have you read this? The output of gold in the Auckland Province is nearly £200,000 less than in the same period last year. This fall-off in production is mainly due to the unfortunate dispute at Waihi."

"I don't quite see what that has to do with the argument."

"Have any of the Waihi managers died at Waihi?"

"Not that I've heard of."

"Have any of the shareholders withdrawn their capital?"

"No! but many of them would like to."

"Then you admit that with the same brains, the same capital, and the same managers, the output of gold is £200,000 less. Why should that be if the gold production is due to the brains and capital of the rich men?"

A Silencer

Mr. Prowser-Wowser was quiet for several minutes, then said: "After all, Mr. Hartley, the shareholders don't get very much!"

"Don't they? Not at Waihi? Why, the capital is less than half-a-million, and the dividends are paid at four-and-a-half millions in 21 years."

"Now, Mr. Hartley, that is just where you are wrong. I know what I'm talking about. I've invested a fair sum in the Waihi Mine and lost money."

"Oh, no!"

"Really, sir! Do you mean to say that I don't know my own business? I tell you I've invested money in the Waihi Mine and lost by it."

"Very well. I tell you that if you invested money in the Waihi Gold Mining Company you have not lost any money. As the dividends paid are four and a half millions sterling, and the paid-up capital under half-a-million, if you got original shares, so far from having lost money, for every pound you put in you will have had nine pounds out, and still have your pound invested."

"Oh, quite so! But, I didn't get original shares."

Investment and Gambling

"Then you didn't 'invest.' You've been gambling in shares."

His face was a study.

"Gambling! Gambling! What do you mean? I'm very much opposed to gambling of any kind. It is sinful."

"Perhaps so. Yet if you didn't get original shares you didn't invest. And if you've been speculating in shares, it's gambling, much like horse-racing, you know."

"Not at all, sir! Not at all. Buying shares is a very different matter."

"As you say, not at all! You put your money on the wrong shares instead of the wrong horse, that is all. Yet it's gambling, all the same."

This finished Mr Prowser-Wowser. He glared at me for a while, then sank back in his seat, and a few minutes later slowly arose, and, reaching his handbag, sought other quarters, without even bidding me "Good-day."

He was mad, and I don't think he's forgiven me yet. I don't think telling the truth always makes friends.

■ Behind the Wall

Schalom Asch, 1913

In the middle of the plain stands a huge black fortress, surrounded by a broad, mighty river. At eve, when all is still and sinks into silence, the waves murmur …

Within the fortress every floor was filled with prisoners. During the day it seemed to be a dead building, a catacomb, the cavities of which were peopled with living, healthy, human beings. The convicts were sleeping on their sacks of straw, or gazing fixedly at the cornice of the stove or some similar object till they were nearly mad.

But towards evening the place came to life. Everywhere knocking began on the walls, and, thanks to the secret alphabet, long conversations were held. Every now and again a heavy step in the corridor plunged the whole house into silence. But, hardly had the warder passed by before all the knocking began again, even more vigorously.

The prisoners got accustomed to their speechless existence. They could now only talk with their fingers, and were at last able to guess by the knocks the character of their neighbour and even his social position. Sometimes, indeed, the desire assailed them to see, to speak a little—just to use once more a sleeping organ, to see if it was still able to fulfil its function.

One evening, when the whole prison was engaged in lively conversation, a fresh, youthful, merry laugh was suddenly heard—the clear voice of a young girl. The prisoners started. Something quite unusual was evidently happening, and the knocking on the walls ceased, the prison lay wrapt in silence. But the merry laugh, which warmed like the sunshine, sounded a second time between the walls ... strange ... as though the dead began to speak.

She was hardly more than a child, she who laughed there. When they brought her away from her mother's house she had not in the least realised the seriousness of her case. She had risen proudly, and followed the gendarmes in a romantic attitude. After such an adventure she expected something very wonderful, something in which she would be the heroine. But once alone between the four walls, loneliness laid heavy hands around her heart.

For a long time she cried silently to herself. Then she got better, and began to feel like a heroine. With clenched fists she raised herself on her couch and presented her chest as if it were about to be pierced by the bullets of the soldiers. Then she suddenly remembered that she was alone, and burst out sobbing like a child.

The warder hurried to the spot and cast an irritated glance through the spy-hole. As the eye appeared at the little opening, the young girl could not help a burst of laughter. When he saw her—the only female prisoner—the soldier was touched, and laughed too. But then his sense of duty got the upper hand, and when he spoke again he spoke in a rough voice, and put on his bearish manner.

Thus was the discipline once broken in the gloomy building. Soon the news spread through the whole prison that a young girl had arrived. How did it get about? Once she was fastened up in the cell, they could no longer hear her voice. Only the knocks of the secret alphabet penetrated through the walls. Neither could she be seen for she was taken alone for her walks. But they probably recognised her as a woman by her step when she passed along the corridor.

Then, too, she was musical, and in order to console herself for having to do without her piano, she sat down, the very first day, in a corner and beat with her foot the rhythm of her favourite songs. The convicts in the dark cells heard her above their heads, recognised the rhythm, and hummed the divine melody to themselves.

The whole gloomy building seemed changed by the presence of this fair creature.

In the neighbouring cell lay a young man. The dungeon walls had already robbed him of eight months of his life, but had not succeeded in stifling his fiery heart. He only felt that it was asleep in his breast. After getting up in the morning, he used to lie down again on his couch and think for hours of scenes from his childhood which now smiled at him as in a dream. Thus the energy which dwelt in him was lulled to sleep. It was a matter of indifference to him whether the sun shone outside or whether the rain came down in torrents. And yet it needed but a breath to awaken his heart once more.

He heard through the wall the step of the young girl, and when in the evening twilight she beat the rhythm of a Chopin nocturne, he became lost in sweet dreams. He saw a young wood in the first days of Spring. Here and there a glint of sunbeams between the little trees … A deserted castle reflected in the blue river, a young girl wandering beneath the pines. Wrapped in mystery, she steps softly between the trunks—she comes from a strange land and wanders into a strange world …

He had already tried to talk to her through the wall: with his fingers he confessed to her his love.[1]

"Who are you? I feel that you are young and beautiful, and I love you … I am as strong as a lion. When night comes I will break down the wall and come to you. I will hide you in my breast like a little bird, and will flee with you far, far away ..."

She listened to the beating of his fingers, but without understanding it, for she did not know the secret alphabet. But she had at least the feeling that behind the wall a heart was beating which belonged to her, and that a voice was there calling to her. And she often laid her ear against the wall to listen, and to try to make out this mysterious language. Sometimes she knocked too, as though her fingers could speak.

Often, too, as night fell, she lay down on the floor close to the wall, and knocked to find out if he was at the same place on the other side of the wall. Thus they waited, and with his fingers he sang songs to her through the wall and told her of his love.

Though she did not understand them, yet the knocks touched her to her heart. She pressed her forehead against the wall.

One day something suddenly happened which sent a thrill of horror through the whole of that dreadful building. One of the convicts had discovered that a gallows had been erected in front of the prison.

Like rain dripping into the gutter the sound of knocking on the wall sighed on the whole night long through the prison. First it passed from wall to wall, then from floor to ceiling. They exchanged advice and comforted each other, asked questions and said farewell. That nocturnal beating was as the beating of the wings of the death-angel against the walls. At last the sounds gradually died away. Each prisoner in his own cell thought once more of his own life.

But during the night the knocking of the young girl's neighbour had assumed a strange tone. His fingers trembled as if in fever. Surely he had something serious and urgent to communicate. His knocks became faster and faster … Then silence, as though a shudder passed over him. She divined that he was pressing his face against the wall; that he was giving her kisses through it; that he grew frenzied and began scratching it. But she could not tell what secret he was trying confide to her.

Outside the wind wept and raved and rattled at the little iron shutters and moaned through the bars. Never had the young girl's cell appeared more dreadful to her.

She had already knocked several times, to call her neighbour; but he remained silent, as if angry with her. Then she became sulky and threw herself down on the bed. An unbounded sadness crept over her. She would have liked to go again to the wall and call him, but she waited that he should come first.

An uncanny stillness lay upon the prison. The knocking had quite ceased … nothing was to be heard but the far-off stop of the sentry. At last horror got the better of her, she sprang up and ran to the wall. She knocked, sought, begged, and even hurt her face against the rough stones.

"Answer me, what are you doing?" she murmured. "What has happened? O, I am so frightened! Answer! Give me an answer! …"

■ Alice in Sunderland. A Baffling Mystery

'Casey', 1914

The author deeply regrets this week's article. The truth about it is that he stayed two hours at the Pentecostal Convention[1] held during Whit-week[2] in Sunderland, and on his arrival at the well-known health resort of Jarrow[3] the daughter of his hostess recited "The Mad Tea Party" from *Alice in Wonderland*. Unfortunately, the two events became mixed—not the author—hence the mystery. He hopes his many friends and enemies, likewise Lewis Carroll, will forgive him.

—WALTER HAMPSON ("CASEY")

Alice was beginning to get very tired. Her mother had taken her to hear the Pentecosters. Her head ached with the uneven singing, so she finally crept to a door at the back of the hall and wandered away in the dark.

Suddenly she felt herself falling and falling, until she lost consciousness.

She was awakened by a voice she thought she recognised. "Who has followed us up here?" it asked.

"Why, it's the Mad Hatter!" said Alice. "Please, where am I?"

"You should not say 'Where am I,' but 'here am I,'" corrected the Mad Hatter.

"But where's here?"

"Oh, here is where—where you are, you know. Still, it does not matter much because you are not now."

"I don't understand you."

"Well, it isn't really necessary now, you Izzer Deadun."

"What is that?" cried Alice, thoroughly alarmed.

"You Izzer Deadun from Sunderland. You have left it far behind."

"Well, thank heaven for that."

"Don't be so heavenly thankful, you might wish yourself back again on earth."

"Rubbish," said Alice, "I am quite tired of listening to those Pentecosters straining discordant unisons thro' their neezy noses. It's too slow."

"Ah," said the March Hare, chiming in, "let me assure you you've jumped from the frying pan into here. We Eternitists sing more hymns in one year than your Earthistes do in a billion."

"Great Scott," said Alice.

"No, no, not Scott, mostly Wesley and Newman.[4] How do you suppose we'd get thro' Eternity if we did not sing hymns?"

"'Ark at 'is science!" said the Mad Hatter, chiming in. "Eternity is not a turnstile or a railway tunnel. You can't get thro' Eternity. It has no beginning, nor no ending. It is all over again."

"But how can it be all over again, if it never began?"

"Treason," yelled the Dormouse, waking up. "She's axing questions."

"Well, if I can't ask questions, I want to go."

"I knew it," sang the March Hare.

She wants to go, she wants to go,
She wants to go right down to Dixie.[5]

"Why, that's not a hymn, that's a song," said Alice.

"Ha, ha, ha," laughed the March Hare, "your knowledge is not worth an old song. Don't you know a hymn is simply a song of praise about Dixie."

"Don't bother with her," said the Mad Hatter.

"And don't you bother with hymn," retorted Alice.

"You are simply arguing about a trifle," chimed in the Dormouse.

"You'll be whipped shortly," said the March Hare, "and you'll find that no trifle."

"Ridiculous," yelled the Mad Hatter. "How can you whip a Wasser or an Isnot?"

"She's a saucy little baggage," yelled the March Hare.

"'Ark at 'is science!" laughed the Mad Hatter. "She is neither a saucy baggage nor has she any. She Izzer Deadun, and an Izzer Deadun is a ghostess; no legs, no arms, no nothing."

"Certainly," said the Dormouse, "she does know nothing."

"Is a ghostess a kind of spirit?" queried Alice.

"So to speak," replied the Dormouse. "A ghostess or ghost is a kind of spirit level. Something on the Astral plane."

"Well," said Alice, "if the Astral plane is anything like Annfield Plain,[6] I prefer to be excused. But I can't make it out. First I am an Izzer Deadun, then a ghost on a spirit level; bless my soul what am I? I do not understand."

"Guddle, Goddle," roared the Mad Hatter. "You are not supposed to understand. No one understands—except—except those who do. And what's the use of these things, for you haven't a leg left to stand on. That is as plain as the nose on your face."

"You're a nasty pasty, calling my nose plain."

"You really 'ave no nose," said the Mad Hatter, "spirits 'aven't."

Alice put her hand to feel—I mean she would have put up her hand if she'd had any.

"You've quite confused her," said the Dormouse. "When he said you had no nose, dear, he used it as a figure of speech. He used figures of speech, while honest John uses speeches of figures."

Tell me not in mournful numbers
That the soul is dead which slumbers
Like a Burnsian speech.[7]

"I am getting still more confused," said Alice.

"Well, you cannot know these things anyway," said the Mad Hatter, "it's all a mystery."

"What, a kind of Maskelyne and Devant?"[8]

"In your case," said the March Hare, "it's a kind of Feminine and Devant. This place is inhabited by spirits who never ask questions."

"Bother," said Alice, "I dunno where I are. First I'm an Izzer Deadun, next I'm a ghostess, then I'm a spirit. Bless my soul, I'm a sausage."

"Treason. Blasphemy. Lay hands on her," said the March Hare.

"Don't be silly," said the Mad Hatter, "there are no hands here, they're all on earth. What do you mean by saying spirits and souls are sausages?"

"Well," said Alice, humbly, "on earth the sausage is a mystery."

"Chuck it," said the Dormouse, "tell us a story."

"I do not know any stories."

"Great expectations!" hissed the March Hare. "I'll tell one myself. There were once three nice little girls who wanted to be angels."

"What's an Angel?" asked Alice.

"Axing again," said the March Hare.

"An Angel is a composite nebula with wings fixed too high for aeroplaning and not low enough for floating," said the Mad Hatter. "For further information study the old masters."

"Ha, ha! Caught yer," said the March Hare. "How can she study when she has no head for study?"

"You lost yours long ago," roared the Mad Hatter. "It's your fault," he said, glaring at Alice, "you've tried to upset our most cherished beliefs."

"Rubbish," said Alice. "All beliefs were cherished until brighter, purer, and better beliefs upset them."

"I am quite sure you've lost *your* head," said the March Hare.

"Why?" queried Alice.

"Because spirits have none," said he, triumphantly.

Alice knitted her brow—at least she would have done had she possessed one—when suddenly she felt herself shaken, and a well-known voice rang in her ears—

"Wake up, darling. Come and have some tea and toast."

"Bless you, dear old mummy, I wouldn't swap you for a million souls."

"Hush, darling," said mother, quite shocked, "You mustn't say such things."

■ It Can't Be Done! A History of Impossibilities

Edward Meyer, 1914

Chapter I.

(STONE AGE.)

Stone Hammer: Look at that crazy gink[1] over there.

Sheep Skin: Wot's he up to?

S.H.: Oh, he's loony. He says it's nonsense to run after deer in order to capture it. He says he can take a hickory stick, a strip of raw hide and another short stick with a sharp stone on one end and a feather on the other end and then send that second stick after the deer and get him! Can you beat it?

S.S.: Gee! He must be a nut! Whoever heard of such bunk? Why, it's against all the laws of nature and human precedent! Don't we know from experience that the only way to get a deer is to run after him and catch him? Hickory stick! Sharp stone! Oh, fudge!

IT CAN'T BE DONE!
(But it was done.)

Chapter II.

(LATER ON.)

First Moss Back[2]: Waddye know about that fool blacksmith?

Second M.B.: What's the idea?

First M.B.: Why, the blamed idiot says he is going to build an iron tube and put a black powder in it and then shoot a lump of lead a hundred times as far as we now shoot an arrow from a bow! Ain't that the limit?

Second M.B.: Why, that fellow must be as crazy as they make 'em! Whoever heard of such a thing? It's against all reason and logic.

IT CAN'T BE DONE!

(However, it came to pass.)

Chapter III.

(A PREVIOUS DATE.)

Tree Dweller: Are you hep[3] to the fool stunts that yap[4] across the lake is up to?

Cliff Dweller: Why, no. Put me wise.

T.D.: Why, the condemned simp[5] says it's all foolishness to straddle a log when you want to paddle your way across the lake. He says the sensible and scientific thing to do is to burn the inside out of that log, and then sit down inside the log instead of on top of it.

C.D.: It's a safe bet he's bughouse,[6] all right. Haven't we and our ancestors always straddled a log when crossing the lake? Now comes the bloke and tells we ought to sit inside the log instead of on top! Oh, piffle.

IT CAN'T BE DONE!

(But the canoe arrived.)

Chapter IV.

(SOME TIME LATER.)

First Fisherman: I've had my laps[7] on that cuss down in the cover. Wot's doin'?

Second F.: Aw, he's off his nut! He's got the dope that he's goin' to quit paddlin' his canoe; got an idea in his think tank that he will put a big stick up in this boat and hang a hide on it and make the wind take him where he wants to go.

First F.: Why, the poor mut. Does he think he can get away with that? Don't we know from experience that the only way to move a canoe is to paddle it? A sailboat! Oh, pshaw!

IT CAN'T BE DONE.

(But she sailed.)

Chapter V.

(LATER YET.)

First Bonehead: Get wise to this guy. He's got an idea that he can put the kibosh on the steam that comes from hot water, and then bottle it up in a machine and make that machine work! Get that? Isn't he bughouse?

Second B.H.: You bet he is! Why, there is no weight, or power to steam! It floats in the air, as light as a fog! Power from steam! Nothing to it!

IT CAN'T BE DONE!

(But the engine turned over.)

Chapter VI.

First Colonist: Say, there is a darned fool over at the Hudson River with a little ship he calls the Clermont,[8] and he had the fool idea in his bean that he can do away with sails and make the steam engine do the stunt.

Second C.: Do tell! Hasn't he any better sense than to know that while the steam engine has a limited usefulness on land it is impractical and a failure on board ship? Take it from me, the Clermont will never move!

IT CAN'T BE DONE!

(But the Clermont did move.)

Chapter VII.

(STILL LATER.)

First American: Say, this fellow Langley[9] in Washington, D.C., is dead wrong. The idea of him saying that a human being could learn to fly.

Second A.: Right! It's beyond the bounds of human possibilities to fly. Moreover, it is sacrilegious to fly. If the Lord ever wanted us to fly He would have created us with wings.

Human beings ever fly? Never!

IT CAN'T BE DONE!

(But they do fly now.)

(Historian's Note.)

Several hundred thousand chapters of the world's history are omitted from this work for the sake of brevity.

What the writer desires to point out is that in the progress of mankind a never-failing series of cycles has taken place. Here is what has happened in a regular rotation:—

One day, Ignorance says; "It Can't be Done!"

Next day, Intelligence does it.

The following day Ignorance says of something else: "It can't be done!"

The day after that Intelligence makes Ignorance back up by doing the very thing that "could not be done!" And so we find it down through all ages, Ignorance trying to hold humanity in darkness and Intelligence lifting mankind out of intellectual night into clear daylight—into ever brighter light.

To the non-Socialist who may happen to read the foregoing the writer wishes to point out that the Ignorance which says the interests of Labour and Capital are identical is the very same Ignorance which says "Socialism is impossible."

On the other hand, it is the extremely superior Intelligence of twenty million (20,000,000) Socialists in the world to-day who say that the interests of Labour and Capital are absolutely opposed to each other. It is this same massed Intelligence that says we are even now about to realise the fulfillment of this "beautiful dream" which would always "remain a dream!"

Now, Mr. Non-Socialist, which way are you betting? Do you back Ignorance to win?

If so, I place my money on Intelligence and give you heavy odds.

And, by the way, if you want to meet up with the highest grade of intelligence on earth to-day just cultivate the acquaintance of the Socialists. They have the history of humanity's evolution at their finger tips.

They and they alone understand why present conditions are as they are. They (the Socialists) and they alone know how to make the future as it should be—and will be.

When anyone tells me (not knowing what they are talking about) that Socialism is "impossible," I think of the "impossibilities" Ignorance has set up all through the ages, and which Intelligence, with unerring aim, has every time wiped away like a set of ten pins on the bowling alley. Then at this point I get real busy brushing the cobwebs out of the cranium of the gink who impersonates a phonograph reproducing a record recorded in his brain by the flutes—"Socialism is impossible!"

■ Notes

Introduction

1. William Morris, 'How Shall We Live', unpublished lecture, given 1889, Bloomsbury, London, first published in *The Unpublished Lectures of William Morris*, edited and compiled by Eugene D. LeMire (Detroit, 1969).

2. William Morris, 'The Decorative Arts, Their Relation to Modern Life and Progress', an address delivered before the Trades Guild of Learning, published London, 1878.

3. William Morris, 'Art and Socialism', lecture to the Secular Society, Leicester, 1884, first published in *The Works of William Morris*, vol. 23, edited by May Morris, 1915.

Aristos and Demos

1. *St Michael*: an archangel charged with fighting Satan. Daniel 12: 'At that time [the end of the world] shall Michael rise up, the great prince, who standeth for the children of thy people.' Demos is taking the same role in an earthly fight.

2. *myrmidons*: a warlike people, from Homer's Iliad. Hannigan is aligning pre-Christian imagery with the aristocracy and Christian imagery with the workers to create a hierarchy of morality in line with biblical teachings. 'Myrmidons' can also be used to mean 'hangers-on', 'sycophants', and 'hired ruffians' (*Oxford English Dictionary* [OED]), e.g., hirelings of an unscrupulous and disreputable kind.

A Dream of Queer Fishes (A Modern Prose Idyll)

1. *Theocritus*: Greek poet (300–260 BC), author of pastoral poetry termed idylls, which were criticized for assigning peasants characteristics of a greater capacity for language and sentiment than was deemed realistic.

2. *Salisbury and Co.*: a reference to Robert Gascoyne Cecil, Lord Salisbury's (1803–1903) Conservative government (1886–92). The story is a thinly disguised criticism of Joseph Chamberlain's (1836–1914) retreat from home rule support for the Irish Unionists after the 1886 general election.

3. *Billingsgate*: Billingsgate market in London, the largest fish market in the United Kingdom. Fish trading on the site dates back to 1699, when an act was passed allowing the general business market of Billingsgate to trade in any kind of fish. The porters working at the market had a reputation for swearing and bad language.

4. *three acres ... and a sea-cow*: 'Three acres and a cow' was a phrase coined by Jesse Collings (1831–1920), friend and political ally of Chamberlain and mayor of Birmingham, 1878–80. The phrase was used in Chamberlain's radical program for the general election in 1885 after the franchise was extended in the 1884 Third Reform Act. Part of the program was to distribute small portions of land to Irish tenants to encourage partial self-sufficiency, and this was seen as a poor alternative to the home rule he supported prior to the election.

Nobody's Business

1. *pocket book*: a small book to be carried in the pocket. The merchant is keeping a record of all his financial successes, drawing more money to himself and his family and away from those who need the money desperately, such as the dying man.

2. *babbles o' green fields*: The hostess describes Falstaff's last moment in *Henry V*, act 2, scene 3: "A made a finer end, and went away an it had

been any christom child; 'a parted ev'n just between twelve and one, ev'n at the turning o' th' tide; for after I saw him fumble with the sheets, and play with flowers, and smile upon his fingers' end, I knew there was but one way; for his nose was as sharp as a pen, and 'a babbl'd of green fields.' Both men return to happier times before their death, but the return to nature is more poignant for the dying man in this story, as he dies in urban squalor far from the green fields of his memory.

The History of a Giant

1. *pleased as Punch*: derived from the *Commedia dell' Arte* character Pulcinella, Mr. Punch is a comedic and violent puppet in Punch and Judy shows. His sense of self-satisfaction gives rise to this phrase.

2. *first Reform Act*: The Representation of the People Act 1832, generally known as the First Reform Act (there were eight 'Reform Acts' between 1832 and 1928, excluding those that dealt solely with Ireland and Scotland), redrew the constituency boundaries in England and Wales and extended the franchise, though the wealth criteria it imposed excluded most working-class men. It also introduced for the first time a system of voter registration. Dissatisfaction with the outcome of the 1832 act led directly to the creation of the Chartist movement (see note 6 to 'Jack Clearhead').

3. *towsy*: disheveled, unkempt, tousled; shaggy, rough; *OED*.

4. *spinning jenny*: Invented in Lancashire by James Hargreaves around 1764–67, the spinning jenny was a revolutionary development in the industrialization of the textile weaving industry, which allowed spinners to fill eight or more spools of yarn simultaneously.

5. *steam loom*: a textile weaving machine powered by steam. Its invention is credited to Edmund Cartwright (1743–1823).

6. *linotype machine*: the proprietary name of a composing machine used in printing, invented by Ottmar Mergenthaler (1854–99), that sets type line by line (*OED*). Linotype was the industry standard for

newspapers and magazines from the late nineteenth century until the 1970s and 1980s.

7. *Cunninghame Graham*: Robert Bontine Cunninghame Graham (1852–1936) was a Scottish politician and writer. He became the Liberal member of Parliament for North West Lanarkshire in the 1886 general election on a personal platform with strong socialist appeal. Becoming more radical during his service in the House of Commons, in 1888 he left the Liberal Party and founded the Scottish Labour Party (SLP) with James Keir Hardie (1856–1915), hence becoming the first socialist MP in the UK Parliament. He stood as the SLP candidate for Glasgow Camlachie in the 1892 general election but lost. He subsequently helped Keir Hardie to found the Independent Labour Party (ILP) in 1893 and was instrumental in the formation of the National Party of Scotland in 1928, which merged with the Scottish Party in 1934 to create the Scottish National Party (SNP).

8. *Bradford*: The founding location of the Independent Labour Party (ILP) in 1893, Bradford, a city in West Yorkshire, was an international center of textile manufacture, especially wool. It grew rapidly as a manufacturing base, leading to a significant increase in its working-class population. The Manningham Mills strike of 1890–91, the impetus for which was the proposed slashing of workers' wages in the face of a downturn in trade caused by increased global competition as well as tariffs on cloth imports into the United States, was most likely a factor in the choice of the city as the site for the conference that ended with the creation of the ILP.

A Terrible Crime

1. *photographic and lithographic*: A photograph is an image copied onto sensitive material; a lithograph is an engraving or print on stone (*OED*). In both senses the money produced by Bullion is only a representation of the real.

2. *paper money … a forger, a scoundrel*: Paper money or bank notes are a form of promissory note where, in exchange for the note, the bank will supply the bearer with the equivalent value in gold. The value of British currency in the nineteenth century was based on the global price of gold (the gold standard), while America and France based their currency on the price of both gold and silver (bimetallism). The exchange of paper money, which in Britain has the words 'I promise to pay the bearer on demand the sum of … ,' began in the seventeenth century and became the standard currency in 1844, when the exchange of metal was replaced by a note promising the bearer metal to the cost of the note. Bank notes were backed by the country's gold reserves until the Great Depression in the 1930s, when Britain ended the gold standard (in 1931), and now all bank notes are fiduciary, meaning the value is based on consumer confidence or on securities; *OED*.

Tom Hickathrift

1. Jacobs notes his source for this story as follows: "From the Chapbook, c. 1660, in the Pepysian Library, edited for the Villon Society by Mr G. L. Gomme. Mr Nutt, who kindly abridged it for me, writes, 'Nothing in the shape of incident has been omitted, and there has been no rewriting beyond a phrase here and there rendered necessary by the process of abridgement. But I have in one case altered the sequence of events putting the fight with the giant last.'"

Jack Clearhead

1. '*Dullards never, never, never shall be slaves*': The Dullards are singing a variation of 'Rule, Britannia!', a British patriotic song derived from the poem 'Rule, Britannia' by James Thomson (1700–1748). The chorus as sung nowadays is: 'Rule, Britannia! / Britannia rules the waves / Britons never, never, never shall be slaves'.

2. *Plumduff*: Plum duff is a rich boiled or steamed suet pudding made with raisins (the 'plums'), currants, and spices (*OED*). Being somewhat heavy, its use here as the name of one of the political parties carries overtones of dullness, stuffy entrenched attitudes, and stupidity.

3. *Piecrust*: 'Promises are like pie crust, they are made to be broken', i.e., promises are not to be trusted. This expression was first used in the political periodical *Heraclitus Ridens* in August 1681, and popularized by Jonathan Swift (1667–1745) in his 1738 book *Polite Conversation*.

4. *ugsome*: horrible, horrid, loathsome; *OED*.

5. *leal*: loyal, faithful, honest, true; *OED*.

6. *"The three colours which you see … Green for nature"*: Social-Ism's colours are those of the Chartist flag. Chartism was a pre-socialism working-class movement in Britain from 1838 to 1858, which sought electoral reform to make the political process more democratic (e.g., extension of suffrage to every man over the age of twenty-one; secret ballots; no property qualifications for members of Parliament, but instead salaries for MPs so that ordinary men could afford to be parliamentary representatives), following dissatisfaction with the 1832 Reform Act, which extended the vote but only by lowering the level of means-testing.

7. *kine*: archaic plural of 'cow', i.e., cattle; *OED*.

Little Red Riding Hood

1. *board-school*: a school under the management of a school-board, as established by the Elementary Education Act of 1870 (*OED*). This act made education compulsory for children from the ages of five to thirteen.

2. *Ting-a-ling-ting-tay*: a popular American song from 1892, written and composed by Harry Dacre (the pen name of Frank Dean) (1857–1922). He is best known for his song "Daisy Bell" ('Daisy, Daisy / give me your answer, do …').

3. *Band of Hope*: a temperance society first established in Britain in 1847.

4. *P.S.A.*: Pleasant Sunday Afternoon was a nondenominational Christian society formed in 1875 by John Blackham, a deacon of Ebeneezer Congregational Church in West Bromwich (near Birmingham, UK). Its aim was to offer Christian instruction in a lighter fashion than church services, usually with other recreations as well, such as musical entertainment.

A Mystery

1. *purple sweets*: violets. The Victorians were fond of associating flowers with certain human attributes, and the violet represents modesty, virtue, faithfulness, love, and the willingness to take a chance on love.

The Golden Egg

1. *Embankment … Temple Gardens*: Opened in 1870, the Thames Embankment, the collective name for the Victoria, Albert and Chelsea Embankments, reclaimed around thirty-seven acres of marsh land at the side of the Thames between Westminster and Chelsea Hospital. The Embankment, like Trafalgar Square, had become a place where the homeless gravitated at night to sleep, and it was an image of the problem of poverty in London at the end of the nineteenth century. Sociological surveys of poverty in the capital included descriptions of the Embankment homeless in works by Charles Booth, George Sims, Andrew Mearns, and others. The image was also drawn into fiction by other socialist authors, including A. Neil Lyons and Robert Blatchford. Middle Temple and Inner Temple Gardens sit beside the Victoria Embankment between the Blackfriars and Waterloo Bridges.

2. *co-proprietors of the Municipal wealth*: a worker; somebody who creates municipal wealth and has a right to its disposal.

The Doll Shop

1. *Penrhyn Anachronisms … Tyrannies*: a reference to George Sholto Gordon Douglas-Pennant (1836–1907), second Baron Penrhyn, who founded the North Wales Property Association in 1886 to resist land nationalization plans promoted in the press. He rescinded the 1874 Pennant Lloyd agreement at his slate quarry, which allowed workers to control wages and management and to set wages by collective bargaining. The Penrhyn dispute between owner and workers, lasting between 1900 and 1903, saw riots and the use of troops against the workers and ended only when the workers' funds ran out.

2. *West Ham … hundred other suits*: clothing associated with the poor working class: the worker in the slums of London, the agricultural laborer, the low-ranking soldier, the police, the sailor and the lifeboatman. All are essential to create and protect the wealth and body of the rich but are regarded as inferior to those they protect. The worker will 'look very well' as an MP, but the public is not yet ready for the worker in a position of power.

3. *Charles Kingsley … William Morris … John Ruskin*: Charles Kingsley (1819–75), the son of a Hampshire country gentleman, was ordained in 1842 and worked to alleviate poverty; he practiced Christian socialism by setting up co-operative workshops as well as preaching the ideas of the movement. He declared himself a Chartist but rejected the revolutionary aspect, and he drew his moral Chartism and Christian socialism into novels such as *Yeast* (1849) and *Alton Locke* (1850). William Morris (1834–96) was the eldest surviving son of a wealthy City financier; he first found fame as a poet and began the move toward socialism after reading Ruskin's chapter 'On the Nature of Gothic Architecture' in *The Stones of Venice* (1853). Morris went on to join the SDF in 1883. Unhappy with the parliamentary direction in which Henry Hyndman, chairman of the SDF, was leading the group, he left the SDF to form the revolutionary Socialist League at

the end of 1884. John Ruskin (1819–1900), son of a prosperous sherry merchant, was a critic of both art and society. Although not a socialist, declaring himself an old-school Tory, Ruskin's work combined both the aesthetic and the social, and he criticized the conditions of manufacture that dehumanized the producer. All three men were from a class of society that benefited from the status quo but who relentlessly criticized the social structure and its effects on the worker.

The Scarlet Shoes. (The Story of a Serio-comic Walking Tour and its Tragic End.)

1. *What do they know of England ... modern poet*: 'The English Flag' (1891) by Rudyard Kipling (1895–1936): 'Winds of the World, give answer! They are whimpering to and fro—/ And what should they know of England who only England know?—/ The poor little street-bred people that vapour and fume and brag, / They are lifting their heads in the stillness to yelp at the English Flag!' Kipling's poem celebrates the global power of England, asserting that those who know only England cannot understand its worldwide strength; Skeat uses Kipling's question as a motivation to discover the beauties of England.

2. *old lad*: not Hargold, Skeat's old friend, but a slang term for the Devil.

3. *Hans Christian Andersen and the Brothers Grimm*: authors of fairy tales. Andersen (1805–75) was the Danish author of tales such as 'The Ugly Duckling' and 'The Emperor's New Clothes'; the Brothers Grimm (Jacob, 1785–1863; Wilhelm, 1786–1859) were the authors of stories such as 'Cinderella' and 'Snow White'.

4. *cocoanut matting*: a rough and hard-wearing material made from coir. The term is used to indicate the unkempt appearance of a person's hair.

5. *Eastgate-street ... Grosvenor Museum*: The historic Roman city of Chester (northwest England, close to the border with Wales) has many sites of interest to Skeat and Hargold. Eastgate Street, running either side of the east gate of the city walls, is the site of the Victoria

Clock, which was erected in 1899 to celebrate Victoria's Diamond Jubilee. Grosvenor Park, on the banks of the Dee, was designed by the renowned landscape gardener Edward Kemp (1817–91) and was opened in 1867. The Rows are covered walkways at first-floor level running along the four main streets of the city above the ground-level shops. The origin of the medieval walkways is unknown, but they are unique to Chester. The city wall dates back to the Roman occupation and is the most complete set of city walls in Britain. The building of the Gothic structure of Chester Cathedral was begun in 1260, although there had been religious buildings on the site dating back to the Druids. The Grosvenor Museum was opened in 1886.

6. *Eaton Hall:* Eaton Hall, about six miles south of Chester and a mile south of the village of Eccleston, is the country house of the Duke of Westminster—hence the reply to the 'red-faced fellow's' question. The house is situated near the River Dee, which runs through the city of Chester.

7. *'Who is Reason? What is she?':* a play of words on the song *'Who is Silvia?'*, act 4, scene 2 of *Two Gentlemen of Verona* by William Shakespeare (1564–1616).

He, She, and It

1. *slavies:* servants, usually female, who carried out general housework instead of being assigned specific duties. 'Slavies' would generally be the only servants employed in a household and were employed to indicate the status of a lower-middle-class family of the 'shabby-genteel' type, as the area is later described.

2. *supper … dinner:* The vocabulary used for the main meals of the day is an indicator of social class.

3. *red-jackets … Crimear:* The Crimean War between the Russian Empire and an alliance of the British, French and Ottoman Empires was fought between October 1853 and February 1856. The British army uniform was the red coat, except for the artillery, rifles and light cav-

alry, and 'red coats' was the general term used to indicate a British soldier.

4. *Soho Square*: a square and park located near Charing Cross Road and Tottenham Court Road, London.

5. *Regent's Park*: a park to the north of Soho Square. It was designed by John Nash (1752–1835) on the orders of the Prince Regent (later George IV), and work began in 1818. The park is Crown property.

6. *Bethnal Green*: a slum area of East London renowned for the Old Nichol rookery used by Arthur Morrison (1863–1945) as the setting for *A Child of the Jago* (1896).

7. *Le-ster Square*: Leicester Square, London.

8. *Alhambra*: Alhambra Theatre and Music Hall, Leicester Square. Built in 1854 as the Royal Panopticon of Science and Arts, it became the Alhambra in 1858 and was demolished in 1936.

9. *Her eyebrows … she paints*: The wearing of makeup was one of the signs of prostitution, which is reinforced here by setting the scene outside a theatre. There has been a historical association between the theatre and prostitution, as Jeffrey Kahan points out in his biography of John Kean (1811–68): 'Prostitution in London was nothing new, nor was its association with the theatre'; *The Cult of Kean* (Aldershot: Ashgate, 2006), p. 84. See also K. Pullen, *Actresses and Whores: On Stage and in Society* (Cambridge: Cambridge University Press, 2005), for her consideration of prostitution and performance.

10. *Frenchies and Prooshians coming to blows*: The Franco-Prussian War was fought between July 1870 and May 1871.

11. *Piccadilly*: Piccadilly, along with Leicester Square, the Haymarket, Oxford Street, and Pall Mall, had some of the highest levels of prostitution in the capital, as 'the West End of London was the epicenter of commercial sex in the metropolis in the decades after 1885'; see J. Laite, *Common Prostitutes and Ordinary Citizens: Commercial Sex in London, 1885–1960* (Basingstoke: Palgrave Macmillan, 2012, quote p. 79), for further information.

12. *Guy's Hospital*: Founded by Thomas Guy and opened in Southwark, London, in 1725, the hospital originally cared for the incurably ill, but by the nineteenth century Guy's practiced medicine rather than simply palliative care.

An Idyll of the Dover Road. A True Story

1. *'Begin, ye Muses …'*: from Theocritus, *Idyll I, The Song of Thyrsis*, translated by Andrew Lang (1844–1912).

2. *Arcady*: meaning poet. The narrator is chiding the churchman for wanting to hear secular songs.

3. *"My goats … among the artintus"*: a series of quotations from Theocritus, *The Fifth Idyll*. Comatas and Lacon are two rural peasants who accuse each of stealing from the other, and settle the difference by a battle of pastoral song. The version quoted is the Andrew Lang (1844–1912) translation *Theocritus, Bion and Moschus* (1880). Blatchford replaces 'Lacon' with 'McGinnis' in the accusation, and 'artintus' should be 'arbutus'.

4. *When Britain … tricks*: a pastiche of the crier's nationalism, making a medley of 'Rule, Britannia!' (When Britain—first—at heaven's command—arose from out—the azure—main), a mnemonic rhyme about Guy Fawkes (and gun—powder—treason was plot) and the national anthem (confound their knavish—tricks, which should read 'frustrate their knavish tricks').

The Peasants and the Parasites. A Fable

1. *clomb*: i.e., 'climbed'; archaic past tense of 'to climb'; *OED*.

The Eternal Feminine

1. *St. Stephen's*: St. Stephen's Hall, on the site of the Royal Chapel where the House of Commons sat until 1834, when the chapel was destroyed by fire.

2. *the shrieking sisterhood*: a derogatory term for women demanding suffrage. The origin of the term is a cartoon published in *Punch*, 17 January 1906, entitled 'The Shrieking Sister'.

3. *Rome was saved by the cackling of her geese*: The cackling of geese woke sleeping Roman soldiers when Rome was attacked by Gauls.

4. *exults over a Boer War … foot the bill*: The successes of the British army in South Africa during the Second Boer War (1899–1902) were celebrated with excessive exuberance, but the £200 million cost to the country was not so well received.

5. *Chinese Slavery*: After the Second Boer War had ended, British companies were importing indentured Chinese labor, who were paid considerably less than British workers would have expected to receive.

6. *Manchester school*: advocates of free trade, opponents of war and imperialism, and the protection of consensual contract between peoples.

7. *Stirling Burghs*: a United Kingdom parliamentary constituency in Scotland, which, until 1918, consisted of Stirling, Dunfermline, Inverkeithing, and Culross.

8. *Plautus*: Titus Maccius Plautus (c. 254–184 BC) was a Roman comedic playwright. His surviving plays are the earliest extant works of Latin literature.

9. *Herbert Spencer … Or Machiavelli*: Herbert Spencer (1820–1903) argued that human beings were controlled by immutable natural laws and that the role of the state was to protect individual freedom; Niccolò Machiavelli (1469–1527) was author of *The Prince*, which showed pragmatic politics based on cunning and duplicity.

The Myopians' Muddle

1. *Coma*: in this context, a reference to the blurring of an object under a microscope due to an aberration in the lens.

2. *Myopians*: Myopia is a condition of the eye that prevents distant objects from being seen clearly. The naming of these people suggests that there is no long-term vision for their lives or society.

3. *Thews and sinewa*: Thews and sinews in this context refer to the bodily vigor and physical strength of the individual, as if the person consists of muscles or tendons alone. Thew is also an archaic term for a slave or thrall and an apparatus of punishment; *OED*.

4. *yclpet*: The correct spelling is 'yclept'; it means 'to name' or 'named', 'called'.

5. *recked*: past tense of 'reck'—to know about, to be aware of; *OED*.

A Martian's Visit to Earth. Being a Literal Translation into English of the Preface to an Account by a Martian of his Visit to England

1. *"Lower" House … "Upper" House*: the House of Lords and the House of Commons in the British parliamentary system, as the Martian goes on to explain. The Martian's account of the House of Lords' history focuses on the 'Lords Temporal' members—peers and noblemen, who in the feudal period would raise and command armies. The House of Lords is also attended by the 'Lords Spiritual'— bishops and archbishops. Parliament in Britain became the two distinct Houses in the fourteenth century. In 1909 the Lords rejected the Liberal government's budget, also known as the 'People's Budget'. This budget was to introduce new tax rates (including heavy land and property taxes), tax allowance for poor families with children, health and unemployment insurance for workers, and old age pensions. The unelected Lords' rejection of the budget, desired by both the electorate and their representatives in the House of Commons, caused a constitutional crisis and led to the passing of the 1911 Parliament Bill, which removed the Lords' right to veto any Commons Bill other than the extension of Parliament beyond five years.

2. *pari passu*: side by side, simultaneously and equally; *OED*.

3. *Vestigial Rudiments*: something remaining from an earlier, less developed period.

4. *7,500,000, of whom 6,500,000*: Footnote to the original article: "Mr. Chiozza Money estimates that there are roughly one million persons in

the receipt of incomes of £160 per annum and over. Making the large assumption that these have all a Parliamentary vote, and subtracting this number from the total number of electors, we arrive at the number above stated." Sir Leo George Chiozza Money (1870–1944), born in Genoa, Italy, was a politician and author who changed his name from Leone Giorgio Chiozza in 1903. He developed a reputation for economic, political, and statistical journalism. He was elected as Liberal MP for North Paddington in 1906 and East Northamptonshire in 1910. He argued for the redistribution of wealth through taxation.

5. *one-twelfth of the whole House*: In the 1906 general election, twenty-nine Labour candidates had been elected to the House of Commons out of a total of 670 constituencies. This makes the proportion nearer to one-sixteenth.

6. *Sisyphus*: In Greek mythology, Sisyphus is condemned to rolling an immense boulder uphill for eternity.

7. *ranked*: i.e., become rancid.

The May-Day Festival in the Year 1970

1. *Stockerau to Mödling*: villages to the north and south of Vienna. The prediction is for Vienna to have grown in size to encompass these two villages, a forecast that has not yet been achieved in the early twenty-first century. Vienna was a socialist stronghold, and the city elected the Social Democratic Party to power after the First World War. Its left-wing politics earned it the name Red Vienna. The author hopes that the strength of Vienna and its socialist politics will grow to greater importance in the twentieth century.

2. *Cotta style*: a small land measure containing eighty square yards; *OED*. The houses have space and land surrounding them, differentiating the socialist attitude to planning from the pre-socialist period described by the old man, who recalls the overcrowded slums of capitalism.

3. *Brigittenau*: an area to the northeast of Vienna's city center. There is a clear geographical separation between work and home.

4. *"poorhouses"* or *"alms houses"*: buildings for housing the poor and needy, often funded by individual philanthropy.

5. *Goethe's "Faust"*: *Faust: A Tragedy* (1808; 1832) by Johann Wolfgang von Goethe (1749–1832). The line is from part 2, act 5, where Faust has died—as the contract with Mephistopheles demanded—when he attained a moment he wanted to last forever. This came as he imagined a free land: 'I willingly would such a throng behold, / Upon free ground with a free people stand'. Faust is taken by angels and redeemed in Heaven despite his contract with Mephistopheles.

6. *Kahlenberg*: a mountain in the Wienerwald, or Vienna Woods, on the edge of Vienna and a popular tourist destination.

Mary Davis; or the Fate of a Proletarian Family. A Lesson Given to the Glasgow S.L.P. Socialist Sunday School

1. *The lesson*: This lesson is given to the Sunday School of Glasgow's Socialist Labour Party (SLP), a Marxist group with a strong membership in Clydeside.

2. *told a lie ... believe it*: 'A lie told often enough becomes the truth'; attributed to Vladimir Ilyich Lenin.

3. *reel and strath-spey*: reel, a traditional Scottish dance of four or more participants; strath-spey, a lively dance or reel, the music to accompany the dance; OED.

4. *quoit*: a game played by throwing rings of flattened iron, rope, rubber, etc., at a peg placed in the ground; OED.

5. *sweay*: also spelled 'swey'—a flat iron rod suspended in the chimney, on which pots and kettles are hung; OED.

6. *waggity we-clock*: also *wag-at-e-wa(a)*, *wag at a-*, *-i-*, *-y-*, *waggitawa*, *waggity-*, *wag o the wa*—an unencased pendulum clock, originally with some wooden mechanism, of a kind made in Germany, and hung on a wall; *Dictionary of the Scots Language*, wag, I. 4. ii.

7. *Gibbon's "Decline and Fall of the Roman Empire"*: Gibbon's *The History of the Decline and Fall of the Roman Empire* blamed the decline

of the Roman Empire on its corresponding decline of civic responsibility, with the Christian focus on an afterlife undermining the motivation for progress. Mr. Davis is intimating that the same situation is being repeated in Western capitalist countries as the rich eschew moral and ethical responsibility to society as a whole, focusing only on the acquisition of money. This is compounded by their insistence that workers look to the afterlife for their reward.

8. *shewed the white feather*: a symbol of cowardice.

9. *"pass" ... tenter or "overseer"*: pass, passageway, or corridor between the looms; tenter, either someone who stretches out cloth to dry after dying or someone who oversees (or tends) machinery; overseer, someone in charge of the workers in a specific area or room of the mill. This scene describes the hierarchy among workers in the mills, as an employee in charge of the machinery (spinners, weavers) would subcontract part of the work to others, their wages being paid out of the spinner's or weaver's wages. Charles Allen Clarke describes this subdivision of labor and the double standards of the unionized weaver or spinner when dealing with their own employees through the experiences of Jim Campbell in 'The Red Flag', serialized in *Justice*, 2 May 1908–12 December 1908, the complete text of which can be found in Mutch, *British Socialist Fiction 1884–1914*, vol. 4, pp. 147–254.

The Lost Vision. A Spring Fantasy

1. *hum and shock*: George Gordon Lord Byron, *Childe Harold's Pilgrimage* (1811), canto 2, stanza 26: 'But midst the crowd, the hum, the shock of men.'

2. *Moloch*: the name of a Canaanite god, the worship of whom seems to have been associated with the sacrifice of children by burning (Leviticus 18:21); OED.

3. *the teeth and claws of nature were red*: Alfred Lord Tennyson (1809–82), *In Memoriam* (1850), stanza 60: 'Tho' Nature, red in tooth and claw'.

The Aerial Armada. What Took Place in A.D. 2000

1. *Goodwood*: a racecourse in Sussex, north of Chichester.
2. *Alhambra matinée … Maud Allen species*: 'Alhambra' was a popular name for theatres in Britain in the nineteenth century. Maud Allen (1873–1956) was born Beulah Maude Durrant in Toronto, Canada, and was a popular music hall entertainer. She was renowned for her scanty costumes, and her 'Salome Dance' was excluded from some performances in her national tours as it was deemed licentious by some theatre censors.
3. *Leicester-square*: an area in London associated with the theatre. The Alhambra Theatre stood in Leicester Square from 1858 (originally opening in 1854 as the Royal Panopticon of Science and Arts) until its demolition in 1936.
4. *Nore observation station*: The Nore anchorage in the Thames Estuary was the location of a naval mutiny in 1797, following the Spithead mutiny at the anchorage in the Solent. The power of the British navy has been superseded by the power of the air force.
5. *dirigible*: a balloon or airship; *OED*.
6. *chewing-gum*: Chewing gum had been used in various forms for centuries, but the use of chicle, imported from Mexico, in the 1860s produced what is recognized as chewing gum today.
7. *Ouida's guardsman*: Ouida was the pseudonym of Marie Louise de la Ramée (1839–1908). The reference to the guardsman is to the character of Hon. Bertie Cecil in *Under Two Flags* (1867), a member of the Life Guards who carries out many heroic acts under the name 'Louis Victor' after having faked his own death to save the honor of his brother.
8. *I mean billiards*: an allusion to Francis Drake (1540–96) playing bowls at Plymouth Hoe while the Spanish Armada was sailing toward England. Drake is supposed to have waited to finish the game before setting off to defeat the Armada.

9. *financiers and Bourse thieves*: A bourse is a meeting place for merchants and the name of the French equivalent of the Stock Exchange. The biggest danger to Britain comes from capitalists and moneymen.

10. *promissory note*: a written promise to pay the bearer of the note the sum stated; *OED*.

11. *propria forma*: in proper form, in a form legally binding.

Mr. Prowser-Wowser

1. *the strike at Waihi*: a six-month mining strike at the goldmines of Waihi. On 12 November 1912 escalating violence aimed at strikebreakers culminated in gunfire, the storming of the miners' hall by police, and the death of striker Fred Evans by beating.

2. *Labour is prior to … not first existed*: from US president Abraham Lincoln's State of the Union Address, 3 December 1861.

Behind the Wall

1. This is not at all improbable. Russian political prisoners have been known to communicate their inmost thoughts by these means.

Alice in Sunderland. A Baffling Mystery

1. *Pentecostal Convention*: Pentecostalism is a revivalist branch of Protestant Christianity that practices radical evangelism and which emerged in Britain and America during the late nineteenth and early twentieth centuries. The annual Sunderland Convention was organized by Alfred Boddy (1854–1930).

2. *Whit-week*: Whitsun is the seventh Sunday after Easter; Whitsuntide is the week following Pentecost, the seventh Sunday after Easter, and a religious holiday for Christians. The holiday was celebrated in the north of England with towns organizing walks or parades of Sunday School children through the town, brass band displays, and competitions to herald the beginning of summer. The Whitsun holiday

is a relic of feudal society when the lord would allow his serfs time away from work.

3. *Jarrow*: a town in the northeast of England associated with shipbuilding. It is most famously associated with the 1936 Jarrow March, when men walked from Jarrow to London to protest against unemployment.

4. *not Scott, mostly Wesley and Newman*: Sir Walter Scott (1771–1832), poet and novelist; John Wesley (1707–91), founder of Methodism, who published a large collection of hymns entitled *A Collection of Hymns, for the Use of the People Called Methodists* (1780); John Henry Cardinal Newman (1801–90), part of the Oxford Movement of the 1830s and 1840s that believed High Church Anglicanism to be one of the branches of Catholicism. The March Hare takes Alice's exclamation to differentiate between the secular poetry of Walter Scott and the hymnal poetry of the churches.

5. *She wants to go … down to Dixie*: a rewording of Irving Berlin's (1888–1989) 'I Want to Be in Dixie' (1912): 'I want to be / I want to be / I want to be down home in Dixie.'

6. *Annfield Plain*: a mining village in County Durham, to the west of Sunderland.

7. *Tell me not … Burnsian speech*: a critical reference to the speeches of John Burns MP (1858–1943). Burns was elected to Parliament in 1892 as an independent Labour candidate along with James Keir Hardie. Burns lost the support of the socialist and Labour politicians and members when he gravitated toward the Liberal Party, accepting a position as president of the Local Government Board in the Campbell-Bannerman (1836–1908) administration in 1905.

8. *Maskelyne and Devant*: Former watchmaker John Nevil Maskelyne (1839–1917) and his friend former cabinetmaker George Alfred Cooke (1825–1904) were stage magicians and illusionists who have been credited with devising some of the most famous illusions, including levitation. After the death of Cooke, Maskelyne formed a partnership with David Devant (1868–1941), a partnership that became even more

successful than Maskelyne and Cooke and lasted until just before
Maskelyne's death. The mysteries of religion and of stage magicians
are all the same to Alice.

It Can't Be Done! A History of Impossibilities

1. *gink*: a fellow, a man; usually pejorative; *OED*.
2. *Moss Back*: a slow, rustic, or old-fashioned person; one attached to antiquated ideas; *OED*.
3. *hep*: well-informed, knowledgeable, 'wise to'; *OED*.
4. *yap*: a fool, someone easily taken in; also, an uncultured or unsophisticated person; *OED*.
5. *simp*: a fool, a simpleton; *OED*.
6. *bughouse*: crazy, very eccentric; *OED*.
7. *laps*: applied to certain parts of the body—of the ear, liver, lungs (c.f. lobe) (*OED*). 'I've had my laps on …' would seem to mean 'I've been listening to …'.
8. *Clermont*: the first practical and commercially viable steamboat, designed and built by Robert Fulton (1765–1815) and Robert R. Livingstone (1746–1813) in New York in 1807.
9. *Langley*: Samuel Pierpont Langley (1834–1906), pioneer of aviation.

■ References

'An Old Fable Retold': William Morris, *Justice*, 19 January 1884, p. 2.

'Fables for the Times—I: The Monkeys and the Nuts': 'Utile Dulci', *Justice*, 11 October 1884, p. 2.

'Fables for the Times—II: The Political Economist and the Flowers': Anon., *Justice*, 18 October 1884, p. 2.

'Aristos and Demos': D. F. Hannigan, *Justice*, 30 April 1887, pp. 2–3.

'A Dream of Queer Fishes (A Modern Prose Idyll)': H.S.S. (Henry Shakespear Stephens Salt), *Commonweal*, 19 November 1887, pp. 372–73.

'Chips': H. Bellingham, *To-Day*, September 1888, pp. 81–83.

'Nobody's Business': Elihu (Samuel Washington), *Labour Prophet*, September 1892, p. 69.

'The History of a Giant': Being a Study in Politics for Very Young Boys': Keir Hardie, *Labour Leader*, 8 April 1893, pp. 1–3.

'The Man without a Heart': F. J. Gould, *Cinderella: A Paper Devoted to the Service of Cinderella Children*, *Labour Prophet*, October 1893, pp. 101–2.

'A Terrible Crime': Dan Baxter, *Workman's Times*, 30 December 1893, p. 2.

'Tom Hickathrift': Edited by Joseph Jacobs, *More English Fairy Tales*, D. Nutt (London), 1894.

'Jack Clearhead: A Fairy Tale for crusaders, and to be read by them to their fathers and mothers': Keir Hardie M. P., *Labour Leader*, 8, 15, 22, and 29 September 1894, p. 11; 6, 13, 20, and 27 October 1894, p. 11.

'The Four Friends': Anon., *Cinderella: A Paper for the Children, Labour Prophet*, December 1894, pp. 173–74.

'The Princesses' (adapted): J. H., *Labour Prophet*, March 1895, p. 44.

'The New Shilling': Dan Baxter, *Justice*, 23 March 1895, p. 2.

'The Harebell's Sermon': 'The Fairy', *Cinderella: A Paper for the Children, Labour Prophet*, June 1895, p. 93.

'Little Red Riding Hood': C. Allen Clarke, *Labour Leader*, 26 October 1895, p. 12; 2 November 1895, p. 12; 9 November 1895, p. 12.

'A Mystery': Caroline E. Derecourt Martyn, *Labour Leader*, 7 March 1896, pp. 80–81.

'Odin and his One Eye': T. Robinson, *Cinderella: A Paper for the Children, Labour Prophet*, August 1896, pp. 132–33.

'The Elves and Fairies': T. Robinson, *Cinderella: A Paper for the Children, Labour Prophet*, October 1896, p. 165.

'A Monkey Story': Dan Baxter, *Justice*, 31 October 1896, p. 2.

'Elfhome (Charlie's Garden)': T. Robinson, *Cinderella: A Paper for the Children, Labour Prophet*, April 1897, p. 61.

'A Fairy Tale for Tired Socialists': C.S.J., *Justice*, 20 August 1898, p. 6.

'The Golden Egg': Joseph Grose, *Justice*, 13 July 1901, p. 3.

'When Death Crossed the Threshold': E. Whittaker, *Teddy Ashton's Northern Weekly*, 28 February 1903, p. 10.

'The Doll Shop': Frank Starr, *Labour Leader*, 15 August 1903, p. 262.

'The Scarlet Shoes. (The Story of a Serio-comic Walking Tour and its Tragic End.)': Harford Willson, *Teddy Ashton's Northern Weekly*, 3 March 1906, p. 6.

'He, She, and It': M. Winchevsky, *Social Democrat*, April 1906, pp. 253–56.

'An Idyll of the Dover Road. A True Story': McGinnis (Robert Blatchford), *Clarion*, 5 April 1907, p. 1.

'His Sister. A Little Spangle of Real Life': Glanville Maidstone (Robert Blatchford?), *Clarion*, 19 April 1907, p. 7.

'"Happy Valley." A Fairy Tale': Anon., *Justice*, 20 July 1907, p. 5.

'The Peasants and the Parasites'. A Fable: R. B. Suthers, *Clarion*, 24 January 1908, p. 3.

'The Eternal Feminine': C. L. Everard, *Justice*, 7 March 1908, p. 5.

'The Myopian's Muddle': Victor Grayson, *Clarion*, 12 March 1909, p. 8.

'A Martian's Visit to Earth. Being a Literal Translation into English of the Preface to an Account by a Martian of his Visit to England': A. L. Grey, *Socialist Review*, November 1909, pp. 232–40.

'Nightmare Bridge': Glanville Maidstone, *Clarion*, 15 July 1910, p. 1.

'The Fool and the Wise Man': W. Anderson, *Justice*, 13 August 1910, p. 6.

'The May-Day Festival in the Year 1970' (translated from the Vienna *Arbeiterzeitung*): 'Optimus', *Social Democrat*, 15 April 1911, pp. 189–92. (The *Arbeiterzeitung* workers' newspaper was founded in 1889 by Vicktor Adler [1852–1918], leader of the Social Democratic Party of Austria.)

'Mary Davis; or the Fate of a Proletarian Family. A Lesson Given to the Glasgow S.L.P.' Socialist Sunday School: Tom Anderson, *Socialist*, January 1912, p. 34.

'The Lost Vision. A Spring Fantasy': Victor Grayson, *Justice*, 4 May 1912, p. 3.

'The Aerial Armada. What Took Place in A.D. 2000': Frank Starr, *Daily Citizen*, 10 April 1913, p. 7.

'Mr. Prowser-Wowser': Edward Hartley, *Justice*, 28 June 1913, p. 2.

'Behind the Wall': Schalom Asch, *British Socialist (Social Democrat)*, 15 December 1913, pp. 573–76.

'Alice in Sunderland. A Baffling Mystery': 'Casey' (Walter Hampson), *Labour Leader*, 18 June 1914, p. 5.

'It Can't Be Done! A History of Impossibilities': Edward Meyer (from the *New York Call*), *Justice*, 6 August 1914, p. 8.

Tom Anderson (n.d.) (no biographical details known).

W. Anderson, William Crawford Anderson (1877–1919), was born in Banffshire, Scotland, to a blacksmith in a community of crofters. He encountered socialism during his apprenticeship as an industrial chemist. A member of the Shop Assistants' Union, he joined the Independent Labour Party (ILP) in 1907 and was elected to the National Administrative Council in 1908. He was a lead writer for, and later a board member of, the *Daily Citizen*, the daily socialist paper, and was able to support himself by his own writing and speaking engagements from about 1908 onward. He won the seat of Attercliffe, Sheffield, for the Labour Party in 1915.

Schalom Asch (1880–1957) was a Polish Jewish novelist, dramatist, and essayist writing mostly in Yiddish. He was born in Kutno, Poland, son of a cattle dealer and innkeeper. He emigrated to the United States in 1910 but at one point moved back to Poland and also lived in France. He wrote a historical novel in Yiddish and wrote the drama *God of Vengeance*, which was performed on Broadway and resulted in the whole cast being arrested and successfully prosecuted on obscenity charges. He carried on writing novels, plays, and articles, exciting controversy on religious and political grounds.

Dan Baxter (n.d.) was a regular contributor to *Justice* and the ILP-affiliated periodical *Workman's Times*.

I I. Bellingham (n.d.) (no biographical details known).

Robert Blatchford (1851–1943) was one of the major figures in the history of British socialism. In 1890 he was based in Manchester, where he founded the local branch of the Fabian Society and launched the weekly newspaper the *Clarion* in 1891. By 1910 the paper was selling about eighty thousand copies per issue. He also set up the Clarionettes, who ran choirs, cycling clubs, the Socialist Scouts, Glee Clubs, and the 'Clarion Van', which travelled the country disseminating propaganda for the movement. The Cinderella Clubs for children were also part of this working-class, socialist, cultural movement. A *Clarion Song Book* was produced in 1906, and the strength of this movement also supported working-class action such as the great lockout of the Penrhyn slate quarry workers in North Wales.

In 1893 he published his famous book of articles on socialism, *Merrie England*, which sold over 750,000 copies across the English-speaking world within a year of its publication. One strong strand of Blatchford's thinking was patriotic and at times militaristic; unlike many on the Left, he supported the Boer War and actively backed Britain's side in trade wars, saying, 'We are Britons first and Socialists next.' In the lead-up to the First World War he was an active supporter of the 'war party' in Britain, advocating conscription against what he saw as the menace of Germany, and in defense of the British Empire.

In 1915, Blatchford formed the National Democratic and Labour Party (NDP) and won nine members of Parliament in the 1918 general election. Following the death of his wife in 1921, he took a strong interest in spiritualism, and by 1931 he declared himself to be a "Tory democrat".

'Casey' was the pseudonym of Walter Hampson (1864–1932), who was a railwayman, poet, and author. His works include 'Who Are the Bloodsuckers' (c. 1907), and the dialect works 'Tykes Abrooad' [*sic*] (1911) and 'Awheel in Wharfeland' (1918). He was the editor of the *Clock Almanac* from 1917 until his death.

Charles Allen Clarke (1863–1935), most widely known as C. Allen Clarke, was an English working-class humorist, novelist, journalist, and social investigator from Bolton in Lancashire, the son of cotton mill workers. As an eleven-year-old, he worked for the first half of the day and went to school in the afternoons. He escaped full-time mill working by becoming a pupil-teacher at the age of fourteen and moved on from there to working for various newspapers. He founded the short-lived socialist periodical the *Labour Light*, published articles for *Cotton Factory Times*, started yet another, the *Bolton Trotter* and another (!), *Teddy Ashton's Journal*. He was a versatile writer, producing a range of articles and stories from polemic to dialect fiction, poetry, and children's fiction, working under the pseudonyms Capanbells, Grandad Grey, Allen-a-Dale, and Ben Adhem.

'Utile Dulci' (n.d.) (no biographical details known).

'Elihu' is the pseudonym of Samuel Washington (n.d.), author of 'Whose Dog Art Thou? An Argument for a Labour Party' (1892), and 'A Nation of Slaves' (n.d.). He published articles in *Justice*, the *Workman's Times*, and the *Labour Prophet*.

C. L. Everard (n.d.) was an author of a good deal of fiction for *Justice*, and he also published under the pseudonym 'Gadfly'. He went on to write for the *Daily Herald*, the first socialist daily newspaper, and for the *British Worker* during the 1926 general strike.

'The Fairy' (n.d.) (no biographical details known) made regular contributions to the *Cinderella* pages of the *Labour Prophet* from March 1895. All contributions appeared under the title 'Our Cinderella Letter'.

Frederick James Gould (1855–1938) was an English teacher, writer, and pioneer secular humanist. He was born in Brighton, the son of evangelical Anglicans, but grew up in London. At the age of seven he was sent to study and sing in the choir at the chapel in Windsor Castle. He then went to school at Chenies, Buckinghamshire, and became a Sunday School teacher. After he was appointed head teacher at Great

Missenden church school, he began to develop doubts about his own religious faith. In 1879 he started working as a teacher in publicly funded board schools in poorer parts of the East End of London. In 1897, he produced a four-volume book of ethical lessons for children, and he helped found forerunners to humanist organizations and publications that survive to this day. He served for a while as a Labour Party councilor, identified himself as a follower of Comte and positivism, and travelled widely through the United States and India promoting secular education while writing an extensive series of books on the subject.

Victor Grayson (1881–disappeared 1920) was born in Liverpool. He joined the ILP in 1905 and was a celebrated public speaker. He was elected as an independent socialist MP for Colne Valley in 1907 and lost his seat in 1910; he tried again in Kennington (London) in the second election that year but failed. He published articles on socialism in A. P. Orage's *New Age*. He spent a short while in Australia before returning to Britain and disappearing from view in September 1920.

A. L. Grey (n.d.) (no biographical details known).

Joseph Grose (n.d.) (no biographical details known).

J. H. (n.d.) (no biographical details known).

Denis F. Hannigan (n.d.) was a reviewer and translator of many works including Gustave Flaubert's *Sentimental Education* and Honoré de Balzac's *The Love Letters*.

James Keir Hardie (1856–1915) was a giant of the socialist and Labour movement. He served as the first Labour member of Parliament. Hardie started work at the age of seven but was rigorously educated at home by his parents and later attended night school. Working in the mines, he soon became a full-time trade union organizer. Having won the parliamentary seat of West Ham South as an independent candidate in 1892, he helped to form the ILP in the following year. In 1900 he helped to form the union-based Labour Representation

Committee, soon renamed the Labour Party, with which the ILP later merged. Hardie was also a lay preacher and temperance campaigner, who supported votes for women, self-rule for India, home rule for Scotland, and an end to segregation in South Africa. At the outbreak of World War I, he tried to organize a pacifist general strike but died soon afterward. As a writer and journalist he founded his own periodical, the *Miner*, which was renamed the *Labour Leader*, and was an active participant in the socialist educational and recreational movement of the late nineteenth century known as the 'Cinderella Clubs'. As part of this, he contributed socialist fairy tales and allegories to the *Cinderella* pages of the *Labour Prophet*.

Edward Robertshaw Hartley (1855–1918) published a series of didactic articles called 'Train Talk' in *Justice*, which were based on actual or imagined conversations about socialism with people on train journeys. These were later collected into one volume and published. Born in Bradford, the son of woolen and worsted spinners, he joined both the Social Democratic Federation (founded in 1881, the SDF was the first organized British socialist political party) and the ILP in the 1890s. He edited the *Bradford Labour Echo* and supported the election campaign of Harry Quelch in 1920 in Dewsbury. He stood as a Socialist Unity candidate in the 1906 election.

C.S.J. (n.d.) (no biographical details known).

Joseph Jacobs (1854–1916) was an Australian folklorist, literary critic, and historian who became a notable collector and publisher of English folklore. His work went on to create the core canon of English fairy tales including 'Jack and the Beanstalk', 'Goldilocks and the Three Bears', 'The Three Little Pigs', 'Jack the Giant-Killer', and 'The History of Tom Thumb'. He published his fairy tale collections *English Fairy Tales* in 1890, and *More English Fairy Tales* in 1894, but also went on after and added to these collections of tales from continental Europe as well as Jewish, Celtic, and Indian fairy tales. Jacobs was also an editor for journals and books on the subject of folklore, which included editing *Fables of Bidpai, Fables of Aesop,* and *The Thousand and One Nights*. He wrote on the migration of Jewish folklore, became an editor of the society journal *Folklore*, and contributed to the *Jewish Encyclopedia*.

Glanville Maidstone—pseudonym, see Robert Blatchford.

Caroline E. Derecourt Martyn (1867–96) was a regular contributor to *Labour Leader* in 1895–96. She was born in Lincoln, the daughter of a policeman. Deeply religious, she became a Fabian socialist and a famed public speaker, travelling widely across the country. She acted for a short while as secretary to the socialist leader Tom Mann (1856–1941). Just after her appointment as editor of the journal *Fraternity*, she died suddenly of pleurisy.

McGinnis—pseudonym, see Robert Blatchford.

Edward Meyer (n.d.) (no biographical details known).

William Morris (1834–96) was an English textile designer, poet, novelist, translator, and socialist activist. He helped to establish the modern fantasy genre and wrote socialist songs, while playing a significant role as speaker and activist in the socialist movement in Britain. Born in Walthamstow in Essex to a wealthy middle-class family, Morris came under the strong influence of medievalism while studying classics at Oxford University. He trained as an architect and associated himself with the Pre-Raphaelite movement. Aside from his long-lasting contribution to interior design, his huge literary output included Icelandic sagas, epic poems and novels, and utopian works like 'A Dream of John Ball' and 'News from Nowhere'. From the 1880s onward, he became a committed revolutionary socialist and Marxist.

'Optimus' (n.d.) (no biographical details known).

Thomas Robinson (n.d.) (no biographical details known) contributed a series of stories to the *Cinderella* pages of the *Labour Prophet* between July 1896 and April 1897, mostly based on the mythology surrounding the Norse god Odin.

H.S.S. was Henry Shakespear Stephens Salt (1851–1939), a humanitarian, vegetarian, and Fabian socialist. His 1897 pamphlet *The Logic of Vegetarianism* was claimed by Gandhi to have converted him to vegetarianism.

Frank Starr (n.d.) (no biographical details known).

R. B. Suthers (1870–1950), more fully Robert Bentley Suthers, was the son of a Chorlton (near Manchester) draper. He was employed at the *Clarion* as an accountant, began contributing to it from 1901, and became renowned as a propagandist for municipal socialism. His first novel, *A Man, a Woman and a Dog*, was published in 1901. He founded his own journal, *Ideas*, in 1910 and also contributed to other socialist journals such as the 1930s *Labour Magazine*.

E. Whittaker (n.d.) was a regular contributor to *Teddy Ashton's Northern Weekly*, writing fiction, poetry, and a children's column.

Harford Willson (n.d.) (no biographical details known) was a regular contributor to *Teddy Ashton's Northern Weekly*. He more usually wrote factual articles rather than fiction.

M. Winchevsky (1856–1932) was born Leopold Benzion Novkhovitch in Yanova (Jonava), Lithuania. After being deported from Germany to Denmark he moved to London, where he founded and edited the Yiddish socialist newspaper *Dos Poilishe Yidl* ('The Little Polish Jew'); he was also instrumental in the development of Yiddish poetry. In 1894 he moved to the United States, where he carried on writing and working for socialism until his death.

British Socialist (1912–13): this was the final incarnation of the *Social Democrat* (see below), which was renamed from January 1912 following the formation of the British Socialist Party in late 1911.

Clarion (1891–1935): the socialist movement's best-selling periodical (around thirty-four thousand copies in the 1890s), it was founded by Robert Blatchford and a small group, was first published in Manchester, and cost one penny. In 1895, it moved to London. Though it was connected to the Independent Labour Party (ILP), it was not its official organ. The periodical had an influence beyond its circulation, as its name was used to head up a range of social organizations all across Britain. It carried a good deal of literary material by such people as Edward Carpenter, as well as much by Blatchford himself.

Commonweal (1885–92): founded by William Morris, it was at first published monthly, then for four years as a weekly, before reverting to being a monthly. Its subtitle changed in 1890 from *The Official Journal of the Socialist League* (the SL being the socialist group that Morris founded) to *A Journal of Revolutionary Socialism* and then again, in 1891, to *A Revolutionary Journal of Anarchist Communism*. It was edited by Morris himself and later by such people as Marx's son-in-law Edward Aveling, Ernest Belfort Bax, and H. B. Samuels. The paper published articles by Eleanor Marx, George Bernard Shaw, Friedrich Engels, and of course Morris, Bax, and Aveling themselves. It was published in London and cost one penny, and though the first issue sold five thousand copies, circulation subsequently hovered between two and three thousand.

Daily Citizen (1912–15): this was the first official daily newspaper of the Labour Party and the Trades Union Congress and was published in Manchester. It was short-lived mostly because it was unable to compete with the *Daily Herald*. It included short stories, a daily poem, and serial fiction.

Justice (1884–1925): *Justice: The Organ of the Social Democracy* was the weekly official periodical of the Social Democratic Federation (SDF). Editors included H. M. Hyndman, the leading figure in the SDF, and Harry Quelch. It published articles by people such as Annie Besant, George Bernard Shaw, John Burns, and William Morris. Its peak sales were four thousand, though most of time around thirteen hundred.

Labour Leader (1888–1987): this was founded in Glasgow by Keir Hardie in 1888 as a new name for his first periodical, the *Miner*. It was relaunched in 1893 as a monthly and ran under that name till 1987. It was the official publication of the Independent Labour Party and carried some fiction on a fairly regular basis.

Labour Prophet (1892–98; 1899–1901): the official periodical of the Labour Church, it was edited mostly by the church's founder, John Trevor. In its second incarnation it was a free quarterly called the *Labour Church Record*. It occasionally carried articles by Robert Blatchford and Keir Hardie, and it included some fiction from such people as the dockers' leader Ben Tillett. The *Labour Prophet* also regularly carried stories for children in its supplement *Cinderella: A Paper for the Children*; this was added in May 1893 in order to expand the church's 'Cinderella Work', which focused not only on the practical aspects of child poverty, for example, feeding and clothing them, but also on the educational and moral growth of such children. Some of these stories were known fairy tales such as those of the Grimm Brothers, which were often reworked to include or reinforce the socialist message, and some were original, written to expound Christian and socialist ideals. The supplement was sold separately at Labour Church services as well as being included within its parent periodical.

More English Fairy Tales (1894): edited by the Australian-born Joseph Jacobs, this followed his successful *English Fairy Tales* (1890); both volumes came out of his work as a folklorist and editor. These two volumes are credited with helping to establish a canon of English or British stories such as 'The Three Little Pigs', 'Jack and the Beanstalk', 'Goldilocks and the Three Bears', and 'Dick Whittington'.

Social Democrat (1897–1912): subtitled *A Monthly Socialist Review*, it was edited by Harry Quelch, who also edited *Justice* (see above). It was one of the longer journals of the time, sometimes running to sixty-four pages, and had a more pronounced internationalist perspective than most other British socialist periodicals. Contributors included Edward Aveling, Eleanor Marx, and R. B. Cunninghame Graham. It regularly published short stories, including some by Quelch himself. It was renamed *British Socialist* in 1912 (see above).

Socialist (1902–24): subtitled *The Official Organ of the Socialist Labour Party*, it was published first in Edinburgh and then in Glasgow. Its editors included leading socialist figures such as James Connolly and Tom Bell. The socialism was influenced by Marxism, and it carried a few stories and a good deal of poetry.

Socialist Review (1908–34): subtitled *A Monthly Magazine of Modern Thought*, this was an ILP periodical, which ran originally from London before moving to Salford in 1909. The journal focused on socialist theory and carried articles by such people as Ramsay Macdonald, H. G. Wells, and the French socialist leader Jean Jaurès. It didn't carry much fiction.

Teddy Ashton's Northern Weekly (1896–1908): originally, this journal ran as *Teddy Ashton's Journal: A Gradely Paper for Gradely Folk*. It was published in Bolton, and the editor and chief writer was Charles

Allen Clarke. He wrote most of the paper himself, using various pseudonyms. He also published the fiction of local authors, many of whom were working-class people doing full-time jobs.

To-Day (1883–89): *To-Day: A Monthly Gathering of Bold Thoughts* changed its subtitle to *The Monthly Magazine of Scientific Socialism.* This was originally edited by H. M. Hyndman, chairman of the SDF, before he passed on the job to Ernest Belfort Bax, then later to Hubert Bland, before Hyndman took control again and changed the name to *International Review.* It carried lengthy articles and debates including a famous series on the 'Woman Question', led by Annie Besant. The paper serialized a translation of Marx's *Das Kapital* and carried a good deal of literary material by such people as Edith Nesbit, Henrik Ibsen, Ivan Turgenev, and George Bernard Shaw.

Workman's Times (1890–94): this was a weekly periodical published first in Huddersfield, then London, and then Manchester. It also published local editions in Birmingham, Hull, Tyneside, Teeside, Sheffield, Staffordshire, and the Midlands. The editor was Joseph Burgess, who wanted the journal to assist in organizing the ILP.